Lew Matthews (the pen name of Matthew Z. Lewin) was born in Johannesburg, South Africa in 1944. After studying social anthropology and psychology at university and training as a journalist, he left the country in 1969 (terrified of spiders, disgusted by Apartheid). After travelling and freelancing for a year in South America he came to London in 1970 and discovered the joys of English local weekly papers. In 1973 he joined the staff of the famous *Hampstead and Highgate Express*, becoming news editor in 1976. This year, he was appointed deputy editor of the newspaper, a job he describes as 'the second best job in journalism in the world'. *Unseen Witness* is his first novel.

the WARE LIBRARY

LEW MATTHEWS

Unseen Witness

HarperCollins*Publishers*

HarperCollins*Publishers*
77–85 Fulham Palace Road,
Hammersmith, London W6 8JB

This paperback edition 1993
1 3 5 7 9 8 6 4 2

First published in Great Britain by
HarperCollins*Publishers* 1992

Copyright © Lew Matthews 1992

The Author asserts the moral right to
be identified as the author of this work

Although Hampstead exists, as do many of the
locations described, all characters are entirely fictitious
and no reference is intended to any living persons,
any more than the *Hampstead Explorer* is intended to
represent the *Hampstead and Highgate Express.*

ISBN 0 586 21777 0

Set in Baskerville

Printed in Great Britain by
HarperCollinsManufacturing Glasgow

All rights reserved. No part of this publication may be
reproduced, stored in a retrieval system, or transmitted,
in any form or by any means, electronic, mechanical,
photocopying, recording or otherwise, without the prior
permission of the publishers.

This book is sold subject to the condition that it shall not,
by way of trade or otherwise, be lent, re-sold, hired out or
otherwise circulated without the publisher's prior consent
in any form of binding or cover other than that in which it
is published and without a similar condition including this
condition being imposed on the subsequent purchaser.

CHAPTER 1

There had been nothing in the omens or portents of the morning to indicate that this day would be anything out of the ordinary. The radio alarm had gone off on time at 8.0 a.m., there had been no major disasters reported on the news, the central heating system had, for once, produced sufficient hot water for my bath, and I had not cut myself shaving.

There were no ravens lying ominously dead on the door-mat. The *Independent* and the *Sun* were on the doorstep, and there was not a single demand for money in the morning's post, not even from Julia my ex- (and unlamented) wife who was threatening to sue me for what she called her share of the value of the house. The milk was not sour.

Shortly after nine o'clock my car did not start. Nothing unusual about that; the starter motor was a bit wonky and I had been waiting until I had a couple of hours to spare one sunny weekend so that I could fix it. The way my weekends were going recently, that would probably be in about the year 2025. The Unigate milkman gave me a push; rather ungraciously I thought, possibly reacting to the fact that this was the second time that week, and the fifth time that month.

Generally Thursdays are relatively quiet at the *Hampstead Explorer*, the weekly local newspaper which employed me as the crime reporter. After hectic Wednesday night dead-lines, we tend to spend the time relaxing and recovering from the frantic activity of the week. If something exciting happens, we can still wind things up and force the type-setters to change a few things, but it is very seldom that we get the opportunity to hear someone shout those famous words: 'Hold the front page!' So it should have been a quiet morning, but that is when it all started to go peculiar.

'Where the hell've you been, Parker?' snapped Arnie

Bloch, the irascible and overweight South African news editor, as I walked into the big open-plan newsroom. Rumour had it that he ate live bunnies for breakfast. I looked at my watch. I was early, dammit.

'Arnie, I'm not actually due in for another five minutes—' I began, using my patient, placatory tone. I hadn't even taken my coat off.

But he was in one of his impenetrable states. Once Arnie Bloch has his teeth into something, whether it is a sandwich or a reporter, it gets swallowed.

'Don't give me a lot of uphill, man, Parker. I haven't got the bloody time,' he said. It sounded more like: 'Doan gimme alorra upheel, men, Porker. Oi hevin't got the bleddy taam.' He'd been living in England for nearly twenty years and he still spoke like a Boer. He looked a bit like his hero, Lou Grant, except that his eyes were closer together and he had a lot more hair. And he was grumpier.

'Arnie, what's the matter?' Still patient.

'Halifax's wife, what's 'er-name, the film star, has been found dead near Jack Straw's car park.'

Some pieces of news are so shocking and appalling that they take a few seconds to sink in, and I remember those exact seconds with pinpoint accuracy. Adrenalin rushed into my veins, and images of Monique Karabekian began to flash through my brain. I think my mouth must have dropped open.

'I'm holding the printers for an hour and a half. So close your bloody mouth and get on to it. We're dropping that stupid story you did about the duck being drowned in Highgate Ponds and we're re-making page one. I want fifteen paragraphs by eleven o'clock. There's a press conference at Hampstead nick at ten. Mike's doing the political reactions, you do the police side. Come on, man, move!' He was right, this was no time for me to be standing around the office with my mouth open.

I glanced at Mike Graham, one of the other reporters, and saw that he was already talking urgently into the telephone. Within a few seconds I was out the door.

I think I actually ran to the car, which I had left parked illegally on a hill on a double yellow line, in case the starter motor wouldn't work. But for once it did, and I turned up Fitzjohn's Avenue and headed for Jack Straw's Castle.

Monique Karabekian murdered. Christ, what a story! She was the wife of Malcolm Halifax, the Conservative MP for Hampstead, the man who had won the seat with a surprise landslide in 1979, and since then had held on to it more and more easily as his political star had risen in the House of Commons. He had become a junior Foreign Office minister the previous year—not quite at the Prime Minister's main table yet, but few believed that a cabinet post would be denied him for much longer. There had even been some who had tipped him as a future premier himself.

He was one of those men who seemed to have everything, from the right background and education to the most perfect set of teeth in the Tory party. When he flashed those ivories whole public meetings full of voters would know where their next X would go on a ballot paper. He was handsome, too, with an elegant and aquiline face, silvery wavy hair just like Robert Redford's, and a skin colour that looked as if he gave his face a 15-minute boost in front of a sun lamp every day.

And then, as if his profile had not been high enough already, he had clinched a publicity spotlight for all time by abandoning his status as Hampstead's most eligible single man and marrying the indescribably exquisite Monique Karabekian, the film star.

I was myself more than a little in love with Monique Karabekian who, despite her exotic Armenian family name, was, like me, brought up in Hampstead, and had once lived in the next street from mine. We had been at the same comprehensive school, she a year behind me, and I had even had a date with her once. She had gone to acting school and had moved quickly from fringe theatre into major films in which she had played a succession of simmering sultry roles which had brought her into prominence in the sexual fantasies of a whole generation of men, including me. I could not conceive of her being dead, let alone murdered.

There was, of course, nothing at all to see in the car park behind Jack Straw's Castle. The pub itself was famous for its age and associates with Dickens and Dick Turpin, and for the fact that it stood at the highest point in London, about 440 feet above sea level. That's the kind of useless knowledge you pick up as a journalist.

The car park was itself was also famous, or notorious, depending on how you looked at such things, it having become a meeting place for homosexual encounters and the site of a number of previous assaults and even the odd murder or two.

This morning it was full of policemen. The tight-lipped, bored sort who stood with their arms crossed on their chest in front of the fluttering tape which cordoned off most of the car park. The type who wouldn't even look at a press card held beneath their noses. The type of policeman who had been warned that if even one reporter got within a hundred yards of the incident their guts would be hung out to dry back at the police station.

There were a number of other journalists nosing around, trying to find someone to question. I saw Woody Corkery of the *Sun*, one of the more degenerate of the tabloid body hunters. Worse still, he saw me.

'Isn't this the place they call "Gobblers' Gulch"?' he oozed as he sort of sidled up to me. I had always thought of Corkery as the sort of person who would squeeze his spots during an audience with the Queen. I ignored the question. He gave no indication of noticing that I had ignored the question, or that I was trying to ignore him, for that matter.

'So, find out anything yet?' he sleazed.

'Christ, Woody, I just arrived. You saw me.'

'Just thought you might know something, you being a local and all that.' Then his neanderthal brow furrowed and he looked at me.

'You got a car here?' he asked.

It still being relatively early in the morning and my brain not yet in high gear, I said yes before I realized that what he really wanted was a lift to the press conference. We drove down to the police station in Rosslyn Hill in near silence. He made only two or three disgusting comments during the whole journey.

We got only marginally more information from the press conference than we did from the scene of the crime itself. An officer who I vaguely knew introduced himself as Chief Superintendent Norman Harrison and gave brief details.

The body of Miss Karabekian (he did not say 'Mrs Halifax') had been discovered at approximately 6.30 a.m. by an early morning walker on the Heath. This person had been eliminated as a possible suspect. It was not possible to release information about the cause of death yet, since the post-mortem examination had still to be done, but he could tell us that it was being regarded as a murder and a full investigation was being mounted. Police were appealing for witnesses who might have seen anything at all in the vicinity of Jack Straw's Castle from around 11.0 p.m. on the Wednesday night to come forward. The inquest would be formally opened and adjourned at St Pancras Coroner's Court in Kings Cross on Monday. Were there any questions?

'Had she been sexually assaulted?' Corkery asked.

The policeman answered: 'We have no definite information about that. But first indications are that no, she was not sexually assaulted.'

'What about Mr Halifax?' asked another reporter.

'Mr Halifax returned to London early this morning from an official visit to West Germany. The news was broken to him when he arrived home at approximately eight a.m.'

'How did he take it?' asked Corkery. The question was ignored.

'Is he a suspect?' asked another hack.

'He is not a suspect,' the Chief Super said, enunciating the words clearly and slowly. I thought I had better ask a question.

'Where was she killed?'

'We do not know where she was killed. We are awaiting the outcome of certain forensic tests and the results of the post-mortem, but we believe that Miss Karabekian was murdered in a place as yet unknown, and her body brought to Hampstead Heath by way of the car park at Jack Straw's Castle, presumably in a motor vehicle of some description.' Typically pompous police-speak. He could just as easily have said: 'No, she was done in somewhere else and brought there by car.'

It was then that I noticed that Sergeant Theo Bernstein was standing at the back of the room and I tried to catch his eye. He studiously avoided my eye and when I looked again, he was gone.

'Are there any suspects at all?' the man from the *Guardian* asked.

'At this stage, none at all.'

'Is there any information about where she was last night?'

'None at this stage. Bear in mind, please, that it is only just over four hours since the body was discovered. The investigation is not yet fully under way.' The Chief Superintendent was beginning to look weary and I suspected that the press conference was nearly over. I was right. He fielded a few more irrelevant questions, then made his excuses and left.

Most of the journalists drifted out slowly, heading no doubt for the coffee bar up the road, since the pubs were not open yet. I was the only one who hurried out, my deadline looming quickly.

Bloch looked at his watch ostentatiously as I hurried back into the office. It was twenty to eleven and he wanted fifteen paragraphs by eleven. I checked with Mike Graham.

'What have you got, Mike?'

He shook his head. 'Nothing, just a bunch of no comments from everyone in sight. Christ, more than half the people I telephoned hadn't even heard yet. God, I hate that!'

So it was all up to me. Contrary to what you see in the

movies and on Lou Grant, the difficult part of journalism is writing. Anyone can go to a press conference, ask questions, take shorthand notes and chase stories around. The real skill is required when you get back to the office and there is this keyboard in front of you, with a blank screen sort of looking at you. That's when the talent and training is put to use.

I did it. I finished at exactly eleven o'clock. Or I would have if I hadn't tried to whip the last sheet of paper out of the printer with a grand flourish. It tore in half, and I had to go back to my desk to print out another copy, while Bloch made loud and sarcastic comments. I didn't mind Bloch's ranting, but what did unsettle me was the amused expression on Andy Ferris's face. There was something about that girl that was altogether unsettling. I would have to devote some time to thinking about what it was.

The said Andrea Ferris had joined the staff about eighteen months before, a trim twenty-five-year-old from Exeter who had become fed up with the boredom of writing fashion pieces and recipes on the *Western Daily Herald* and had come to London where, rumour had it, she had to focus her translucent green eyes only once on Arnold Bloch before he gave her a job.

Those eyes had captivated half the office as well, but I had not really noticed them. I had been an unhappily married man during most of her time at the paper.

Besides, she was a political reporter and, I suspected, probably felt that sneer of superiority with which her breed regarded people like me—the fire-engine chasers and loiterers in police stations. I had thus not paid much attention to the way she held her head when she typed, sometimes putting the back of her left hand to her mouth in a kind of thoughtful repose that decidedly improved the layout of the office.

I had hardly noticed that she seemed to glide across the floor when she walked, and that when she smiled little lines around her mouth and eyes seemed to dance with excitement. I had never really registered that deep in those icy clear pools of green there were little specks of battleship grey. And I had paid little attention to the husky sexiness of her voice. I don't think I had spent more than two or three hours a week thinking about her and wondering if she would come out with me.

I made myself a cup of coffee, black no sugar, and while I stood by the kettle waiting for it to boil, I watched Bloch and the editor reading my copy. They made very few changes. Then I watched it disappearing into the computer modem, the words being minced into electronic pulses that ended up, finally, in the typesetting computer a hundred miles away.

I went back to my desk with my coffee, exhausted. God, it was only half past eleven, I hadn't even opened my mail, and I felt as if I'd done a whole day's work. The phone on my desk rang.

'Is is possible to speak with Mr Horatio T. Parker, please?' said a man in a very precise voice. It was not an unpleasant voice, but my heart sank anyway. Someone else had discovered my first name.

'It is I,' I admitted.

'Mr Parker, my name is Ambrose Pendleton of Pendleton and Pendleton, a firm of solicitors in Lincoln's Inn.'

'Yes?' I said.

'Well, I will be as brief and as clear as I can. I am the executor of the estate of the late Mrs Edwina Llewellyn, whom I believe you knew, and well . . . I was hoping you would be free to come and see me this afternoon.'

'This afternoon?'

'Well, as soon as possible really.' The faintest trace of something half way between excitement and a buzz of alarm began to stir in my soul.

'What is this all about, Mr er . . . Pendleton?'

'Well, to be blunt, Mr Parker, you are the chief beneficiary of Mrs Llewellyn's estate, and there are a number of matters which I would like to discuss with you.'

Chief beneficiary. Words to get your teeth round and chew. Chief beneficiary. Say them slowly. Let them circulate easily in the mind and roll around the tongue before issuing from the lips. Noble words. Words of promise. I liked the way Mr Pendleton enunciated them, so crisply and precisely, but without hurrying them, giving them their full meaning, but without stressing them; letting them take their rightful place in the sentence and exert their control over the meaning in their own subtle way.

'How about two o'clock?' I suggested.

'Two o'clock would be ideal,' he said, and he gave me the address in the Inn.

I spent the next hour vaguely pretending to do some work, and actively wondering what it was that Edwina could have left me. I knew it couldn't be the house, that splendid house in Downshire Hill with its wonderful high ceilings and excellent black iron balconies. She had told me once that the house would eventually go to her family. So what else had she had to leave anyone? Some furniture, a few pictures, perhaps. Maybe a few hundred pounds in the bank. It couldn't be more than that; the dear old lady had been pretty short of money. I remembered I had once even picked up a newly arrived gas bill off her mat and, in an ill-timed fit of philanthropy, paid it.

Shortly before one 'clock I told Bloch I wouldn't be back immediately after lunch as I was going to 'poke around on the Halifax murder'. I had him at a disadvantage. He was half way through a triple-decker Reuben club sandwich from the Waitrose delicatessen, and there was coleslaw mingling with his beard. All he could do was grunt.

By some miracle there was a parking meter exactly where I needed one at Lincoln's Inn. And by an even bigger miracle I found that I had sufficient of the correct coins to buy half an hour of freedom from the clamp. I heard some ancient clock somewhere strike two. As usual, I was on time.

Pendleton's office was on the second floor up a narrow staircase that looked as if it hadn't been painted, or swept, for a hundred years. At the top there was a door, on which I knocked politely. With a sound like a gunshot, a small hatch next to the door was snapped back and part of a face peered through. The sound had given me a terrific shock, and for a nasty moment I thought it was Peter Lorre looking through the hatch at me.

'Yes?' demanded a querulous voice.

'My name is Parker. I have an appointment with Mr Pendleton,' I said in my most modulated tone. Only a lie-detector would have registered that I had been shocked rigid.

'Come in!' he barked, and as he spoke there was a buzz and a click and the door opened. Peter Lorre was sitting at a vast roll-top desk of a kind I had thought existed only in the imagination of Portobello Road antique dealers. It must have been six feet wide and five feet deep, and there wasn't a square inch not covered in untidy piles of paper.

'Mr Pendleton is expecting you. Go through,' he said through his nose. He had half-glasses which he wore on the end of his nose, and he wore those woollen gloves through which one's fingers poke. When he gestured towards a door, it was with an ancient claw of a hand, and the fingers actually pointed towards the floor.

But Mr Pendleton was indeed expecting me. He was standing, beaming, just inside the door, and extended his hand.

'Well, well. So pleased to meet you, Mr Parker, come in and do sit down.' He waved me to a chair which wheezed air when I sat on it. The funny thing was that he seemed more nervous than I was. He disappeared round the side of his desk, which was piled high with envelopes and papers on the edges, and then sat down in his leather swivel chair. He put his elbows on the desk, locked his fingers and rested his chin on his hands. 'You must be eager to know what this is about, Mr Parker, so I won't keep you in suspense. The point is that Edwina Llewellyn left you all her money.'

The fluttering in my stomach began. How much money? To justify this kind of meeting it must be hundreds of pounds, I told myself. Projects began to flash through my mind, beginning with a new starter motor for the car, a new tape-deck, possibly pay some of the legal bills already mounting under the onslaught from Julia.

'How much money is there in the estate, Mr Pendleton?' I was keeping very calm.

'A great deal of money.'

Thousands! It must be thousands! Perhaps there were some shares somewhere, a long-forgotten building society account. I began to think more in terms of a new car, pay all the legal bills, carpet the living-room. I could feel my heart pounding in my chest.

'Approximately how much, in round figures?' I asked.

'Fifty-two million pounds.'

I sat in that gloomy dusty room, with the sunlight creating almost solid sheets of light as the rays reflected off the millions of particles drifting in the air.

'Sorry, did you say fifty-two million pounds?' I had to force the words out; my mouth was as dry as a bone.

'I did.' Ambrose Pendleton sat perfectly still. He had a small beaky face, and beady eyes that glistened sharply as they looked at me above his old-fashioned wire-framed half-glasses.

I was rigid in my chair, the words he had spoken having given me that deep chilling sensation one feels in moment of panic or shock, as if a block of ice had suddenly formed in one's bowels and was now fighting its way back up the alimentary canal. I must have sat like that, not moving, for well over thirty seconds. I definitely was not breathing properly.

'Yes, it's around that figure, give or take a hundred thousand here or there.' He leaned forward as he spoke, his even and precise voice a little louder this time, as if he wondered whether I had heard him.

But I had had no problem with the volume. I had heard every astonishing syllable, and my problem was that I then had this instant fantasy that if I moved a muscle the whole room and its contents would disintegrate into a billion shards of mirrored glass, with the image of me and Mr Pendleton, and what he had just said, completely irretrievable for all time. Then I noticed that my heart was beating very fast, and I seemed decidedly breathless. Then I broke into an icy cold sweat and . . . well, to put it simply, I fainted.

CHAPTER 2

I couldn't have been unconscious for more than a few seconds, because when I opened my eyes Pendleton was still hurrying towards me with a worried look on his face. I was lying on a carpet that smelled of mouldy litigation, and I remembered wondering vaguely whether I had had a heart attack. God! No more pastries from Louis' Patisserie. Ever. I swear.

I felt decidedly awful. My shirt was drenched in sweat and clung to me coldly, my heart was still pounding loudly in my ears, I had the beginnings of a monster headache, and my breathing could be described as ragged. My thoughts in those few seconds of awakening were slow. Had I heard what I thought I had heard? Was it before I fainted or was it something I dreamed down here on this musty carpet? And if I had heard what I thought I had heard, why wasn't I jumping around the room and whooping for joy instead of lying here feeling ill?

'Oh dear me, dear, dear me!' Pendleton was muttering in some distress. 'Here, Mr Parker, let me help you up. Do you feel all right? Or perhaps I should send Spanner to summon a doctor?' I shook my head with a weak smile. Once I was back in the chair and had taken a few deep breaths, I began to feel a lot better.

'Are you sure?' I nodded again. 'Well then, I shall ask Spanner to make us some tea. Just sit there, Mr Parker, and perhaps put your head down between your knees. I think I read that somewhere.' I did so, and it was good advice, and after a minute or so I began to experience a distinct lifting of the spirits.

Fifty-two million pounds. That's what he had said. Could it for one wildly inconceivably improbable and impossible moment be true? Would he ever come back into the room again?

He did, followed by Spanner who was carrying a tray. A minute later I was sipping sweet strong tea and eating chocolate biscuits, and I felt decidedly better. I realized that I had eaten nothing that day since a bowl of muesli at breakfast. Never become a multi-millionaire on an empty stomach, that's my advice.

Mr Pendleton was talking again. 'I am so terribly sorry, Mr Parker. I really should have known that this was going to be the most terrible shock to you, but I'm afraid that I was rather excited myself. You see, I have never before told anyone anything like that. I do hope you will forgive me.' He was rubbing his hands together, obviously quite distressed.

'Mr Pendleton, I will forgive you anything. Just tell me that what you said is not a joke or a trick of some sort or some kind of legal gobbledegook that actually means something else. Are you telling me that Edwina has left me fifty-two million pounds?' Just saying the words made my head swim a little again.

'Well, I assure you that that is exactly the situation. I am pleased to tell you that you are now a very wealthy man indeed.'

I have to admit that there were little bubbles of elation beginning to pop in my mind, but the dominant thrust was still a powerful dread that this was all impossible, that it was a hoax, that it could not possibly be happening to me, that candid cameras would suddenly be thrust in my face.

'Mr Pendleton, forgive me, I don't want to sound unduly suspicious but . . . well—' I clawed for the words—'I just don't know who you are, and I don't know . . . have no way of knowing . . .'

'. . . whether I am telling you the truth?' He finished the sentence.

'Yes.'

'Well, I had thought that this sort of doubt might arise, and I take no offence, I assure you. You are correct to be cautious. It is, after all, an extraordinary situation. I can, however, do two things which might help you with this. I can show you Mrs Llewellyn's will, and I can put you in touch with the person at Rothschild's Bank who has been in charge of administering the financial part of her estate. I have spoken to him, and he was warned that you might be telephoning for just that form of confirmation, and he will be delighted to speak to you if you care to ring him. His name is Mr Douglas.'

'Now?'

'Yes, now.' He handed me the telephone directory, and I understood that I should look up the number myself. There it was: Rothschild N.M., Asset Management Limited, Investment Advisers, Mrcnt Bnkrs, in St Swithin's Court, EC4. I dialled the number.

'Rothschilds, good afternoon,' said a woman's voice.

'Mr Douglas, please.' My voice was slightly shaky. Pendleton nodded encouragement.

'Douglas.' It was the kind of voice to which one would entrust millions.

'Mr Douglas, my name is Parker and I am in Lincoln's Inn with a Mr Ambrose Pendleton who has given me some rather breathtaking news which, I gather, you are in a position to confirm.'

There was no hesitation. 'Yes, indeed, Mr Parker, I am more than happy to do so. I have known Mr Pendleton for a very long time, and I knew Mrs Llewellyn very well, having handled her financial affairs for more years than I care to remember. I can assure you that the situation is precisely as he has no doubt outlined it to you.' Now the thing was beginning to penetrate.

'I am worth fifty-two million pounds?'

'Approximately that, yes. I made a rough calculation of your assets this morning, and that is correct to within two or three hundred thousand pounds. It is, of course, the sum remaining after the payment of substantial death duties to the state. If you want to know exactly how much, I'll need a day or so to work it out.'

'Thank you, Mr Douglas, I think the round figure will suffice.'

'Not at all, I am delighted to be of service, and I look forward to continuing to be of service, should you decide to remain with us.'

'Thank you. Goodbye.' I put the telephone down, and looked at Pendleton. He was sitting quietly and looking squarely back at me and I think that is when I first allowed myself to believe, really to believe, that I now had more money than I could reasonably spend in three lifetimes.

He handed me a sheaf of stiff paper, bound with a red ribbon, and I realized it was Edwina's will. It was open at the third page, and I read:

> Since 1984 the quality my life has been immeasurably enhanced by the friendship of a young man, Horatio Thorpe [I winced] Parker of 142 Estelle Road, London NW3, to whom I give and bequeath the total sum of my financial assets currently held and managed on my behalf by N. M. Rothschild Limited, to be used by and/or disposed of at his absolute discretion. I make this gift out of gratitude for his attentions and kindnesses over the years, which were more precious to me than he could have known, and in the belief that he will be better able than I was to use these resources both for himself and for the benefit of the community. My only request is that he should accept the bequest in the spirit in which it is made, without burden or guilt, and in peace.

Then the will relapsed into incomprehensible legal jargon and I handed the document back to Pendleton. There were, I swear, tears in my eyes.

'Did you know about this before she died?' I asked.

'Of course. As her solicitor, it was I who drew up her will. I will confess that when she first came to me to change her will in your favour, my alarm knew no bounds.'

'I can imagine.'

'Well, yes. Then we made certain inquiries, and eventually we were persuaded Edwina knew exactly what she was doing and that she was, as the saying goes, "in sound mind".'

'What inquiries were made, exactly?' My question flustered him a little.

'Nothing sinister, I assure you. The inquiries were, ah . . . more to do with whether there was any possibility that you could have been aware of Mrs Llewellyn's financial situation at the time than into anything else, although I must confess that we did also check to see whether you had a police record. Oh, and I suspect some confidential inquiries were made into your financial status by Rothschilds. It was all very discreet.'

'And?'

'It was obvious almost immediately that you knew nothing. May I say, Mr Parker, that my own conversion to the cause, the moment when I became convinced that Edwina was acting sensibly and within her rights, was when you took a statement from North Thames Gas from her home and paid it out of your own funds. I understand that it put you current account into overdraft.'

'Oh, you knew about that?' I said.

'Of course.'

Then something occurred to me. 'I know she had no children, but there is other family—I remember seeing them at her funeral. Won't they be jumping about all over the place when they find out about this. They'll want to challenge the will, surely?' As the thought occurred to me, the feeling of alarm was heightened by the very short time that I had been rich.

'Indeed, there is family, but not on Edwina's side. She has no living relatives that we have been able to find, and I assure you that we have looked. And, to be blunt, the handful of relatives on her late husband's side are almost as wealthy as she was.' I began to realize just how much more money there was in the world than I had ever dreamed existed.

He continued: 'In any case, Edwina told them what she was going to do, and extracted their written agreement to the concept. She has left them the house, in order to assuage family honour, together with her furniture, personal possessions and her paintings, some of which I understand were extremely valuable. There were also other properties, both in London and in Wales, that have also been left to individual members of the late Mr Llewellyn's family. There will be no legal challenge to the will.'

'Where did all the money come from?' I asked. Pendleton lifted his shoulders in a shrug and grimaced.

'After this amount of time it is not always possible to know exactly where money like this comes from. One relies on information of that sort from one's client and, to be honest, Edwina didn't know too much about it all. I know a little, however. It seems that Mr Llewellyn's grandfather was a Welsh coal baron, and clearly did very well, making some sound investments along the way.

'Mr Llewellyn's father eventually took his share and put it into shipping, and did equally well. The world of shipping was, you may be aware, an extremely lucrative business in the early part of this century.

'Mr Llewellyn himself didn't do much at all—which is why the family was not better known. He was an only child and seems to have taken everything he inherited and put it in the care of Rothschilds before the war. As it happens, it was a very wise move, and the value of his investments has been quietly, but substantially, increasing over the years. I believe it has more than trebled in value since the mid-nineteen-thirties.'

'Please excuse what may sound like a stupid question, but I am rather new to all this. In what form is this money? Is it in cash sitting in a bank account?' Pendleton never lost patience for a second, and I began to realize that he was now enjoying the scene immensely.

'It is, of course, all rather complicated, but I will attempt to simplify it. I understand that approximately half is invested in interest-bearing stock and deposit accounts which attract a rate of interest of around nine per cent a year. The rest is in equities.'

'Equities?'

'Forgive me. Equities are shares listed on the stock exchange.'

Pendleton paused for a second, and then continued. 'I understand that the current income on capital is in the region of seven per cent a year.'

Income! Until that second I had not grasped the obvious fact that there would be, on top of the inconceivable sum of fifty-two million pounds, an annual income as well . . .

'How much is that a year?' I asked. His fingers darted around the keys of a desk calculator.

'About three million, nine hundred thousand pounds a year. Of course you would have to pay tax on that at the maximum rate of forty per cent, so the actual net income would be—' the fingers flew again—'about two million, three hundred and forty thousand pounds.' I was beginning to feel weak again.

'How much is that a month?'

'One hundred and ninety-five thousand pounds.'

'A week?'

'Forty-five thousand pounds.'

That, in a way, was the stunner, the one that really brought it home to me. Fifty-two million pounds was a very remote concept. An income of forty-five thousand pounds a week was something someone like me could begin to understand. I stood up abruptly, perhaps rather too abruptly because Pendleton seemed momentarily alarmed.

'I'm sorry, Mr Pendleton, but I think I've had enough for one day. Forgive me if I seem rude, but my feeling is that I have to take all this away and do some thinking about it. Sort of let it go down and get digested before we carry on any further.' Besides, I thought to myself, absurdly, my parking meter had probably expired. 'Can I come back and see you tomorrow?'

'Of course, of course, at any time. Just telephone first to see that I'm here, and I would be delighted to speak to you at any time.'

We shook hands, and suddenly I wanted to get out of that dusty room rather urgently, perhaps to see if the whole thing would evaporate when I got out into the open air. But when I got to the door something occurred to me. I stopped.

'Sorry, just one more question. When does this all happen. I mean, when does all this become available to me?'

'Well, we have to go through all the process of probate and because it is a rather large and complicated estate, that could take quite a few months. On the other hand, there is absolutely no reason why you cannot borrow against your inheritance from Rothschilds. You can afford the interest, and the bank, I am sure, will advance you whatever you need. Your standing with them, after all, could hardly be higher.'

When I got outside it was about half past four, and the sun was shining. Nothing evaporated.

I walked to the car and before I got there I knew my meter had in fact run out. I knew that because there was a traffic warden standing next to my car, writing out a ticket. But I knew nothing could spoil this day.

When I got to the car the warden smiled at me in a genuine sort of way and shrugged, as if to say: 'Sorry, but I have to do it.' That's why I gave her the car. The registration document was in the glove compartment, and I signed it and gave it to her along with the keys.

'It needs a new starter motor,' I told her, but I'm not sure if she heard. She was looking a little panic-stricken. 'Oh yes, and you'll have to pay the parking fine.'

I got my Keith Jarrett cassette out of the car and started looking for a taxi. I considered that I could probably afford one.

CHAPTER 3

That Friday morning I bought almost all the papers. Most had regarded the murder of poor Monique Karabekian as warranting front page treatment, although in their own inimitable ways, of course. *The Times* reported it fairly straight at first but ended up devoting much more space to the current, and possible future, career of Malcolm Halifax, MP, even going so far as to quote a senior Tory back-bencher proclaiming that this 'terribly unfortunate personal tragedy' would not mar his political career in any way. Not much it wouldn't.

The *Sun*, on the other hand, had let the hounds off the leash entirely.

SEXY
FILM
STAR
SLAIN
SHOCK

was the screaming headline down the right-hand side of the page. The left-hand side was a full-length photograph of Monique in one of her most provocative poses. Underneath was the secondary headline:

TORY MP'S WIFE FOUND DEAD IN
HAMPSTEAD HOMO HAUNT

The report itself was brief and lurid and full of fabricated innuendo. Woody Corkery at his best. Or worst. Inside the paper there was another page full of photographs of Monique and reports on her film career, early love-affairs, consorts, and marriage to the MP.

It being Friday morning, there was also the *Hampstead*

Explorer and my own piece, which was an object lesson in balance and style.

I should have been riveted by all of it, but I wasn't. For one thing I seemed to be seeing everything through a red mist in which there were dancing blood spots. Something to do, no doubt, with the fact that I had not slept a great deal the night before.

I had tried, of course, and then attempted every means known to me of summoning drowsiness. I had tried relaxation exercises, meditation, deep breathing, shallow breathing, camomile tea, mental arithmetic, thinking about proportional representation and the single transferable vote system and even counting sheep. But I was kept powerfully awake by constant visions of cascades of money which would not go away even when I attempted to count the fifty-pound notes.

I had also spent a long time thinking of Edwina Llewellyn.

I had met her on a bitterly cold day in January, 1984. It was a Tuesday. I know that because it was after the routine weekly press briefing at Hampstead police station.

Calls at some of the police stations were boring, but the Hampstead call was always enlivened by the presence of Sergeant Theodore Bernstein, the middle-aged crime prevention and community liaison officer who went through the crime books and reports with the reporters. I hadn't come across too many Jewish policemen before, and Theo made the experience all the more interesting because he was something of a scholar of Jewish law and the Talmud, the written version of the teachings of the early rabbis.

On this occasion there was the usual mixed bag. Burglaries in posh Hampstead homes, a spate of car radio thefts in Belsize Park, a cycle stolen from a teenager in broad daylight on Hampstead Heath, money snatched from a till at a butcher's shop, a policeman injured in an incident outside a pub at closing time on Saturday night. The usual sort of criminal endeavour in NW3. But there was also a particularly nasty case of what the police call 'burglary artifice', or what anyone else would call 'conning pensioners'.

It happens in a variety of ways, but the end result is usually a very distressed elderly person. The bastards, who range from quite young kids to seasoned teams of vicious con men, worm their way into pensioners' home on a variety of pretexts and then steal money and valuables.

Theo Bernstein told us of the case of an 82-year-old woman around the corner in Downshire Hill who had been conned out of £700 and various personal items only the day before. A widow by the name of Edwina Llewellyn.

'Why is it,' I asked him as the assembled hacks dispersed, 'that there is such wickedness in the world?'

He grinned at me. 'The Talmud tells us that the evil impulse is at first like a passer-by, then like a lodger and finally like the master of the house. It is a force from within us rather than an influence from without. Now, sod off and let me do some work.'

I decided to go round to the house and see if the widow wanted to be interviewed. Horatio T. Parker was nothing if not thorough. And besides, I had nothing else to offer Bloch.

The front garden of the splendid house was unkempt, but not wholly neglected, and the front of the building needed more than a lick of paint here and there. I rang the doorbell. It was opened within twenty seconds, without hesitation and without a door chain, by an elderly woman with short grey hair and large spectacles wearing light blue slacks and a cream cardigan. I don't always remember what people were wearing, but I remembered her clothing because it was not the usual rather dull uniform of the average 82-year-old. Her face was lined, but she looked ten years younger than that.

She was about five feet six inches tall, maybe a little less, and she stood leaning on the door handle. There was no walking stick, and she wasn't bent over. She was quite poised and erect, and she looked me straight in the eye. It was a steady gaze, and I think our relationship started right then and there, on her doorstep.

It was very cold, and there was an icy breeze blowing but she was too polite to try to hurry the encounter.

'Yes, may I help you,' she said in an unexpectedly clear voice, with only the faintest trace of a quaver.

'Good afternoon, I'm sorry to bother you, but I'm from the *Hampstead Explorer* and I was wondering if I could talk to you about what happened yesterday.' I was speaking clearly and patronizingly, as one does to old people.

'Oh, the *Explorer*. I always read the *Explorer*. Yes, of course, come in and close the door behind you.' She had let go of the doorknob and was walking away from me, towards the front reception room.

'Mrs Llewellyn!' I said, quite sharply and quite loudly. She stopped abruptly and looked at me in surprise, but with no alarm showing in her face. I continued, still standing on the doorstep: 'It was only yesterday that someone came to your house and robbed you when you let them in! Don't you think you should ask me for some form of proof of identity before you let me in?' I really was feeling the frustration I expressed. She took the point very quickly.

'Oh dear, that's exactly what the detective said when he came.' She smiled and sighed: 'The trouble is, young man, that after doing something as simple as opening a door for eighty-odd years, one tends to get into the habit of doing it in a particular way. But you're quite right. Show me your press card or whatever you have . . . and then shut the door behind you. It's terribly cold.'

Then she turned her back on me and walked into the living-room. I was left speechless on the doorstep, grinning to myself and shaking my head.

She had lost, it turned out, in addition to the £700 in cash, all her late husband's medals and campaign ribbons from the Second World War and, most precious of all, his letter of commission as a colonel in an infantry regiment personally signed by King George the Fifth.

When speaking to me she said all the right things: how

silly she was to have let in the men—who had claimed to be from the Gas Board, how she would never do it again, and how she hoped other vulnerable people would learn from her experience. But all along I knew she was just saying the words. At one stage she winked at me, and I realized that for her this was already history. It had happened and she was not the kind of person who was going to let it spoil the rest of her life, or even the rest of her week.

She made tea and suddenly I found that the tables had been turned in stages imperceptible to me, and it was I who was now being interviewed—about the newspaper, my life as a reporter, my love-life, and my parents (both dead). We spoke about my late mother until I realized with a shock that it was already five o'clock. I had been due back at the office by four, and Bloch would be looking for blood. My blood.

But before I left she looked at me in her direct way again and said: 'Please come and visit me again.' I said I would, and I meant it, and I did.

At first I just dropped in occasionally to see how she was. She was fine. Then once or twice we had lunch together—a glass of white wine and a salad at the wine bar in Rosslyn Hill. Each time we would chat animatedly about everything under the sun, and I would invariably be late getting back to the office. She showed none of the conservatism of old age, none of the entrenchment of attitudes I had always come to expect from old people. She was interested in things, new things, and when she asked questions it was because she genuinely wanted to hear the answers and she listened to them. And she stretched me, too, never being satisfied with silly statements, half-baked ideas or evasions.

One night I had press tickets to a fringe play at the King's Head pub theatre in Islington, and she was delighted that I asked her. Then we went to the Hampstead Theatre one evening, and it wasn't long before the relationship had developed into a regular Thursday evening outing to the cinema or the theatre. Most times I insisted on paying, although there were times she stood her ground and demanded to be allowed to pay for tickets, or a meal.

How does one explain a relationship like that? Perhaps there are a host of Freudian explanations lurking somewhere. It is true that I had never really known any grandparents, and my own parents had died when I was relatively young, but I maintain that I was responding primarily to the personality of the woman, not to what she was. I liked her, and we had fun together.

We would occasionally go to art galleries on a Saturday afternoon, and there was even one time when we drove down to Bath to see an exhibition and spent the Saturday night in a hotel. I remember worriedly telephoning her room in the morning when she didn't come down in time for breakfast, only to find that she was still fast asleep. So I took her to the Pump House for tea and pastries where I teased her unmercifully about her slothful habits.

I paid for that trip. It was, you understand, when I was still a single man, unencumbered by Julia the wife or the house we were to buy later, and I was modestly solvent.

For reasons that I understand now, she studiously avoided talking about money, but at the time I assumed that it was because she was rather short of the stuff and the subject worried her. I made lots of assumptions, such as that she was struggling to keep the house going and that was why she had four or five university students living there to help with the expenses. I know now that they were all, on the contrary, living rent-free, referred to her by an agency which helped find accommodation for less well-off students, and Edwina was even giving them pocket money.

There are times, now, when I wonder what I would have done, how I would have felt, and what would have happened to that quiet and unruffled relationship of ours had I discovered her immense wealth. I never find any definitive answers, but it does lead me to understand why she never dreamed of telling me.

I never liked her rather baroque furniture and paintings and in my arrogant way I therefore assumed that they were not worth very much. When her relatives finally sold it all, I was staggered at what it all fetched at Sotheby's.

She would tease me about my disastrous love-affairs, and although I sensed that she wasn't crazy about Julia, when all that happened, she never said a word against her. Julia, on the other hand, hated Edwina. Our first, our biggest and always our most spectacular rows were about the amount of time—and money—I spent with the 'poisonous pensioner', as Julia called her. But it was an issue on which I would not budge. Thursday night Edwina night, and Julia could join us or not, as she wished. She seldom joined us.

When Julia walked out, Edwina was quietly supportive. She was never crass enough to gloat or tell me that there were other fish in the sea.

Then, a few months ago, and at the age of 89, Edwina simply failed to wake up one Monday morning. Theo Bernstein rang me at work to tell me. I remember keenly the sweeping sense of loss and the sharp grief I felt, but they were also emotions tampered by the philosophical understanding that she had, after all, lived a long and, by all accounts, interesting life.

She was cremated in Golders Green on the Thursday afternoon, one of those perfect mid-winter days in which the sky is so clear and the air is so still that there is warmth in the rays of the sun despite the iciness in the air. The short service was conducted by a man who clearly hadn't known her, and who had to refer surreptitiously to a piece of paper whenever he needed to remember who it was we had all gathered together to mourn.

That night I went to the Barbican Theatre on my own, and the empty seat next to me spoke more poignantly and eloquently than anyone on the stage.

The phone rang. It was Bloch.

'Arnie, it's my Friday off,' I protested, but it was as if I hadn't spoken.

'Halifax phoned. He wants to speak to you. Wouldn't speak to anybody else.'

Every journalistic nerve-ending in my body twitched, and my nose sensed that most exquisite newspaper phenomenon—a scoop. The cream of the crime reporters in London would be clamouring to speak to Halifax, and would be rebuffed by reams of lawyers and policemen. Clearly I had underestimated his thirst for publicity in his constituency, and here he was asking to speak to me. Only me.

'Where was he when he rang?' I asked quickly.

'At home.'

'I'll go round there right away,' I said. After all, what's a mere day off compared to a scoop?

CHAPTER 4

Just for a moment when I came out of the house, I thought my car had been stolen. Then I cursed myself for giving it to the traffic warden. I could see that I was going to have to curb any propensity towards grandiose impulses; this particular one had left me without transport.

I started walking, and finally managed to get a taxi in South End Green. It was one of those new ones with a mobile telephone for use by passengers, so I rang Pendleton. Certainly he would be able to see me that afternoon, he said, any time I cared to come, although he usually left the office at 4.0 p.m. on a Friday afternoon. He also gave me Douglas's number at Rothschilds. I rang him too.

'I need some money,' I told him.

'Of course,' he said simply (I had half expected him to say: 'Don't we all?'), and added: 'How much do you need?'

'Well, I'm not sure. I need to buy a car, and I have some bills to pay, and I have a few ideas that I want to discuss with Mr Pendleton this afternoon, and I suppose it might be useful to have a bit left over . . .' My voice sort of tailed off.

'Would twenty-five thousand pounds be the sort of figure

you had in mind?' I swallowed, loudly. 'Good,' he continued. 'I will organize the transfer immediately, and the funds will be in your current account at the Midland Bank in Hampstead by midday.' I swallowed again, loudly.

'You understand that this is an advance by Rothschilds against the funds held by us comprising your inheritance, which will only be released to you when the formalities of probate have been completed. I will arrange for all the necessary documents to be sent to Mr Pendleton, and it would be useful if when you see him this afternoon, you could consider giving him some limited power of attorney which would enable him to arrange transactions such as this on your behalf.

'Of course,' he added hastily, 'that is assuming you intend to continue using the services of Mr Pendleton and, for that matter, Rothschilds. You don't have to, you understand.'

'Mr Douglas, I would not dream of taking my business elsewhere. If you were good enough for Edwina, you're good enough for me.'

An idle speculation that absorbed me as I sat in the taxi was about how much I had earned in the twenty-four hours since I had discovered I was rich. I didn't have a calculator, but it wasn't that difficult. One seventh of forty-five thousand a week was about six thousand five hundred, say about six thousand, taking the four missing hours into account. It sounded quite absurd, utterly unreal, and all I could do was grin happily. I was earning nearly £4.50 a minute.

I was, I thought, a very nice new taxi, and then another thought struck me. I slipped over to the seat behind the driver and opened the glass slide. 'Are you an owner-driver?' I asked him.

'It's the only thing to be, guv.' There was a surprised, inquiring look on his face. But I was thinking hard and I didn't answer his unspoken query.

When I got out, and paid the £3.50 fare and a pretty steep £3 for the phone calls, I tipped him a fiver. He grinned broadly. I grinned back, broadly, and asked: 'What do you earn?' His grin disappeared. Mine was still in place, but that wasn't what was stopping him from driving off in a cloud of diesel fumes. What was stopping him was the five-pound tip and the fact that I was leaning in the window. I could see that he was wrestling with himself. Part of him wanted to tell me to fuck off, and the other part was for humouring me. Eventually he said, succinctly:

'Why?'

'I need transport during the day, and I'm offering you the job.'

'I've got a job, and I don't need an employer, thank you.'

'No, I'm not offering to employ you. What I'm suggesting is a sort of block booking. You drive me around wherever I want to go between nine in the morning and six in the evening on weekdays. At any other time you do what you like.' I stepped back from the taxi. He didn't drive away.

'Think about it,' I said. 'Wait for me here. I'm going into this block of flats, and I'm going to be there about an hour. Think about the position, and think about what you would charge me a week for the arrangement. If you're still here when I come out we'll talk figures. If not, that's OK.'

'I'll think about it,' he said, and he switched off the engine. That, I thought, was a good sign.

I was standing in front of a large and modern block of flats in Prince Albert Road, St John's Wood, aptly named Park Vistas since the flats on this side of the building at any rate had the most stunning views of Regents Park. Halifax had a flat on the third floor.

It was a modern building, built in the late 'seventies, with lots of landscaped garden in front and a babbling fountain feeding a little pond with goldfish and water-lilies in abundance. The flats towered above, with lots of glass to make the most of the view over the park. Each seemed to have a large picture window off the living-room and, to the side of it, a balcony, so that the inhabitants could almost pretend that they lived in the park itself.

In front of the entrance lobby there was a very large police constable standing with thick arms folded across his chest, who was also obviously blind, deaf and dumb, just like the ones at Jack Straw's Castle.

I discovered these disabilities very quickly. He seemed unable to see my press card, he apparently did not hear me when I told him Mr Halifax was expecting me, and he declined to speak to me.

'Are you a resident here, sir?' he said finally, using that slow sing-song rhythm in which all words are enunciated precisely that policemen use when they want to insult you politely.

'No, I'm a newspaper reporter and I told you, Mr Halifax is expecting me. He telephoned my office about an hour ago and said he wanted to see me.' I was being very patient.

'I know you reporters.' He allowed himself a half-smile here, and a kind of a strangled chuckle. But then the face darkened again: 'My orders are to admit only residents and bona fide visitors, and you, I am afraid to say, are staying out.' I looked at him hard. Piggy eyes glared back.

I was about to deliver him a stunning snub by turning on my heel and storming away, when his dignity was saved by the arrival of the porter, a lithe black man wearing a beautifully fitting maroon suit with lots of gold braid on it and the Park Vistas logo on the breast pocket.

'It's OK, mon,' he lilted in a strong Jamaican accent. 'This is Mr Parker from the *Explorer*, and Mr Halifax is expectin' him, mon.' He said Halifax more like hully-fucks, with a little more pause on the hyphen to emphasize the last syllable. There was something about the man that rang a bell, but I couldn't put my finger on it.

The bobby didn't admit defeat or even apologize. He simply stepped aside. As I walked past him I glared triumphantly.

He leaned forward and with his piggy eyes close to mine, said: 'Just doing my job, sir,' before I disappeared into the building with the porter.

The black man punched the button for the lift, and while we were waiting he flashed me a face full of brilliant white teeth and said: 'How's it goin', Horatio?' I winced. 'You remember me, of course?' My mind raced, but came up with nothing other than that his face was vaguely familiar.

'Of course! How are you?' I said brazenly. He peered at me cheerfully, and then shook his head.

'Nooooo, you don't remember nuttin' about it.' There was disappointment but no anger in his voice. 'Remember, a couple'a years ago, you wrote an articule—' that's how he pronounced it—"bout me. I was beaten up by the pigs, mon, and I took the bastards to the cleaners?'

Then I remembered. And the name came to me: Nathaniel Jackson. He had been walking quietly along Finchley Road in the early hours of the morning when a swarm of uniformed police had poured out of a police van and beaten him to a jelly. They had mistaken him for another black man who had assaulted a WPC near Swiss Cottage underground station. He was left with a broken arm, broken cheekbone, a chipped vertebra, numerous cuts and bruises caused by boots and truncheons and he had spent six weeks in hospital. There he was visited by an embarrassed senior officer from Scotland Yard who offered him an official apology and five hundred pounds compensation. He told the policeman to fuck off and he found himself a lawyer.

Seeing the writing clearly on the wall, the police quickly settled out of court, and sent him a cheque for £10,000.

Then I remembered something else: Halifax had become involved. He had not missed the potential political mileage to be made out of an issue like that in a place like Hampstead, had climbed enthusiastically on the bandwagon, asked questions of the Home Secretary in the House and called for a public inquiry. The request was gently but firmly turned down, as Halifax had known it would be.

'Nathaniel Jackson,' I said, and he grinned broadly. 'What the hell are you doing here?' But I think I already knew the answer.

'What do you think? I work here, bro'. That nice Mr Hully-fucks got me this job, just after that time, you know. But I'll tell you somethin', mon, it was the lady made him do it. He was just full of hot air, but she was the one found me the job.'

'You mean Mrs Halifax?' By this stage we were in the lift.

'Monique Karabekiaaan,' he said, gently stressing the last syllable of the surname. He said it sadly, like a two word obituary, and it was more heartfelt than most that I had read.

The lift door opened on the fifth floor. There was a small lobby and two doors. Jackson pointed at the one on the left and I stepped out. 'See you in a while,' I said, as the lift doors closed. I pressed the bell.

To say that Malcolm Halifax looked rough would be a grave whitewash of the situation. The man was wasted. His hair, which usually flowed with a graceful flourish across his forehead, seemed thin and greasy and hung in his eyes; eyes that were themselves sunk in sockets so deep and dark that the usual blaze of clear blue was all but extinguished by the gloom. The skin on his face was the deathly white of a feverish child's, except that there were high points of colour on his cheekbones. Only his teeth remained their usual gleaming selves, being revealed to me in what was probably intended to be a smile but emerged as a rather strained grimace. His hand shook slightly as he held it out.

'Parker.' It was less of a greeting than an acknowledgement that I had indeed come.

I followed him into the kind of room ordinary people normally only see in the cinema and in the colour supplements. It was at least thirty feet long, and the wall overlooking the park was made entirely of glass, part of which, I could see, would slide aside to provide access to the terrace outside. Light flooded in and I looked around, taking in a gorgeous white carpet covered here and there with oriental rugs, tasteful brass and glass tables and apparently endless banks of low settees and armchairs covered in soft white leather.

There was a pile of newspapers on the floor. It looked as

if he had read every one. He waved me to a couch and I let the white hide caress me.

'Mr Halifax, what can I say? We were all absolutely devastated at the news. All my colleagues send their sincere condolences.' I was lying, of course. They were all mourning the beautiful Monique Karabekian, but they hadn't given Halifax's feelings a thought. He nodded dully.

'You knew her, didn't you? I mean personally.' His voice was rather flat, as if he was exhausted.

'Yes, we were at school together; she lived in the next street; we knew each other then,' I acknowledged.

'She spoke about you more than once, you know. Said you were a very good journalist and that she couldn't understand why you hadn't moved to Fleet Street.'

'I am very flattered, and honoured.' I was, too.

'Did you write today's report in the *Explorer*?' I nodded. 'I thought so. You seem to have been the only one to get everything right.' I shrugged, modestly. Then he added: 'Will you write the obituary?'

The issue of the obituary had not yet crossed my mind, but I did not hesitate: 'Yes, I'll be doing that personally.'

'Good, I was hoping you would, and that's what I wanted to see you about.' He paused, and I just sat quietly, waiting for him to find the words he was searching for. Eventually he said: 'She wasn't just some bimbo, you know.'

'I know.'

'I mean, she wasn't like all those other actresses. She was an intelligent woman, and clever, really clever. She was a thinker.'

'I know that.' I didn't, but I said it anyway.

'She kept a diary, you know.' My heart missed four beats, fibrillated a bit and then resumed pumping erratically. Diaries, as every journalist knows, contain that vital drug called 'human interest', information about people written by themselves which gives us insights into how they lived, what they thought, how they made their decisions, who they knew and who influenced them. A diary written by

Monique Karabekian would, at this particular juncture, have an incalculable value.

'Really? No I didn't know.' The late Lord Olivier would have been proud of me, the way I got the words to come out so calmly and so naturally.

'No, of course, how could you have known. Stupid of me. Anyway, she did, and it occurred to me that you might want to have a look at them—for the obituary, you know.' Now it was my lungs that were failing. Monique Karabekian's diaries were being offered to me, and every hack nerve ending in my body was firing at random. Inside it felt as if I was jumping around in excitement. I tried to sit still and look mildly interested and not tear holes in the leather couch.

'I'll go and get them,' he said, and he walked out of the room. I think I held my breath until he came back and that was probably why I was feeling so light-headed when he walked over to me and handed me two A4 size ring bound notebooks with black covers. He actually put them into my sweaty hands. No one was going to believe this, I thought. Everyone would think I had stolen them.

'She started writing the diary when we got married, four and a half years ago. You're welcome to use them.'

All I wanted to do was get out of the flat before he changed his mind and took them away from me. My instinct told me to get up and run like the clappers. But I sat quietly. I still had work to do. I got out my own notebook.

'Mr Halifax,' I said softly, 'I hope you don't mind if I ask you a few questions about the . . . er . . .'

'The murder,' he said. He was sitting down now, looking gaunt and haunted. 'No, I don't mind. I've told the police everything I know already so I can't see what harm there would be in talking to you. The trouble is that I don't know anything at all. When I arrived back yesterday morning the police were waiting for me here and they told me what had happened.' His voice was shaking. 'I have no idea where she was on Wednesday night, or with whom, no idea at all.'

'Did she have any enemies that you knew of?' I asked.

'There were actresses and other women who would willingly have scratched her eyes out, but not enemies, not real enemies, not that I knew of, anyway. Most people loved her.' There were, I swear, tears in his eyes.

'I'm sorry if this is impertinent,' I said, 'but it is relevant, I think. Can I ask how successful your marriage was?' That is what is called taking the bull by the horns. Only journalists with balls ask that kind of question. He answered meekly.

'Our marriage . . .' he hesitated . . . 'worked. Yes, it worked. We are . . . were, very different. We had different lives and backgrounds, and sometimes we were going in different directions, me in politics and she in the cinema, but it worked, it really did. We got on well, and we enjoyed each other's company.' I wrote it all down in shorthand.

'There's not a lot more to ask about, is there?' He was beginning to look pretty desperate.

'No,' I replied. 'Just one more impertinent question, if I may. Obviously there's going to be a lot of speculation, and lots of it will be nasty, so I may as well ask before anyone else. Was there any insurance on Mrs Halifax's life?'

'The police have already asked me that,' he sighed. 'Yes, there was. Quite a big policy, I think, but I don't know the details because she arranged it herself and the beneficiaries are all members of her family.' There was a pause. 'I was aware of that, of course, and I was quite happy about it. I am not in need of money, as you know.'

'No, I don't know,' I said.

'Oh. Well, I am what they describe as well off, thanks to energetic and industrious parents who left me a great deal of money. It happens, you know.' I nodded. That I did know.

I couldn't think of any more questions, and the diaries were beginning to scorch the couch, so I picked them up and made my exit, once again expressing our condolences. He smiled sadly and closed the door behind me.

The lift arrived with Nathaniel Jackson inside it. He looked frankly at the books squeezed tightly under my arm, and asked: 'He give you anythin'?'

'Just some old diaries for the obituary.' Then I changed the subject. 'You been interviewed by the police yet?' I asked him.

'Hell, yes. I been talkin' to dem all day yesterday, nearly. Dem aksing the same questions, and me givin' dem the same answers. I don't tink dem like me.' He grinned.

'What answers?'

'Like nooo, I didn't see or hear anyone or anythin' strange or unusual. Like nooo, I didn't see or hear Miss Karabekian after she got back from work at about half past six. And yes, that's right, I didn't know anythin' a'tall and couldn't help dem a'tall.'

'Were you on duty on Wednesday night?' The lift reached the lobby and we got out.

'All night, mon.'

'Where were you?' I asked. He pointed to the desk in the foyer, behind which there was a comfortable chair.

'I was there. Maybe I slept a little, that's allowed, but the door is locked at night and no one could have come in without me seein' them and buzzin' them in.'

'Unless they had their own key.'

'Sure.'

'Is there another way in?'

'Dere's the car park, but you need a key for that too.'

'Does the lift go to the car park?'

'Yes.'

'So she either left here of her own accord, or whoever came for her had their own key?'

'That's the way the police see it, mon.' It was the way I saw it too.

As I came out of the door, PC Piggy Plod was still standing there, glowering at me.

I was pleased to see that the taxi was also still there. I went over to the driver's window and said: 'Hi.'

'Three 'undred and eighty quid a week. That's twenny grand a year. I don't work weekends or bank 'olidays and I take six weeks' paid 'olidays a year. After six p.m. I do what I like and I can ply for hire if I want. I don't carry anything heavy, and I don't do anything illegal. OK?' He paused, then: 'Also, I want some sort of guarantee that you've got the money.'

'What's your name?'

'Francis Price. You can call me Frankie.'

'Frankie, you've got a deal. Now let's go and have lunch. Take me to your favourite pub in the Hampstead area, and then we'll go to the bank for your guarantee.'

CHAPTER 5

Our reception at the bank impressed the hell out of Frankie. To be honest, it impressed the hell out of me too but I handled the surprise better.

For sixteen years they had been writing me letters informing me that my account was overdrawn, refusing my requests for loans, bouncing my cheques and asking me to drop in to speak to the manager about my financial affairs. Now, as we walked through the door, something like an instant guard of honour formed and we were ushered through to the manager's office before the front door had even swung shut. I half expected a brass band to start playing.

I didn't beat around the bush with Mr Berry, the manager who had been particularly snide and condescending with me for the last three or four years.

'Have you been contacted by Mr Douglas at Rothschilds?' I asked him.

'We certainly have,' he beamed, 'and I would like to say how pleased we are for you—'

I interrupted him. 'That's OK. Just tell Mr Price here that I'm good for his salary of three hundred and eighty pounds a week.' As I said the words it struck me that Frankie's annual salary would amount to less than half of one week's income.

'Oh, I can certainly vouch for that,' he said to Frankie, 'In fact—'

I cut him off again. 'Thank you, that's fine. Frankie, could you wait for me in the cab, please?' When he'd gone I turned to Berry again. 'Has the money been transferred into my account?'

'Twenty-five thousand pounds,' he said.

'Were you given some indication of my er . . . situation?'

'Yes, Mr Douglas has led me to conclude that you are a particularly valuable customer to us and that your resources are, shall we say, considerable, although he did not mention any figures.'

'Good. I suspect, Mr Berry, that you are going to see a lot more activity in my account from now on, and I want to get a few things straight. I don't want any foul-ups. I want my bank statements regularly and on time. I don't want to see any bank charges on the statement. And in no circumstances will you refuse payment on any cheque I issue—you know I'm good for the money even though it may not be in my account at a particular moment. You and your staff will provide positive credit references for me promptly to any bona fide inquiry, and otherwise I expect to have my affairs handled with discretion and complete confidentiality. Is all that clear?'

It was unnecessary, certainly, and uncalled for, probably. But I packed a lot of revenge into those few sentences, and I felt good. He was still smiling unctuously. 'Of course, Mr Parker.'

'OK, you can start by making sure I get a few extra cheque books. I have a lot of payments to make. Presumably you can organize that this afternoon and get them into the post to me tonight?'

'Certainly,' he said. He was still smiling, but I could see

the strain was beginning to tell on him and there was a little tremor in the muscles around the eyes.

I withdrew seven hundred pounds in cash from a woman teller who smiled brilliantly at me, and I left the bank.

Back in the cab, I gave Frankie Pendleton's address and we set off for Lincoln's Inn. I was pleased with myself about the transport arrangements. Constant personal use of a nice new taxi with a telephone was a stroke of genius, and I congratulated myself. Hours spent searching for parking would be a thing of the past, as were the pounds spent on parking fines. And besides, I had discovered that I liked Frankie.

He was a funny-looking geezer in a pleasant sort of way. Rather like a clown, with the top of his head being bald and shiny and tufts of springy ginger hair sticking out almost horizontally from just above his ears, and he had a sense of humour. Most interesting of all was the fact that he was taking courses in psychology through the Open University, and the new arrangement could not have suited him better. Whenever I didn't need him, he would sit happily in the cab swatting up his Pavlov and Freud.

Lincoln's Inn hadn't changed at all since the day before but I, of course, was in a different frame of mind. I tripped up the stairs to Pendleton's office and pressed the buzzer. Spanner did his trick of snapping back the shutter again, but this time I was ready for him, with my face right next to the opening with a manic fish-eyed grin and I think he looked startled. Pendleton, however, looked delighted to see me and called for some tea. We made small talk for a minute or two, and then I outlined my thinking on the subject of suddenly being thrust into the status of multi-millionaire.

'Clearly, such a large amount of money is going to change my life quite dramatically, I have no illusions about that,' I said. He nodded. 'But there is a limit to how much change I can handle.

'It seems that I will never lack for funds, but I am determined to carry on working at the *Explorer* in the same capacity. Now, perhaps you think that's unrealistic and the result of wishful thinking, but I hope not, and you may see why when I have outlined the rest of my plans.

'Apart from ensuring a steady flow of funds in my own direction, I would like to set up two organizations: One will be the Edwina Llewellyn Memorial Trust, suitably endowed from my funds, which will have a handful of trustees—myself, you and Mr Douglas if you both agree—and a small staff to run it. The object of the trust will be to disburse funds as we see fit and to consider applications for assistance from anyone who gets to hear about us. What I have in mind is a source of assistance for people in desperate straits who have either been turned down by other agencies or who don't qualify under others' criteria.

'The other will be a company, wholly owned by me, which will endeavour to buy the *Hampstead Explorer* from its present owner. In both cases my wish to remain unidentified is paramount. I really must stress that: if we are successful I particularly don't want my colleagues on the newspaper to know that I am their employer.' Pendleton was listening intently, making pyramids with his fingers.

'You see, Mr Pendleton, one of the few real achievements in my life has been managing to end up in a job which I actually, positively, enjoy. I have a level of job satisfaction that most people only dream about, which is why I have stayed with the newspaper for so long.

'My immediate problem is that I need expert assistance. I need someone with the knowledge and expertise to set up the two enterprises, and I need someone to organize and then head the day-to-day management as a kind of chief executive or general manager or whatever, and I really was hoping, Mr Pendleton, that you would agree to take on that task.'

It had been quite a long speech, and throughout he had sat in silence, making no move to interrupt. When I finished, we just sat there looking at each other. I wondered just how foolish I had sounded, and he actually looked a bit misty-eyed. Eventually he said: 'Do you know, Mr

Parker, that what you are proposing is broadly similar to what Mrs Llewellyn forecast that you would do?'

I felt a chill run down my spine. He continued: 'She said you would move to buy the newspaper, and that you would set up some sort of charitable organization, although she did not envisage that you would want to do so anonymously. I think she would have been delighted with what you have just said.

'As far as your offer to me is concerned, I have this to say: I am three or four years away from retirement, after a long and modestly successful career in a general legal practice. My son and other younger partners now handle the bulk of the firm's business, leaving me in charge of the affairs of a few long-standing clients, most of whom are by now personal friends. The task you are offering me would be a splendid way for me to bring to a close my working life, and I accept with enthusiasm.' He was literally beaming now.

'However,' he added quickly, 'you must be aware that this will only be a short-term arrangement. I will help set up these organizations you want, and I will run them for you—but only for a couple of years, three at most. Then it will be time for me to retire to Devon, and time for you to find someone more in touch with your own outlook on life and your own motivations than a rather conservative old gentleman like myself.'

We threw these kinds of compliment at each other for another few minutes. Pendleton promised to begin hiring the necessary staff, preparing the paperwork and research necessary so that everything would be in place as quickly as possible.

I told him about my arrangement with Frankie Price, and asked him to arrange for a credit transfer to his bank account every week. I also gave him a limited power of attorney to enable him to deal with funds from Rothschilds on my behalf, as suggested by Mr Douglas.

It was three o'clock when I came outside. Frankie was

quietly double parked and being ignored by everyone. The system worked perfectly.

'Where to now, guv?'

'I need one of those printing shops that do photocopying, preferably a big one with at least two copying machines. Know one?' Of course he did, and we were there a few minutes later.

I waved a wad of money about and that galvanized the staff into action. Working flat out, they managed to make two copies of the hundred or so pages of Monique Karabekian's diaries in about twenty minutes. The thought of the diaries still made my pulse race, but I hadn't even had a chance to glance at them yet. This was going to be my weekend reading.

On the way home we stopped again, this time at a safe-deposit place in Baker Street where I impressed the hell out of them by paying three years' rent for a safe-deposit box in advance. I left one copy of the diaries in the newly rented box.

Then I made another telephone call to Rothschilds. 'Mr Douglas, my wife is divorcing me and is threatening to sue me for half the value of our house,' I explained succinctly.

'I am sure Mr Pendleton will be able to arrange for an effective defence of that suit,' he replied.

'No, you don't understand, I don't want to defend it. I want to pay her. Not quite half mind you, but what I have estimated is her share, which is seventy-two thousand pounds by my calculations, and that's being very generous.'

'I understand.'

'Any problem about getting that kind of money?'

'None at all.'

'Today, perhaps?'

'Certainly.'

'In two cheques, each for thirty-six thousand, made out to Julia Parker?'

'If you wish. I will send them to you by messenger. Where are you?'

'I'm in my taxi, but I'll be at home in about twenty minutes.'

'He'll be with you in about an hour.' He didn't even ask: What taxi? That's discretion.

And that's how easy it was to get seventy-two thousand pounds. When we got to my house, I gave Frankie the rest of the day off, and arranged to have him pick me up at nine on Monday morning. I saw him turn on his 'for hire' light as he drove off. Greedy bastard.

I made some mango tea and then sat down at my trusty Amstrad to write to my wife:

Dear Julia,

You may perhaps notice that enclosed with this letter is a cheque for thirty-six thousand pounds.

It will not bounce. It is from Rothschilds, the merchant bankers.

This sum represents half of what I consider is fairly owing to you in settlement of your claim to part of the value of this house.

I have another cheque for the same amount already in my possession. If you move swiftly towards a divorce, agreeing at every stage with the arrangements to be set out by my solicitors, I will send you the other cheque on the very day that the divorce becomes absolute.

On the other hand, if you fight me, create delays, dispute the amount I am offering or in any other way cause trouble, I will tear up the second cheque, and you will be faced with a long, extremely expensive and bitterly defended alternative route for the money through the courts.

Be smart. Take the money and sprint out of my life.

Your former loving husband,

Horatio T. Parker.

I had proposed to Julia while drunk, she had accepted while in shock, and we had each gone through with the wedding in the belief that to cancel would lead to the other's suicide. About a year after we first started bickering and sniping, which is to say about a year after the marriage, she met Gareth, the dark-eyed Welshman who could do things to her carburettor and differential that no other man or mechanic had ever done before. I came home one night to find her things gone and the proverbial note on the mantelpiece telling me she wasn't coming back. The pain and anger I felt at having been deserted was quickly dulled by the relief I experienced from her absence.

The messenger from Rothschilds arrived just before five o'clock, enabling me to post one of the cheques with the letter to Julia before the last collection at the sub post-office around the corner. With a bit of luck she would get it in the morning.

It was shortly after five o'clock, and my first weekend as a millionaire yawned emptily in front of me. I decided to be bold, and I looked up Andrea Ferris's telephone number. I dialled, but there was no answer. Probably gone out with Mick Jagger or Sting, I thought.

Then I rang British Airways. The Concorde flight to New York was due to leave at seven o'clock, they told me, and I could still catch it if I was at the airport shortly after six. I threw a few things into an overnight bag, managed to find a cab in Mansfield Road, and just made it before the gates closed for the flight.

In Manhattan I indulged myself. I stayed at the Waldorf Astoria, ate in fancy restaurants, went to a Broadway musical, nearly got mugged in Times Square, looked in on four art galleries, bought clothes until my credit cards showed signs of melting, read Monique Karabekian's diary and then flew back on Concorde on Sunday night.

It was the first time I had ever done anything like that and everything was exciting. Everything except for Monique Karabekian's diary. That, as New Yorkers would have put it pithily, was a crock of shit.

CHAPTER 6

Monique Karabekian's diaries were exquisitely boring. I don't know what I had expected to find, but whatever it was, it just wasn't there. There were no revelations about her life or Halifax's, no scandals, no sex, no thoughts even, let alone any philosophical examination of the human psyche.

The entries, handwritten in an obsessively neat script, each on its own half page, and always in the same colour ballpoint pen, read as follows, to give you an example at random:

> *Monday, June 8, 1986.* Malcolm still in Brussels at EEC Commission meeting. Rehearsing outdoor scenes for *Hot Hotel*. Taxi arrived late. Lots of people watching. Had lunch with John Schlesinger. Rehearsals ended 4.36 p.m. Wrote letters to family. Watched *Singing Detective* on TV.
>
> *Tuesday, June 9, 1986.* Malcolm back from Brussels. Rehearsals for outdoor scenes for *Hot Hotel* continuing. Taxi on time. Had lunch with film crew. Rehearsals went on late. Malcolm not required in Commons. Dinner with Malcolm at Camden Brasserie (calves' liver).

It was exactly what we all, in our most cynical moments, fear a film star's life might be like—and it was all like that, except that some parts were even more boring than others. She mentioned people she went out with or had meals with but never wrote a word about them. Never a hint of a feeling about anything or anyone. No interpretation or evaluation of events. No indication of depression or elation.

I had forced myself to read the lot, nearly a hundred pages of the stuff, containing some sixteen hundred similarly short entries, and apart from the agony brought on by the sheer tedium, my overall feeling was puzzlement as to why she kept a diary like this in the first place. I imagined her making these entries meticulously every night and I wondered about her.

I had always wondered about her, ever since that day I saw her arriving at our primary school clutching her mother's hand, an expression of sheer terror on her face. She was painfully thin, but my memory includes a note of how beautiful she was even then, when she was nine years old. Big dark eyes peering out vulnerably at the world, and a soft Armenian accent.

Years later, at secondary school I became desperately, though distantly, obsessed with that face, but it took me nothing short of five years to summon up the courage to ask her out. But eventually inertia was transcended by one supreme burst of courage one Friday afternoon. With a wildly beating heart I somehow managed to ask her whether she would come to the cinema with me the following evening. And she said 'Yes', just like that, without even appearing to consider the matter.

No seventeen-year-old ever prepared a body more thoroughly for a date than I did that Saturday. It was washed, scrubbed, powdered and even subtly perfumed. Its fingernails were clipped, hair shampooed and conditioned. Its teeth were flossed (twice, just in case), and it was then adorned with clothing chosen after hours of tortured doubt.

Monique, I remember, was wearing a long and subtly embroidered Afghan sheepskin coat, the sort of thing kids had stopped wearing four or five years before, but which she bore with a grace and confidence not expected from a sixteen-year-old. She was also wearing lots of dark eye make-up, and she was heart-stoppingly beautiful.

The date, however, came close to disaster. My mistake was a surfeit of ambition. I should have taken her half a mile up the road to the cinema in South End Green and then to the coffee bar on the corner of Pond Street where the old men played chess until the early hours. But I had delusions of grandeur and took her on the No. 24 bus to the West End to see some popular epic film of the day whose name and plot escapes me now, but which went on for hours.

When we finally emerged from the cinema, I realized to my crippling horror that we had missed the last bus back to Hampstead. I prayed for swift death.

'I'll phone my father to come and fetch us,' she said.

I had seen her father a few times, a huge smouldering man with a swarthy complexion, piercing black eyes and the most enormous black moustache I had ever seen. The idea of him coming to our rescue was so horrific that my stomach heaved at the very thought.

'No,' I gasped, 'we'll take a taxi.' But I had spoken before checking with the treasury department. A frantic search revealed the sum total, gleaned from wallet and trouser pocket, and including a coin discovered in the lining of my jacket, was one pound note and forty-two pence.

Monique stood behind me when I approached a cab at the rank in Leicester Square. 'How much would it cost to go to Hampstead,' I asked the driver. He summed me up in an instant, and he said:

'Two pounds.'

'I've got one pound forty-two,' I said, trying to look appealing.

'Owrl right, ge' in,' he said grumpily, and my heart sang. I gave him the money. That, of course, was a mistake.

In the taxi, I felt the evening had been retrieved by the skin of its teeth, and I relaxed a little, trying to look as if I frequently took my women home by taxi. Her hand was on the seat, and I astonished myself by putting my own on top of it. I was even more astonished when she didn't take hers away, and I wondered if my ribs could take the battering they were getting from my heart. Would it last? I asked myself.

Of course not. The taxi-driver stopped suddenly outside Chalk Farm tube station. 'That's it,' he said.

'What?' I leaned forward, appalled.

'That's as far as you get for what you paid me.'

Ten seconds later we were standing on the pavement and he had driven away, leaving us with a lengthy uphill walk home.

Even worse, we were no longer holding hands.

I was mortified. Apologies tumbled abjectly from my tormented soul as we started walking. I hated that taxi-driver. I had memorized his driver number and vicious fantasies were passing through my mind about how I could wreak terrible revenge on him. I would find out where he lived, I would wait until he had forgotten all about me, then I would lure him to a lonely place and torture him. Or maybe just kick him to death if I happened to be in a good mood.

Monique, who hadn't said anything since the taxi stopped, walked in silence for about half a block, and then gently took my arm. 'It's not serious,' she murmured.

How to describe the way anxiety ebbed and fled swiftly before the glow of heat that emanated from that part of my arm held by her fingers? Is this the relief and euphoria heroin addicts experience a second after the drug rushes up the vein towards the heart and brain? I put my arm around her, she leaned her head against my shoulder, and we continued walking. The sky was clear, and the stars were brilliant. There was just enough of a cold breeze to keep Monique pressed closely to me, and I called on God to bless that taxi-driver. I think I may even have had tears of ecstasy in my eyes.

Her house was dark and quiet, and as she opened the door quietly with her key, warm air scented with the spices of exotic cooking touched my skin. She was standing in that dark hallway, the light from a distant streetlamp playing softly on her face.

'You can kiss me but don't touch my breasts,' she whispered. The words are carved as if on tablets of stone in the most secure reaches of my memory, and I can to this day still hear her voice saying them, and see the precise movement of her mouth and lips when she said the astonishing words: 'my breasts'. I had hardly dared think of them, let alone hope to encounter them.

I was not entirely innocent sexually. I had done my share of kissing and fumbling, but nothing had prepared me for the intensity of kissing Monique Karabekian. It was partly the extraordinary softness of her lips, the way they gently searched mine in tiny nibbling movements and then opened slowly as if giving access to her entire body, her tongue meeting mine in delicate flurries of exploration, and then expressing the full passion of our embrace. Then she would break away, look deeply into my eyes and then start again, perhaps touching the corners of my mouth with her lips, brushing them across my cheeks and, just once, kissing the deliciously sensitive part of my neck which made me shudder and hold her even more tightly.

It was also the way she embraced me with her body, her hands never still, moving from my face to my shoulders, fingertips pressing into my back and then moving to another spot, and finally her hands in the small of my back, pulling my body into hers with a boldness and sensuality of contact entirely new to me.

I drowned in that embrace. My lungs filled with the musk of excitement, and when it was over and the oxygen came flooding back, my body coursed with the knowledge of adult sexuality.

Monique whispered: 'Thank you,' in my ear and led me by the hand back to the doorstep. One small squeeze of my hand, one shy smile that was echoed in her eyes, and then the door was closed and I could hear her quiet footsteps disappearing into the body of the house.

I went home with explosions of memory blasting my mind. And I lay in bed wallowing in sensations of love and tremors of desire which focused again and again on my aching groin. It was many hours before my body was washed with relaxation and I slept.

On Sunday morning I telephoned but she was out. I left a message with her mother but she did not ring back. I telephoned again in the evening, but was told she was still out. Warning bells tinkled somewhere in my being, but I ignored them, and it made Monday morning's hatchet blows that much harder to bear.

It started as I approached the school in the morning. A group of girls at the gate dissolved into a jelly of giggling and sniggering as I passed, and one of them called out: 'Want to borrow taxi fare, Parker?' Part of me died. Well, that part of me that would have died anyway with the cynicism of adulthood a few years later.

The entire school seemed to know the whole story. I faced everything from catcalls to sincere commiseration from my friends. At one stage I passed Monique in a corridor. I stopped, but she just gave me a small, triumphal smile and disappeared quickly.

That afternoon an envelope was pressed into my hand by a breathless first year who giggled and ran away. I didn't have to look at it to know who it was from. I put it in my pocket, and it was only much later in the secure privacy of my bedroom that I slit it carefully open. It was very short, and written on a piece of paper torn from a school exercise book in that precise handwriting that I would later come to know so well. It read: 'Why didn't you touch my breasts? I wanted you to touch me.' The pain mingled with frustration and left me dry-eyed and sleepless.

I never spoke to her again at school but later I followed her career with interest, and without rancour; I think I learned eventually that we mortals have no right to touch the gods who feed our fantasies.

The fact that I had kissed Monique Karabekian became part of my own private mythology, and something I never mentioned to anyone at all. Of course, when she married Halifax we began to meet at various local functions at which she would be playing the role of the MP's wife while I was the local reporter. On the very first such occasion she made a point of approaching me, greeted me as a long lost school chum, and chattered gaily for a few moments about common acquaintances, schooldays and the old neighbourhood. She was defining the ground on which we were to walk, and I accepted it gracefully. From then on we were always distantly friendly, and often found ourselves together on the sidelines while Halifax made his speech, planted his tree, cut his ribbon, crowned the fancy dress winner or presented his cheque.

My name did not appear in her diary. The last entry was written on the Tuesday night:

> Malcolm in West Germany. Weather bad. Had lunch with Oliver Trippier and his wife. Read Oliver's latest script. Will probably accept.

Trippier was one of the giants of the film industry. Monique had been about to reach the very top.

CHAPTER 7

Bloch was pleased with me. I could see that because it was half past eleven on Monday morning and he had not yet been irritable with anyone, especially me.

He was delighted with the interview with Halifax and utterly chuffed about the diaries. He didn't care that there was nothing in them. 'The point is,' he said patiently, 'that we have Monique Karabekian's diaries, and the whole of fucking Fleet Street hasn't.

'We'll run little extracts of the best bits, implying that we are leaving out everything sexy, interesting or scandalous only because this is a family newspaper. It will be a sensation,' he said happily. Nothing, but nothing, pleased him more than kicking the big boys in the balls, and he did it with a pleasing regularity.

It had been a good morning so far. Frankie had been outside the house on the dot of nine o'clock with a cheerful greeting and a pile of textbooks at his side. The sun was shining brightly with a hint of real warmth, and Andy

Ferris had given me a kind of smile when I winked at her. Best of all, there had been no telephone call from Pendleton or anyone else to say that the news of my inheritance had been an unfortunate mistake.

Emboldened by spring sunshine and Bloch's approval, I approached Andy's desk. 'What are you doing for lunch?' I asked, in a casual sort of way, only half aware of the precise way her sensual fingers danced around the keyboard of her computer terminal.

'Why, Parker? Have you run out of money again?' Her cheerful reply made me cringe. There had indeed been an occasion when I had taken her out for a lunch-time drink only for me to discover I had no cash on me. The difference between us was that I was trying hard to forget the incident, and she just loved remembering it.

'No, I've come into a little, as a matter of fact, and I've definitely got some of it on me. So, how about lunch?' I said.

'What are you offering, Parker? Tempt me.' What a delicious idea, and how I wished I did.

'Well, how about the Villa Ruffino, in Highgate? We could start with whitebait, or prosciutto with black pepper and melon, and proceed to something exotic like an enormous zuppa di pesce, all washed down by the most presumptuous yet succinct dry white wine imaginable. Perhaps one of those slightly fizzy Lambruscos.' That did the trick. I could almost hear her salivating.

'Wow, you sure know how to tempt a girl.'

'Ah. Tempting is easy, it's the conquering that's difficult.'

'Really? You look like you know a thing or two about conquering.'

'Looks can be deceiving,' I said darkly, in a deep voice.

She grinned. 'OK, you've got a date. Give me a shout at one o'clock.'

I floated back to my desk and rang Alfio at the Villa Ruffino. I told him that if he could give me that isolated table for two in the alcove I would give him the biggest tip he had ever seen. That he had ever seen from me, that is.

Then I rang Sergeant Theodore Bernstein at Hampstead police station.

'Bernstein.'

'Theo, it's me, Parker.'

'Oh Lord,' he intoned, Job-like, 'what have I done to deserve these afflictions?'

'Afflictions? What afflictions? Don't I always mention your name in the paper? Don't I always tip you off about crime and skulduggery?'

'Yes, like last time,' he said bitterly. I had to admit he had a point there. I had told him that I had heard from a very unsavoury contact of mine that there was to be a raid on a sub post-office in Willesden. Theo had organized a large ambush complete with all kinds of Scotland Yard types, many of them armed to the teeth, and we had all hung about shivering on the coldest day of the year, while the raid had gone down unmolested—in Harlesden. I had misread my shorthand notes. Willesden, Harlesden, it was only one syllable different, I had explained to the livid throng of coppers.

'Come on, Theo, don't bear a grudge. Doesn't the Talmud tell you to forgive and forget or something?'

'What the Talmud tells me, Parker, is why God gave us fingers which are tapered at the ends.'

'Why?' I asked, intrigued.

'So that we can insert them in our ears if we believe we are about to hear something improper. Something tells me that's what I should be doing now.'

'You don't want to hear about the diaries, then?' From the depth of the silence that followed I knew I had him solidly hooked.

'What diaries?' he said eventually. I knew Halifax couldn't have told the police about the diaries because he had still had them. The police would have taken them away immediately.

'Monique Karabekian's diaries.' There was another deeply silent pause.

'You have Monique Karabekian's diaries?'

'Yep.'

'Parker, if I find that you've—'

'Halifax gave them to me,' I interrupted.

'Bring them down here immediately!'

'Sure, Theo, as soon as you answer a few questions I have here about the murder.'

'I said now, Parker.'

'Theo, please don't take this as a threat, but unless you cooperate with me you are going to have to go for a court order to get those diaries. We obtained them perfectly legally, and they can be hidden away very securely indeed. On the other hand, you can have them by lunch-time if you will only answer a few simple questions.'

'Go ahead then,' he said, with a long-suffering tone in his voice.

'The first question is: what was the result of the post-mortem?'

'Death was by strangulation, no question about that, and took place some time between two and four o'clock in the morning. They can't be more accurate than that.'

'Any other injuries?' I asked.

'Yes, the pathologist said there were bruises on her back and on the back of her head, which would be consistent with the murderer sitting or lying on her and pressing her down towards the floor. The pathologist also said that considerable force had been used, much more than would have been necessary.'

'Had she been raped?'

'He's pretty sure that there was no rape. There were none of the injuries and bruising associated with rape. But she had had sexual intercourse no more than two or three hours before she died, no doubt about that.'

'But Halifax only got back the following morning,' I noted.

'Yes, Parker, even us policemen managed to work that out.'

'Do you know anything yet about her movements on the Wednesday night?'

'The film company tells us that she left the studio at about six o'clock in the evening, using their regular minicab company. We've checked with the cab firm, and established that she went straight home. The doorman who was on duty at the flats, man by the name of Jackson, says she arrived home at about half past six, and he did not see her go out again.'

'OK, Theo, I'll drop in the diaries just before lunch.'

'You're too kind.'

We didn't need the originals. We had photographed them thoroughly, and we had the copy I had made. There was also my own copy that nobody knew about stashed away in the safe-deposit box. And it was always wise to cooperate with the police.

'Only one thing, Theo.'

'What's that?'

'Not a word is to be said about the diaries to the other newspapers until Friday when we've already come out. Not a single word. Not a hint, even. OK?' He agreed, reluctantly.

Just before one o'clock I went over to Andy's desk and stood behind her. She was writing something and I had to say her name twice before she realized I was there and looked up.

'Oh, sorry, I was concentrating.'

'Lunch?' I said cryptically.

'Let's go. I'm hungry and I can hear an Italian meal calling me.' She smiled again, and I almost missed watching those tiny creases around her eyes get to work. Going down the stairs, she asked: 'Is your car working for a change, or should we go in mine?'

'It's OK, I've got a taxi waiting outside.' Her eyebrows went up, and her eyes widened slightly and I got a full blast from the icy green lasers which turned my knees to jelly.

We drove via the police station where I left the diaries for Theo Bernstein and then Frankie dropped us outside the restaurant. I was about to go in through the door when I noticed that Andy was still standing on the pavement, a puzzled look on her face. 'Parker, you haven't paid the driver,' she said.

'Ah, yes, well . . . he's going to wait for us,' I said taking her arm soothingly. 'I told you, I came into a little money.'

'And no doubt you're trying to spend it all in one day,' she said.

'Not quite.'

Alfio had done his stuff magnificently. The table in the alcove was ours and in the middle of it was a slender glass vase with three superb red roses, at the very peak of their brilliance.

'Ooh,' said Andy, 'I didn't know this was going to be a *romantic* lunch.' I let the remark pass because I couldn't think of any suitably witty reply.

Andy ordered the prosciutto with melon with grilled trout to follow. I had the fish soup, without a starter. I also ordered a £42 bottle of wine, a very fancy vintage Château Mersault. Alfio coughed nervously, and discreetly pointed to the price on the wine list. I patted his hand reassuringly and winked at him, but he still looked worried as he walked off.

The food was good and the wine, as was to be expected, was excellent. During the meal we chatted inconsequentially about this and that and one thing and another, the way people do who don't know each other very well. She told me a bit of her background, about her family, where she'd worked before. She even squeezed a few personal details out of me. I liked everything I heard, and everything she did. I loved the way she held the cutlery, almost with the tips of her fingers; the way she lifted a wine glass and looked at me over the top while she sipped. I found myself fixating on the movements of her lips, wondering perhaps . . . whether . . .

'Parker?' She was looking at me strangely, and I realized that she had been saying something while I was day-dreaming about her mouth, and I had missed it.

'Sorry, I wasn't paying attention. What did you say?'

'For a minute there I thought you had gone into a trance.

I was saying that it's nearly two o'clock and we'd better be getting back. I've got a lot to do this afternoon.'

I paid the bill with a credit card and left Alfio a fifteen-pound tip in cash. When we came out the sun was shining warmly and we were both feeling mellow from the food and wine. I could see Frankie's cab parked a little way down the road and we started walking towards it. Andy slipped her hand behind my arm, just above the elbow, and it felt like a red hot poker. I tried not to scream. Then she leaned over and pecked me on the cheek.

'Thank you, that was lovely, and I didn't even have to pay!'

I spent much of the rest of the afternoon remembering what it felt like when her hand slid behind my arm and those ever so slightly damp lips touched my cheek. I think I also did a little work on the obituary, the story about Monique Karabekian's diaries and my interview with Halifax. I couldn't get the picture of his haggard face out of my mind. The man, usually so poised and assured, had looked positively haunted and desperate, and I felt sorry for him.

Then, at about five o'clock, my telephone rang. It was Theo Bernstein at the police station. 'Those diaries are very boring. Nothing there at all, is there?'

'Oh, you noticed,' I replied.

'The Talmud tells us to engage not in much gossip with women. Now I know why.' He sounded really tired.

'Theo, you didn't ring me to tell me the diaries were boring. I know that already.'

'No,' he said, 'I telephoned to tell you that we have just arrested Malcolm Halifax.'

'WHAT?' I know it sounds corny, but that's what I shouted. Everyone in the office stopped work; they were all looking at me. 'Why, for heaven's sake?'

'Because he murdered his wife,' Theo said, with a kind of mock patience. He was enjoying this, getting me back for the way I told him about the diaries.

'Stop pissing about and tell me what's going on,' I said,

the frustration spilling out into my voice. There was a silence. Then I added: 'Please, Theo.'

'Well, on Saturday morning there was an anonymous telephone call to Scotland Yard from a man with a heavily disguised voice who suggested that we check with Lufthansa about which plane Halifax travelled on.

'I have to admit that we had not actually checked that. We had taken him at his word when he said he had caught the early morning flight to Heathrow, because we'd actually seen him arrive home, or that's what we thought anyway. But when we checked, the airline confirmed that he had caught the ten-fifteen p.m. flight the night before, which had landed at Heathrow just before midnight.

'The next step was that we put out a call to all radio-controlled cabs asking them to report if they had been to Halifax's address and we had three responses. One was from the driver who picked him up after he got out of the airport at about twelve-fifteen a.m. and took him home. Another tells us he was flagged down by a man of Halifax's description outside Park Vistas at approximately five-thirty in the morning and then took him to the airport, where he dropped him at Terminal Three. Finally, the driver of the taxi that we saw him arrive home in confirms that he picked Halifax up outside Terminal Three, and not Terminal Two or One, as one might expect if he'd just flown in from Europe. The first two drivers are due to look at him in an identity parade tomorrow morning, but there's not much doubt about it all.'

I was beginning to get over my astonishment and my brain was beginning to work again. No wonder Halifax had looked gutted when I saw him. He had murdered his wife and had not slept at all that night and probably not much the next, since he knew he had made a host of mistakes and that the police would close in on him in days, as soon as they started checking things.

'So you think Halifax came home at about one a.m. on the Thursday morning, killed Monique, took her body to the Heath, went back home, picked up his luggage again, caught a cab to the airport, and then took another one back home, arriving to discover police all over the show and his poor wife murdered, whereupon he throws a wobbly and breaks down? I'm not surprised, after the night he'd had.'

'That's the current theory.'

'It sounds logical, Theo, but isn't it all too circumstantial?'

'There's more. Stop talking and listen. The Talmud tells us: "Silence is good for the wise; how much more so for the foolish."'

'OK, get on with it. Enough of this folksy wisdom.'

'Our forensic investigators are now sure they have a positive match between one of the tyre impressions found near to where the body was dumped, and the offside front tyre of Halifax's Jaguar.'

'Whew!' I said.

'There's more. When we searched the car we found traces of human fæces in the boot.' Theo sounded triumphant. I couldn't think why.

'What's the significance of that?'

'Well, a real crime reporter would know that one of the body's responses to the extreme trauma of strangulation is, ultimately, a sudden relaxation of all the muscles, including the sphincter of the anus, and . . . well, the bowel evacuates. The tests are being carried out at the moment, but we're pretty sure that the fæces will turn out to be hers.'

'Wow!' I said.

'There's more. When we searched the car, we also found the missing jewellery.'

'What missing jewellery?'

'The missing jewellery we didn't tell you irresponsible scribblers about at the press conference. Our hope was that somebody might start trying to fence it if there wasn't a big hullabaloo going on about it in the press—and thereby lead us to the murderer.'

'Where did you find it?'

'It was sprinkled around the spare wheel well, underneath the tyre.'

'How much jewellery?'

'About a million pounds' worth.'

I had already said 'Whew!' and 'Wow!' so I just whistled. 'It looks like a fair cop, guv'nor, you seem to have got him bang to rights. What happens next?'

'At the moment he is, as they say, helping us with our inquiries, but he'll be charged later tonight and will appear at Hampstead Magistrates' Court tomorrow morning for his first remand. That's about it, for now.'

'Theo, thanks for ringing me, I really appreciate it. But would you do me one favour?'

'What's that?'

'Don't let any of this leak out to the media.'

'Fuck off, Parker.'

'Does it say that in the Talmud?' He had the grace to laugh before he hung up.

I told everyone in the office what had happened, and then I headed for home. I was looking forward to a hot bath, a light supper and an early night, but it was not to be. I opened the front door, and then nearly went out again because I thought for a second that I'd come into the wrong house. But only for a second. I knew with a growing feeling of foreboding that this was indeed my house, and that the person or persons who had ransacked it had been experts.

It didn't take long to establish that it hadn't been a burglary, because nothing had been taken. The hi-fi was still there, as was the television, video-recorder, radio, camera and other valuables. The place had been searched, and searched thoroughly by someone who had not been content to open drawers, but had also felt constrained to empty them out on to the floor. Every cupboard had been turned out, every box overturned, every bookshelf emptied, every chair seat slashed. The sofa had been disembowelled and the bed looked as if it had been attacked by a crazed knifeman who had a particular hatred for down-filled duvets. Someone had spent the afternoon here, at least. It was a scene of feathers and devastation through which I picked my way carefully towards the telephone.

It was only when I was actually dialling the police number that I began to wonder what it was that the intruder had been searching for. Luckily, Theo Bernstein was still there, and although he grumbled a bit he agreed to come round immediately with CID officers, and while I waited for them to arrive I made two deductions.

The first was the method of entry. The intruder had climbed the locked gate which shielded the passage around the side of the house and had then simply kicked in the back door. The door jamb was in splinters.

The second was the realization that whoever it was had been looking for the diaries. It clearly hadn't been an opportunist burglar, and I couldn't think of anything else that I owned that anyone else could have wanted. For a moment I thought about the likes of Woody Corkery and the other Fleet Street vultures who could quite easily have done this sort of thing, but then I decided against it. They would have first tried offering me money—had they known about the diaries. But I couldn't think of anyone else to suspect.

Nor could Bernstein and his men, when they arrived. One of them dusted here and there and took fingerprints, but he announced that some obvious surfaces such as door handles and stair rails had been wiped clean and he was therefore not optimistic about getting anything of any use. They wrote down details, took a statement and apologized for being unable to do much more than that. Bernstein thought about my theory about the diaries, and then rejected it.

'I can't believe anyone would go to such trouble to get those diaries. There is nothing in them that would interest anyone, let alone incriminate them,' he said. But I wasn't so sure. I had a gut feeling about it.

Anyone who has ever had a break-in will confirm that after the initial alarm about stolen goods, the enduring reaction of the victim is one of shock at the invasion of one's private personal space, the violation of home territory, the penetration of security. I was sitting in the remains of an armchair about an hour after the police had left, experiencing the peak of that violated reaction, when the telephone rang. It was Andy Ferris.

'I'm phoning to thank you for a lovely lunch,' she said cheerfully. But I just wasn't up to replying in the same vein.

'Thanks, you needn't have.' I tried not to sound too depressed but the mournfulness crept through.

'Hey, Parker, what's wrong?'

'I've just had a burglary, I mean a break-in. The place is in a bit of a mess . . . nothing stolen though.'

'You OK? You want some help?'

'No, really . . .'

'I'll be there in five minutes.' At another time I would have whooped for joy at news like that, but on this occasion I just felt listless.

Almost exactly five minutes later she was there, ringing the doorbell. Her eyes widened when she saw the mess, and when she saw my face, she took my hand. 'Oh how awful. You must feel terrible.' Actually, I was feeling a lot better, with my hand in hers.

'I've had better moments.' We picked our way through the debris to the kitchen where, after some searching for the kettle, cups and other things, I managed to put together two cups of tea. Andy asked me the same questions I had been asked by the police, but more sympathetically, and after a while I realized that I wasn't feeling so bad at all.

'Let me help you clear up a little,' she offered.

'It's really not necessary, I'll do it tomorrow.'

'Well, let me help you straighten out your bedroom at least, so you've got somewhere to sleep.' There was no arguing with her. She almost pushed past me and we went upstairs, but we both paused at the entrance to the bedroom. The scene really was quite spectacular, with mattress stuffing everywhere, feathers drifting around, and the floor knee deep in clothing, books and everything else which had just been tossed from the cupboards and drawers.

'Oh my goodness,' she gasped, and turned towards me. She was so close I couldn't stand it any more and I reached out for her. She came to me in a single flowing motion and as my arms wrapped themselves around her she put her head on my shoulder and her arms went around my waist. It was the most perfect fit; it was almost as if we had been made as templates for one another, so exactly did our two forms find corresponding contours in each other. My face was buried in her silky hair which smelled faintly of conditioner. She turned her face up so that I could kiss those lips I had thought about all through lunch.

We made love on the slashed mattress, beneath the shredded duvet, our activities sending sending flurries of the best goose down into the air until the room resembled one of those glass things old aunts give one for Christmas which cause snowstorms when you turn them upside down. And I'm damned if the earth didn't move.

After a few minutes, when my breathing was beginning to show signs of returning to normal, I dared to open one eye. It had not been a dream. Andy Ferris was indeed there, next to me.

'You run the bath, I'll get the champagne out of the fridge,' I suggested softly.

'Mmmmm, yes,' she murmured in my ear.

I threw a piece of clothing on, and went downstairs where I searched through the wreckage and prepared a tray with a bottle of champagne, glasses, a candle, and some wholewheat crackers topped with smoked salmon, ground black pepper and lemon juice. The sort of thing I always keep in the fridge for just such an emergency.

When I got upstairs Andy was already running hot steamy water into the bath. I poured in an overdose of bubble bath solution and we got in as it foamed up enthusiastically. I turned the light off, and lit the candle, and in the mellow flickering light we fed each other sips of Dom Perignon and nibbled smoked salmon on cream crackers.

We were both lying facing the taps, Andy leaning back on my chest, with the warmth, the soapiness and the mistiness of the air in the bathroom creating a special soporific atmosphere in which we whispered to each other.

'That wasn't bad, for a crime reporter,' she said.

'Not bad? C'mon, woman, be more specific. How did I score?' I demanded.

'Twenty-two.'

'What do you mean, twenty-two? Twenty-two out of what?'

'Aha! That's the big question. You'll just have to try harder, and look for the answer.'

'Where should I look?' I asked.

'Everywhere,' she murmured. So I started looking then and there, and trying harder too.

A lot of water spilled out of the bath.

CHAPTER 8

I couldn't believe it. She was still there the next morning when I woke up a few minutes before the radio turned itself on at eight o'clock. I watched her breathing gently, one arm locked around the edge of the duvet, her shoulder rising and falling with her chest and her eyelids flickering silently as she dreamed her last dream of the night. Then I threw caution to the winds and I put my lips to that special place where the neck meets the shoulder and I kissed her awake.

Her eyes opened without consternation and they focused on me with dreamy recognition. The sun was forcing its way past gaps in the curtains and light caught the flecks of those translucent green corneas. She smiled.

But then she got up, moving with the unsure modesty of being in a new lover's house, quickly picked up her clothes and went into the bathroom. I heard her use the lavatory and wash her face and two minutes later she was back in the room, dressed but looking slightly crumpled. 'I'm going home first, to change. I can't go to work like this. I'll see you there later.'

I shook my head. 'No. I'm going to take one of the days off that I'm owed and clear up this mess. I'll ring you there later.' She nodded, and then leaned over the bed and kissed me warmly, but briefly, on the mouth. She was about to go, then she hesitated.

'Parker?'

'Yes?' She hesitated again, and then:

'Don't broadcast this.'

'Of course not.'

'It's just . . .'

'I understand.' And then she was gone. I heard her go down the stairs, and when the front door closed. Then I got up, showered, shaved and sang 'Oh What a Beautiful Morning!' in the bathroom, giving a special emphasis to the line '. . . everything's going my way!'

I had breakfast cheerfully amid the chaos, and at half past nine I telephoned Bloch at the office.

'Arnie, I'm not coming in today. I had a break-in here yesterday and the whole place is in a hell of . . .' He did not wait for me to finish.

'Are you trying to be funny, Parker?'

'I'm serious, Arnie, the house is in chaos here.'

'And what about the chaos here?' he demanded.

'How chaotic can it be? It's only Tuesday, and there's no one on holiday and in any case I'll do the Halifax remand at the magistrates' court for you—'

'I'm not talking about that kind of chaos!' he snapped. 'This place has been broken into as well! There's piles of fucking paper everywhere, all the desks have been turned over, and no one can find a fucking thing!'

I felt a chill run down my spine, and I knew that I had had been right the day before. The intruder, having failed to find what he wanted at my house had tried the office next. 'Arnie, does it look like a lot has been taken?' I asked.

'I don't think anything's been taken. That's what's so bloody strange; there's all kinds of stuff lying around that you would have expected them to take, although we're not sure yet.'

'I know what's missing,' I told him, 'and it's the only thing that's disappeared, you'll find.'

'What's that?'

'Your photocopy of the Karabekian diary.'

'Shit, fuck and damnation!' he said sweetly. There was a pause, during which I could hear him rummaging furiously through drawers and piles of papers, and then he was back, slightly breathless. 'You're right! I can't see them anywhere. But why? Who the hell would want them so bad?'

'Well, there's obviously something about them that we've missed, Arnie. But the good news, and this is for your ears only, is that I have another copy, stashed away somewhere slightly more secure than the drawer of your desk, so don't panic. What you need to do is ring Bernstein at Hampstead nick and tell him that my theory is correct. See what he says. And in the meantime I'll cover the court appearance and then go and have a look at my copy of the diary. If anything comes up, I'll let you know, otherwise I'll be in tomorrow first thing.'

'OK,' he said, and then he added, 'But I'm buggered if I'm going to clean up the mess on your desk. You'll have to do that yourself.'

'Arnie, you're a real brick.'

'Wossat? Wodgoo call me?'

'That's an English word, Arnie, spelled with a "b". Means "nice fellow".'

'OK,' he said again, and hung up.

I found a carpenter in the Yellow Pages who agreed to come round that afternoon to fix the back door and replace the lock. I stuck a chair under the door handle, reassured by the knowledge that the intruder had now found at the office what he had been looking for in my house, and would not be coming back.

Frankie had been waiting outside for me since nine o'clock, but showed no irritation when I emerged at ten to ten. Only sarcasm: 'A nice early start, eh?'

'Enough of your lip, driver. I am your paymaster, he of the moneybags.'

He didn't seem intimidated at all. 'Where to, guv? The office?'

'No, Hampstead police station.'

'Going to turn me in, then?'

'That thought becomes more and more attractive.'

We arrived at the police station, which shared a building with the magistrates' court, at exactly ten, and it was only when we got there that I realized with some consternation that I should have come earlier. There must have been a hundred or more journalists, photographers and television cameras crowded around the entrance to the court which, I knew, had only a small public gallery and one small press table.

I rushed round to the police station entrance and asked for Sergeant Bernstein. 'He's up at your office, investigating the burglary,' said the constable on the desk, who recognized me.

'Can you do me a favour, then?' I asked.

'What?'

'I have to get into the court for the Halifax remand, and there's a vast crowd of reptiles trying to get in. Take me through the police cells to the prisoners' entrance. Please,' I pleaded.

'I'll say one thing for you, Parker, you've got chutzpah,' he sighed (Bernstein's influence was everywhere). 'OK, come on,' he said, lifting the flap on the counter to allow me through.

We went through the station and down into the police cells, reeking faintly of urine and vomit. Halifax was behind one of those locked doors, I knew, and I wondered what he was feeling. Then we climbed the staircase that led directly into the well of the court and I was relieved to find that court had not started yet.

'You owe me one, mate,' the PC said.

'Absolutely,' I said. 'What's your name?'

'Turner, Mark Turner.'

'I'll remember it.' He left the way we had come.

Then the public doors were opened, and seeing the look on Woody Corkery's face when he burst through and found me already sitting on the only chair at the press table was worth more than whatever favour it was that I would end up doing for PC Mark Turner. 'How the fuck did you get in before us?' he hissed at me.

'I've been here since yesterday,' I whispered solemnly. He didn't get a chance to reply because the court officer was firmly herding all the reporters into the public benches. Then the magistrates came in and everyone had to stand up.

They called the Halifax case first, and the MP was brought up from the cells. There was a rustle of excitement in the court before he appeared, and I braced myself to see a wreck of a man.

But he was immaculate. Halifax had the kind of figure which enabled him to look well dressed in a pair of pyjamas, and on this occasion he was wearing a perfectly pressed double breasted navy blue suit, with a pale blue silk shirt and a subtly coloured paisley silk tie. The cuffs stood out exactly half an inch from the sleeve of the jacket, and the trousers broke perfectly and cleanly above shiny black brogues. He looked like something out of *Vogue*. The haunted look was gone completely, and he was as erect and confident as I had ever seen him. He stood in the dock, with strong hands gripping the rail, looking directly at the chairman of the bench as if there was no one else in the court at all.

'Your honours, I am appearing for Mr Halifax.' All eyes raced to the man on the lawyers' bench who had spoken. He was tall and cavernous, and standing there in his black suit and waistcoat, barrister's wig on his head, he looked like something out of an old black and white B-movie.

'You are . . . ?' said Peter Strand, the justices' clerk.

'Sir Harold Burton.' There was a murmur of excitement in the room. I did not recognize him, but I knew the name of one of the most famous criminal silks in the country.

And when Strand put the charge to Halifax that he had murdered his wife, etc., etc., it was Sir Harold who replied: 'My client wishes to enter an emphatic plea of not guilty.' There was a pause while the clerk wrote down the words, and then Burton astonished everyone by making an application for bail.

Chief Superintendent Harrison, who had conducted the press conference on the morning after the murder, then astonished us further by announcing that the police were prepared—because of what he described as the 'unique situation' and the standing of the accused—to waive objection to bail, providing that Halifax surrendered his passport, undertook to go on living at his stated address, reported twice daily to Hampstead Police Station, and that there was a surety in the sum of a hundred thousand pounds.

The surety was called from the waiting-room outside. He was another knight of the realm, Sir Aidan Wycherley, a well-known Hampstead property millionaire and former chairman of the Hampstead Conservative Association, who solemnly agreed to stand surety for Halifax and said he understood when Strand explained to him that he could forfeit the full hundred thousand pounds if Halifax failed to appear at his trial. Sir Harold said his client accepted all the conditions of bail, the magistrates approved the deal and the hearing was over without Halifax uttering a single word.

He and his lawyer scuttled down the stairs, and the reporters all started fighting to get out of the courtroom they had just fought their way into, hoping perhaps that Halifax would talk to them outside, or that they might be able to take photographs of him leaving. I didn't join them. I already had an exclusive interview with Halifax, not to mention Monique's diaries, and as many pictures of him as we needed.

I sat in the court, thinking, for about thirty minutes, hardly aware of the rich pageant of human life being paraded in front of me: prostitutes, shoplifters, drunks and disorderlies, people who hadn't paid their fines, and those who had been arrested for violence in pubs the night before. They were sent their various ways by the system, and the court was just beginning to hear a contested case about a driver who had refused to provide a breath specimen, when I left.

By the time I got out, there were no journalists around. Except Corkery, who had clearly been waiting for me, sitting on a bench about fifty yards down the road. He came running up. 'What are you up to, Parker? How did you get in there like that?'

'I told you already, I arrived a day early.'

'Bullshit.' Then he paused. 'OK, so you've got some influence around here. It is your patch, after all. But what else have you got? You look much too relaxed.'

'Aha!' I said mysteriously, tapping the side of my nose.

'I can make it worth your while,' he said, and he was so sincere that it didn't even sound like an attempted bribe.

'How much?'

'I could get you a couple of hundred quid if you had something good.'

'I'll tell you something,' I said seriously. 'You could offer me a hundred times that amount, and I still wouldn't give your paper shit in a sewerage farm.'

'OK, how about five hundred quid?'

'Woody, read my lips: fuck off.'

'Jeez, you middle-class Hampstead types really get up my nose! You seem to forget that four million people a day read my paper. Real people, that is, not the kind of ponces who live around here. How many of them read your pathetic local rag anyway?'

'Hey,' I said patiently, 'I have no intention of standing in the street and having a discussion with you about newspaper ethics. Right now I have something to do, so you'll have to excuse me.' At this moment Frankie, who had been parked nearby and who had seen me emerge from the court, drew up next to us. We left Corkery standing on the pavement, looking angry.

'Where to now, boss?' said Frankie.

'The safe-deposit centre that we went to on Friday.'

Using Frankie's taxi-phone I dialled the *Hampstead Explorer* number and the phone was answered, laconically as usual, by Paul McNipper, our roads and traffic expert, whose desk is next to mine.

'Allo, A would like to spik to Mees Ferris,' I said in the most outrageous guttural French accent I could muster.

'Who's calling, please?' McNipper asked, intrigued.

'Ma name ees Monsieur Jacques Legrand,' I said, pronouncing the surname with a proud flourish.

'Oh, just a moment, please,' and I knew he would report to Andy that there was a strange Frenchman on the line before putting the call through.

'Hello?' said Andy hesitantly.

'Hello, yummy lady,' I said in my own voice, and I heard her peal of laughter.

'Oh, Monsieur Legrand, I'm so pleased you telephoned!' We both knew that the whole office would be hanging on to every word she said.

'How are you this lovely morning?'

'Oh, Monsieur Legrand . . . oh, all right then, Jacques, what can I say? There have been worse times in my life,' she said.

'Things not too chaotic there after the break-in?'

'Well, goodness me, how sweet of you to say so, and I must say you people have such a lovely way of saying things. But no, things are not too bad.'

'Do you want to know why I rang, or do you want to play this game all morning?'

'Well, Jacques, perhaps not the whole morning, but it is fun, isn't it? You go ahead and ask me whatever you want.'

'I rang to say that I will be running a hot bath at six o'clock this evening, and I am inviting you to join me. Dinner may even follow.' There was a longish pause, and when she replied she sounded just a little taken aback.

'My, my, you are direct, aren't you, Jacques?'

'It's the best way to be.'

'I . . . I'm not absolutely sure, Jacques, can we leave it open?'

'Of course. There's no pressure on you at all. If you don't

arrive, I will simply eat the caviar and lobster and drink all the champagne myself. No problem.'

'Well, I must say, that is a rather tempting offer, but I'm still going to have to think about it.' Minds would be boggling in the office, I knew.

The safe-deposit centre in Marylebone was quiet and efficient, and it only took me a few minutes to get access to my box and retrieve the pile of papers that was my copy of Monique's diary. Then we headed for home.

'How good are you on the psychology of cleaning?' I asked Frankie.

'Eh?'

'I'll be honest with you. My house was burgled yesterday and the place is in a hell of a mess. I could do with some help clearing up. Then you could have the rest of the day off.' He was looking at me and shaking his head.

'You journalists! Always taking advantage.' He paused, then: 'Well, OK, I'll help out. I know what it's like. We had a burglary a couple of years ago, kids I think, and they near wrecked the place. Bastards pissed on my books. I wonder what Freud would have said about that!'

And on the way home I also telephoned Mrs de Santos, who came in every Wednesday morning for a few hours to do basic cleaning in the house. She was free and more than willing to come and help for twice her usual hourly fee.

In the end it did not take that long. Once we started to put things back on the shelves and in drawers and cupboards, there wasn't all that much actual cleaning to be done, and we were finished by about four o'clock. I would have to replace the furniture and bedding that had been slashed open, but otherwise things were pretty much as they had been before. The carpenter had arrived at about three o'clock and had repaired the back door.

Then, alone again, I made some tea, sat down at my desk and started reading Monique Karabekian's diaries again. More carefully this time.

The trouble was, reading them slowly and carefully was even more excruciatingly boring than reading them quickly.

Ploughing through the entries again made me drowsy, and I was startled when the doorbell rang.

It was a beautiful fair-haired girl with incredible green eyes who said it was six o'clock and asked was there anybody here offering a hot bath to a tired and dusty traveller. Naturally, I asked her in. Manners maketh man.

Actually, she was quite scathing when she discovered that the bath had not yet been filled. 'It seems I have been lured here under false pretences,' she complained. 'The invitation clearly stated that a bath would be run at six.'

'Well now,' I said soothingly, 'I'm sure we can think of something to do while the water is running.'

'Like what?'

'I'll think of something.'

In the end I thought up a few ideas, and Andy even added a few of her own. We got wet again, the bathroom floor got wet again, and we ended up breathing heavily on the bed again. Andy had a funny look in her eye.

'What are you thinking?' I asked her.

'I am thinking about my dinner. Caviar, lobster and champagne if I'm not mistaken.'

Oh Lord! I had completely forgotten about that part of the invitation, and I groaned inwardly as I realized that my stock was about to drop rapidly.

'Er . . . champagne I've got, but . . .'

'But what?' she demanded.

'I didn't have time to get the other stuff,' I confessed.

'You mean there's no caviar and lobster?' Her eyebrows were way up, and she was looking about as outraged as one can be while sitting up naked in someone else's bed. I decided to make a clean breast of it.

'No.'

'I see,' she said archly. 'It seems as if I have indeed been lured here under false pretences, you bounder.'

'Yes.'

'You cad!'

'Yes.' Then there was a pause.

'There's only one way you can make up for this unforgivable deception.'

'And that is?'

'Go downstairs and open the shopping-bag I brought with me. I suspected that you didn't have any lobster and caviar, so I picked up a few things at the delicatessen on my way here. Some pastrami, a little potato salad, taramasalata, sesame seed rolls and a bottle of Côtes du Rhône. Are you hungry?'

I began to realize that she was close to being a perfect human being.

We ate, ravenously, at the kitchen table, me in a tracksuit and Andy wrapped up in my towelling dressing-gown which was much too big for her and made her look like a little girl. We began to talk about the Karabekian murder, and I told her everything I knew. Everything. Including my own escapade on Monique's doorstep all those years ago, at which Andy laughed happily. She offered to help read some of the diaries, and I leaped at the chance to reduce that tedium, and she started to page through them while I brewed the coffee.

She had been reading for only a few minutes when she asked, 'What are these "T"s?'

'What?!' I said.

'Here, look,' she said, pointing to a small symbol near the bottom left hand corner of one of the entries. It was a capital letter T, with a circle drawn around it. 'I saw one a few pages back, but I didn't think anything of it until I saw another one.' Now my heart was racing.

'So,' I said solemnly, 'you are not merely a pretty face after all. I have read through this crap almost twice and I didn't even see them.'

'It looks like the old Telecom logo. Maybe it means that she telephoned someone.'

'No, I don't think so,' I said. 'When she telephoned people she wrote it down. It's all over the diaries, things like "phoned Malcolm", "phoned Veronica", "phoned Grandpa Pamboukian", all the way through. No, it must be something else. What we need to do is go through them all again and see if there is any pattern connected with these symbols. Are you game?'

'Try and stop me.'

It only took us an hour because we didn't have to read them all again. We just paged through the diaries, looking for the symbols and noting the content of the entry.

We found sixteen. Each was on a day she had lunch with one or other of the top names in the film and entertainment business—famous directors and producers, money men, impresarios, actors and even one journalist, a leading film critic and showbiz reporter.

They were all men. And every date was one on which Malcolm Halifax was out of town or out of the country.

CHAPTER 9

Wednesday is not usually a good day. Wednesday is deadline day, which means one has to stop messing about at the office and get everything written by five o'clock, and that means actually working hard all day.

But this particular Wednesday was a distinct improvement on most that had gone before, because my breakfast-table had been graced by the presence of Andy Ferris, and it had gone well. No, I have to say it, it had gone perfectly.

It had been with some trepidation that I had approached the table bearing coffee, toast and marmalade from the kitchen and the newspapers from the front doorstep. I put them all down and waited to see what happened. She reached for one of the papers and started to read. I poured the coffee and she felt for it absent-mindedly. The toast went cold. She did not say a single word to me. My heart soared.

My breakfasts with ex-wife Julia had always seemed to be the beginning of each new battle day, with the first volleys being fired at me in the form of bitter complaints that I seemed to find the newspapers more interesting than she was. Other women with whom I had had occasion to have breakfast had merely looked hurt and sulky at my compulsive preoccupation with the papers and the almost complete lack of conversation.

Shortly before nine she glanced at her watch and put the paper down. 'Well,' she said, 'we can't sit around here all day chewing the fat like this. The *Explorer* beckons.'

As we left the house, she asked: 'Where's that dreadful car of yours?'

'I gave . . . er . . . got rid of it.'

'About time, too. Come, I'm parked over there.' We had reached a sticky moment. I touched her arm and pointed to where Frankie was waiting with the cab. She recognized the cab, and Frankie, and her exquisite eyes widened in surprise. 'What is it with this taxi? This must be costing you a fortune!'

'No, it's just that I have this arrangement with the driver . . . actually he passes this way every morning and . . . well, he sort of picks me up.' It sounded dreadfully unconvincing.

'So I see,' she said a little coolly. I knew that, eventually, Andy would have to be told about what had happened to me. 'Oh well, it's your money, or at least I hope it's your money and that you haven't robbed a bank or something. See you at the office.' She was smiling.

In the cab, Frankie couldn't contain himself. 'That a friend of yours, Mr Parker?'

'Correct.'

'She's a lovely-looking girl.'

'Correct.'

'But you don't want to talk about it?'

'Correct.'

'You shouldn't repress your feelings, you know, one of my lecturers was saying only the other day—' I leaned over and shut the window. Frankie gave an irritatingly understanding shrug and turned the radio on, just in time for the nine o'clock news. It told us, among other things, that Halifax had resigned his Foreign Office portfolio. Surprise, surprise.

I worked hard all morning. I wrote up my interview with Halifax for an inside feature page. I wrote the obituary on Monique, extracting an interesting line or two from the diaries here and there, and I wrote the major page one news story about the arrest of the MP and the court hearing. We also slotted in the short report we had received from a freelance agency to the effect that the inquest on Monique had been opened and then immediately adjourned following evidence of identification by one of her family. I knew that our coverage knocked that of our rivals and the national papers into a cocked hat, and I felt good.

Then I went over to Arnie Bloch, told him what I had discovered in the diaries, and showed him my list of 16 names. He put down the tuna roll and whistled. Well, he tried to whistle, but it's not easy with a mouthfull of tuna roll.

'Whadjoo think?' he asked. Crumbs sprayed everywhere.

'I don't know. It could be nothing, of course. On the other hand, we know that someone was very anxious indeed to get hold of the diary, or at least a copy of the diary, and these symbols are really the only inexplicable thing about them.' He nodded, and I continued. 'And then when you look at the names they are associated with you find that it is a Who's Who of the top people in the film industry. That alone makes it worth looking into.'

'I agree, it's worth a look around. Drop everything else you're working on and get on to it.'

'I don't have anything else that I'm working on.'

'Well then, get on with it! You won't find out anything standing here, that's for sure.' Bloch was such a cutie.

'OK, Arnie, but look, there are sixteen names here, and I'm going to be moving around a lot, so you may not see me in the office for a few days.'

'That's all right, just as long as I know you're working. But listen here, Parker, I don't want to see any ridiculous expenses claims from you. They tell me you've started going everywhere by taxi . . . well, don't expect us to pay for that. There's nothing wrong with buses and tubes. And no fancy lunches either, hey?' I wondered which well-wisher had told Arnie about my taxi rides.

Before I left the office I telephoned a nearby florist and using my credit card I ordered a huge bouquet of flowers to be delivered to Andy. I also dictated the wording for the card which, I specified clearly, should be very large and should not be in an envelope. It read: 'Andrea chérie, with fondest memories of that sunrise in the desert, Love, Jacques.'

Then I rang Pendleton who said he had news for me and could I come and see him at about half past four. I said yes.

In the taxi I asked Frankie to head for Wapping, and I looked again at the list of names. Five were household names, famous film directors, including two Americans, who had made films featuring Monique Karabekian. There were four names I recognized as belonging to producers. Then there was Eduardo Adolfini, a well-known owner of a chain of cinemas who was also known to be a major film financier and rumoured to be a major mafia-type figure. There were also five top male film stars with whom she had appeared in pictures—and I was on my way to see the sixteenth name, *Sunday Times* film critic Bertrand Blake.

Bertrand Blake was the most influential film critic in the country. His column in the *Sunday Times* could make and break careers and frequently had a dramatic effect on the success or otherwise of films. He had also been given a weekly film news and reviews programme on television which had quickly achieved vast viewer attention and made him even more influential. His career had not been hindered by the fact that he had something of the look of a film star himself—he was tall, with one of those handsome, chunky, square-jawed faces on which a neat fair moustache looks very good indeed. On television he always wore tight, light-coloured trousers, cowboy boots and an open neck shirt.

We had met once, years before, and when I telephoned he had remembered me vaguely and agreed to see me at the *Sunday Times* office at half past three. We arrived at Fortress Wapping just before one, and from the taxi I called Ian Birkett, a former colleague on the *Explorer* who now worked as a reporter on the *Sunday Times.*

'How would you like a juicy steak and a good Burgundy at a City steak house of your choice?' I asked him.

'Who's paying?' Ian asked, a trifle too suspicious, I thought.

'I am.'

'In that case, such a steak sounds like an excellent idea,' he replied. 'What do I have to do for it?'

'All you have to do is emerge from the building. You will find me in a taxi and we will whisk you to the restaurant of your desire,' I said.

He emerged, we whisked, we ate, I paid. During the meal we spoke about this and that and one thing and another, as journalists do when they meet up after a period of absence. Then we took him back to the News International building where I surprised him by accompanying him to the foyer.

'What's up?' he asked, that suspicious tone creeping back into his voice.

'I need a favour.'

'Oh yes?' He looked as if all his illusions had collapsed about his ears.

'Oh c'mon, Ian, you know there's no such thing as a free lunch.'

'One lives in hope, always.'

'Don't hold your breath,' I advised. I then explained that I was meeting Blake at three-thirty, and I asked him to let me see the *Sunday Times* cuttings file on Monique Karabekian.

He sighed, deeply. 'OK, wait here, I'll get it.'

I sat down on one of the comfortable chairs in the foyer and watched all the famous and important people coming and going. Actually I didn't recognize anyone, but they all behaved as if they were famous and important. After about five minutes Birkett was back, carrying a large green file. He put it on the low table in front of me.

'Hand it in at the reception desk when you're finished with it, and they'll send it back to the library. And Parker . . .' He paused, and I knew exactly what he was going to say. I put on my most innocent look. 'Don't . . . er, remove anything from the file on a permanent basis, OK? If you want anything they'll photocopy it for you at the desk.' I looked wounded.

'You're surely not suggesting that I would actually steal something?' I said, feigning shock. 'That is a base slander.'

'Yeah, well, it's just that I don't fully trust anyone who is working for Arnie Bloch. Thanks for lunch, anyway.' He was grinning too.

I still had an hour before Blake expected me, and I opened the file. It didn't take me long to find what I wanted because I knew exactly what I was looking for. I skipped over all the showbiz froth and all the gossipy trash from the tabloids, and I pulled out all the pieces about Monique that had been written by Blake for the *Sunday Times*. There were seventeen clippings, fourteen of which were reviews of films in which she appeared, and the other three were interviews he had done with her, and all were clearly marked with the date of the paper in which they were printed. I put the clippings into chronological order, put my feet up on the table, and started to read.

The first four were reviews of films in which Monique had played minor roles, and Blake had gone out of his way to flay her acting. In one he wrote: 'Miss Karabekian relies almost completely on body language to get her lines across; which is just as well, since no one could possibly understand what she actually says with her voice.' In another he wrote: 'The admittedly delicious Monique Karabekian was sadly mis-cast as the younger sister. She would have made an excellent statue at the bottom of the stairs.' I wondered about the effect such comments had had on the dark and impenetrable personality that was the Monique I knew.

The first interview with her was even more nasty. It was part of a general piece he had written about the scene at the film festival in Cannes about six years before. He had been sitting in a street café, surveying the promenading multitudes, and she had approached him. He wrote: 'The beautiful dark-eyed lady introduced herself as "Monique Karabekian, the actress". I racked my brains. I could remember Monique Karabekian the scantily clad wench in *Huns and Hordes*, and I knew the Monique Karabekian who had taken her clothes off so often as the chambermaid in *Hot Hotel*, and I could even recall the wooden Monique Karabekian who had been the mistress of the ambassador in *Dirty Diplomacy*. But I certainly couldn't remember any actress of that name. "I'm sorry," I said to her, "but have we met before?"' Ouch. And it got even more vitriolic after that.

But then, suddenly, his attitude towards her changed dramatically. There was another interview, this one at the time of the release of *Holding Hands*, a mushy and sentimentally romantic sex romp in which she played the passionate girlfriend of the boy who ultimately goes back to marry the girl next door, leaving Monique's character sitting, bereft, in a pub. The gist of Blake's piece was that the exquisite Monique Karabekian had finally been given a part which could use the talent which had hitherto been imprisoned in very bad roles in even worse films. Miss Karabekian's talent, he wrote, deserved to be taken more seriously by quality film-makers.

From then on, Bertrand Blake was Monique's greatest fan, and he never let pass an opportunity to praise a performance, plug her films or suggest her for parts in major movies known to be on the drawing-board. My puzzlement knew no bounds.

I went over to the desk and asked if I could use a telephone. The receptionist smiled politely and pointed me to a bank of public telephones along one wall. I called Bloch.

'Yeah?'

'It's me, Parker.'

'Yeah?'

I gave him the date of the clipping of Blake's first complimentary write-up and asked: 'See if Bertrand Blake appears in the Karabekian diaries around that date.'

'Hang on.' A minute later he was back. 'Yeah. That date you gave me was a Sunday. She had lunch with him on the Tuesday before, and there's a "T" on the entry. Halifax was in France. Why? What've you found out?'

'I don't know yet. 'Bye.' I hung up.

I went back to my table and chair and neatly put all the clippings back into the file. All, that is, except a list Blake had once published of all Monique's films and the dates on which they had been released. I took that to the desk and asked the lady to photocopy it. She smiled again and charged me twenty-five pence. No wonder Murdoch was a millionaire. Then I went back to my chair again to think. Something black and unpalatable was beginning to nudge my consciousness, and I was trying to work out what it was.

'Parker?' Blake appeared to have crept up on me while I was deep in thought. I jumped up and we shook hands. I also noticed that he was carrying a notebook. He pulled up another chair and sat down. 'I hope you don't mind if we talk here. The management is still a little paranoid about letting outsiders into the inner sanctum, especially other journalists.'

'I understand,' I lied.

'So, you want to talk to me about poor Monique Karabekian?'

'Yes.'

'Well, what have you got?' His pencil was poised over his notebook, and he was giving me that unthreatening open look with an encouraging smile attached that all journalists give to informants and interviewees. Except that I wasn't an interviewee. I had been hoping to be an interviewer.

'Me? I don't have anything,' I said, unable completely to mask my surprise.

'Well, what have you come here for?' He was clearly confused.

'Umm . . . Actually, I was hoping to ask you a few questions about her,' I said.

'Me?' This was getting a bit ridiculous.

'Yes.'

'What sort of questions?'

'Well, like for instance what you thought of her acting abilities.' My own notebook was out now, and my pencil poised.

'What's that got to do with anything? She's dead, for Christ's sake.' There was definite irritation in his voice and he had put his notebook away. 'She won't exactly be making any more movies, will she?' There was nothing charming and engaging in his demeanour now, and I wondered what his millions of fans would think if they saw him like this, his eyes cold and his lips drawn in tight, thin lines.

'I'm just interested in what you thought of her, that's all.'

'Why?' He was being defensive and I was getting nowhere. The time had come to cease beating about the bush and to take the bull by the horns, grasp the nettle, put my cards on the table, and perhaps even run my colours up the flagpole and see who saluted.

'All right, I'll try to be as direct as I can.'

'I would certainly appreciate that.' There was no warmth in his voice at all.

'It is obvious that there was a time when you did not regard Monique Karabekian as much of an actress . . . No, it was more than that, you were positively vitriolic about her performances.' He did not reply. He didn't do anything in fact. Not a muscle moved. I continued: 'And then, quite suddenly, you changed your mind about her. Miss Karabekian became, almost overnight, a woefully underrated talent in your eyes who deserved much more serious attention. It would not be an exaggeration to say that your change of direction on this subject was in the nature of a hundred and eighty degree turn.'

He still said nothing, and the cold eyes continued to scan my face. I pressed on with the punchline. 'I also happen to know that this U-turn coincided almost exactly with a lunch appointment you had with her,' and I gave him the date.

He was good, I'll give him that. There was no flicker of concern, no narrowing of the eyes, no sharp intake of breath nor even tremor of the hand. There was no reaction at all, except the one he could not possibly control. He paled, visibly.

'How do you know about this alleged lunch appointment?' His voice sounded quite normal, if cold.

'She noted it in her diary.' This made his head incline sharply.

'Diary?'

'Yes, she kept a diary in which she wrote very brief, and also very boring, accounts of her activities. It was shown to us by Malcolm Halifax, and you will be able to read all about it in the *Hampstead Explorer* on Friday.'

'What does it say about me?' And then he swallowed. It was discreet, and disguised, but it was nevertheless a nervous swallow.

'It says almost nothing. If I remember, the exact words in the entry for that day were: "Had lunch with Bertrand Blake".'

'That's all?'

'That's all it says.'

'Nothing else?' He was now very pale, and he was leaning forward a little.

'Should there have been?' I asked. He didn't answer, but he leaned back in his chair. I continued: 'There were no other words about you at all, but there was something else. At the bottom of that entry there was a symbol, a "T" with a circle around it, rather like the old British Telecom logo. Do you have any idea what that signifies?'

Again there was no apparent reaction at all. He gazed at me steadily, but I could see reddish blotches starting to appear high on his cheekbones as the skin became almost glassy. And there was a vein pulsing in his neck rather faster than it should have been. But he said nothing at all, and there was total silence for about half a minute. Then he stood up abruptly.

'I have no idea what that symbol is, and I have no intention of justifying my opinions about any actor's career to you or anyone else. I am sorry you came all this way for nothing, but had you made clear what you wanted in the first place, I would have been able to save you the journey. I have to go now. Goodbye.' There was no ranting or raving. He spoke politely but firmly, and then he strode off towards the lifts.

But after a few steps, he turned around and came back. I was still sitting in the chair. 'I will, however, warn you, Parker, to take due care about what you write about me, if you do intend to write about me, that is. If there is even a hint of impugnment of my professional judgement I will hit you with a writ for libel so fast that it will make your head spin. I hope that is clearly understood.' Then he turned again and headed for the lifts and I watched him until almost silent doors closed behind him.

Then I noticed that my own pulse was racing.

CHAPTER 10

At four-thirty, Ambrose Pendleton was waiting for me in his office with a middle-aged fat man who sat in a chair with a brown cardboard file clasped under his arms across his belly.

'This is Mr Anthony Morley, an accountant I asked to look into the question of your buying the *Hampstead Explorer*,' Pendleton said. The fat man put out his hand, without attempting to get up, and as expected it was slightly clammy. But he had a warm, dry smile, and he sort of inclined his head in a non-verbal greeting.

'Mr Morley is well known to me and we have had many

dealings in the past in which he has given us unfailingly accurate and reliable information and advice.'

'If Mr Pendleton thinks highly of you, then I'm delighted to meet you,' I said. Morley beamed. 'Please go ahead and tell me what you found out.'

'Thank you.' He had a rather high-pitched tenor voice, like many fat men. 'You know of course that the newspaper is wholly owned by Heathlands, Limited, a private company in which all the shares are held by Arthur Ernest Blackstock.'

'Yes.' I nodded.

'And of course you know that it is a very successful and profitable business with a very sound financial base and substantial assets, not least of which is the very valuable building owned by the company in the heart of Hampstead.' I nodded again. 'My inquiries at Companies House and elsewhere have revealed that the annual turnover is in the region of two million pounds, the large majority of which is generated by the sale of advertising space.

'In recent years the company has made a pre-tax profit in the region of one hundred and thirty to one hundred and fifty thousand pounds a year and it is likely that this year's figures will be around ten per cent up on last year's. Normally when one is calculating the worth of a company with a view to arriving at a figure with which to make a bid for that company, one multiplies the last available reasonable profit figure by a factor of eight or ten—although that is over-simplifying the situation somewhat.'

'Go on,' I said.

'In this case, ten times an expected hundred and sixty-five thousand pounds pre-tax profit comes to one million six hundred and fifty thousand pounds. To this must be added the estimated value of the building—around nine hundred thousand pounds, I am informed—and a sum for the considerable goodwill established by the company, say a hundred and fifty thousand pounds in this case. All that amounts to two million, seven hundred and fifty thousand pounds.' He stopped, and folded his arms across his belly again.

'That's how much you are suggesting we offer for the company?' I asked.

'That's what I estimate it should be worth, although we would naturally expect to start negotiating at a somewhat lower figure than that.'

I thought for a few moments, and then I said: 'Offer him three million for an immediate sale, and if he doesn't go for it, add another two hundred thousand to the offer, and another two hundred thousand on top of that, if necessary.'

Pendleton cleared his throat but didn't say anything. Morley looked at me shrewdly. 'I suspect you have some very good reasons for this approach.'

'Yes,' I said, 'quite a few. First, I know old Mr Blackstock well. I have worked for him for nearly sixteen years and although he is now well past retirement age and no longer plays much part in the day to day running of the business, he is fiercely sentimental about the newspaper—he absolutely loves the idea of being its owner. A straightforward offer at the market price is not going to impress him. If we are going to interest him, we are going to have to offer more than he would be expecting to be offered.

'Secondly, I believe a higher bid can be justified by the fact that the company's potential is immense. I have ideas which will increase the readership of the newspaper. I also have plans which, if I am right, will increase revenue dramatically. So in the long run, the price we are offering is fair.

'Thirdly, I have enough money not to need to see a return on the investment over the usual period of about ten years —fifteen would be fine by me. And lastly, I want it bad, and I'm prepared to pay whatever it takes.'

'You are, as they say, the boss,' Morley said. He was not mocking; just stating his compliance.

'Yes, and that reminds me—I don't want that to be known. We need to find a way of arranging things which will give me instant powers of decision-making, but which will protect me from the most strenuous inquiries that will no doubt be made by some of my colleagues in an attempt to find out who the new owner is. I don't care how you do it, as long as it's legal, but that is a fundamental requirement. The closest they can get to me is Mr Pendleton here who I know will protect my anonymity.'

'I don't see any problem with that,' said Morley, who went on to explain how it would be done. I don't remember all the many details, but the gist of it was that the paper would be owned by an offshore company registered in Jersey, which would in turn be owned by a holding company in London, and the whole arrangement would make it impossible for anyone to trace specific ownership further back than Jersey.

'How quickly can it all happen?' I asked.

'Very quickly indeed,' Morley replied. 'We can buy a limited company off the shelf in Jersey and make the bid through that almost immediately. To set up the holding company in London will only take a day or two. What do you want to call it?'

'Parker Inc. Ever since I was a kid I wanted to own a company called Parker Inc.'

'Parker Ink?' asked Pendleton. 'You mean like the pen company?'

'No, Inc. with a "c",' I said.

Morley chipped in: 'I don't see any problem with that, except that the formal name will probably have to be Parker Inc., Limited, but if that's what you want . . .'

'It is,' I said.

'What about staff?' Pendleton asked. 'I hope, for your sake, you are not anticipating that I will run the company. I know nothing about newspapers, and come to that, nothing at all about running companies.' He looked a little alarmed.

'No, all I want you to do is be the nominal managing director of the Jersey based company,' I said soothingly.

'Will you want to keep on the present general manager, this Mr Mitchell, I believe you said?'

'God forbid.' I shuddered. 'No, I have someone in mind for the job. His name is Robert Price, and he was once Mitchell's assistant on the *Explorer* before he got fed up with working for an idiot and walked out. He's running a newspaper in Tottenham called the *Gleaner*. We'll make him an offer he can't refuse, and I believe he'll come sprinting back to Hampstead, especially if he knows Mitchell has gone. He's bright, he's up to date, he was popular with the staff, and he knows the business inside out. He's exactly what I want. Perhaps you would approach him, Mr Pendleton, and offer him forty-five thousand pounds a year, say, as long as he's available to start immediately. Tell him as much as you think necessary, but my name is not to be mentioned. Let him think you are the owner. There are other changes I will want to make, but we'll leave those until the whole thing is settled.'

'Very good, I will approach him immediately. Incidentally, Mr Parker, we are in the process of registering the Edwina Llewellyn Memorial Trust with the Charity Commissioners with myself as employed director of the organization, and although that is still going to take some time, Rothschilds have said they are willing to make available whatever funds are required. So we can . . . er . . . start receiving applications for assistance. Do you have any ideas about how this trust might be advertised?'

'Leave that to me,' I said. Then I turned to Morley. 'Let's press ahead with the bid to Blackstock as quickly as possible, and let me know the instant you hear anything.'

Back in the cab, I telephoned my office and said to the reporter who answered: 'Allo, eet is ma desire to spik with Mademoiselle Ferris,' putting a heavy accent on the word 'desire'. Andy came on the line.

'Jacques?'

'It is indeed I.'

'Thank you for the flowers, my love. But listen, my little bouillabaisse—' she was getting the hang of this—'perhaps the message on the card could have been, how should I put it, a little more discreet . . .' I laughed.

'You see the flowers arrived when I was out, and there was a great deal of interest in them.'

'Ah, but it was indeed a special night in the desert,' I said.

'Yes, well, never mind that now, Jacques, I'm afraid I have to go. I need to contact one of my colleagues who is being urgently sought by the news editor.'

'Oh shit, is Arnie after me?'

'You could say that. In fact I would say that the mood here is one of passionate hysteria.'

'OK, I'll ring him in a minute. I really called to find out what you were doing tonight. I thought I could stop off and get this lobster I cheated you out of last night and we could—' She interrupted, gently.

'I'm sorry, Jacques, but I can't make it.' There was a disappointed silence from my end. 'I have another engagement.'

'Oh.'

'I'm sorry.'

'No, really, it's all right.'

'I'll see you soon.'

'Yes.' She hung up.

Then I took a deep breath, dialled the same number again, and asked for Bloch, who exploded on to the line.

'Where the almighty fucking hell have you been?' he demanded.

'Arnie, you know where I've been,' I said soothingly.

'Yeah, well, I told you to keep in touch!'

'No you didn't, Arnie. In fact I said you probably wouldn't see me for a few days, remember?'

'Well, forget that now, man, something important has come up.'

'What?'

'Halifax called again. He wants to talk to you. He's at his flat, and he wants to see you as soon as possible.'

CHAPTER 11

It was nearly six o'clock by the time we arrived at Park Vistas. But the sun was still shining that Wednesday afternoon and what had all week been glorious spring weather had received a touch of summer into its intensity.

As I got out I noticed that Frankie was looking at his watch. 'Do you want me to wait?' he asked, although the look in his eyes said: 'I hope you don't want me to wait, it's six o'clock.'

'Tell you what,' I said, 'put the meter on, and whatever it clocks up I'll cover.'

'Fair enough,' he nodded.

The same PC Piggy Plod was guarding the entrance lobby and I had this rather absurd fantasy that he had been standing there unrelieved for three days and nights because his colleagues had forgotten all about him. It wouldn't be hard. I also wondered whether his presence there was designed to keep unwanted visitors out or whether he was there to keep an eye on Halifax's movements. He didn't say a word to me, however, but just looked at me with his little piggy eyes and moved aside.

I expected to see Nathaniel Jackson at the porter's desk, but it was another man, white, middle-aged and seedy-looking. 'Where's Nathaniel?' I asked him.

'I don't know.' There was a pregnant pause, and then he said: 'It's his night off. We alternate you see.' I nodded wisely. 'You come to see Mr Halifax?'

'Yes, my name's Parker.'

'He's expecting you. Go straight up.' I did.

Once again, Halifax opened the door himself, but he looked nothing like the wasted figure who had received me on the last occasion. He was wearing an expensive-looking cream polo shirt, crisp fawn slacks and Gucci loafers. His hair was impeccably groomed, his teeth gleamed as he smiled at me, and he appeared to be perfectly relaxed. Except that there were signs of strain around his eyes—little lines I had never seen before, and dark bags below them.

'Parker, thank you for coming. Come in,' he stood aside to let me in.

We sat in that splendid lounge, and he wasted no time. 'Well, how did you get on with the diaries? Were they of any use to you?' His face was bland and inquiring, and I have to admit that I was impressed. There was no sign here of the man who had lost his wife a week before; who had probably murdered the woman; who had appeared in court the day before in front of the world's press and been charged with murder and had escaped being remanded in custody by the skin of his teeth. I began to wonder if there was a psychopathic side to his personality. Did the man feel no emotion at all?

'Not an awful lot of use, I'm afraid,' I replied. 'As you probably know, there's almost no personal information or reflection in them at all, and that's the sort of thing we were hoping for. For the obituary, that is,' I added quickly. 'But we have used some bits, and they'll be in tomorrow's paper.'

'Yes, they are rather dry and impersonal, aren't they? I gather the police have them at the moment?' I nodded. 'I wonder if they'll find anything interesting.'

I was sure, now, that he was fishing. He had noticed the 'T' symbols, probably immediately, and he wanted to know if I had as well. But I was not ready to tell him the truth about anything, and I said nothing.

'So, what do you think of all this hullabaloo?' he said, after a pause.

'To be quite honest, Mr Halifax, I don't know what to think.'

'Do you think I'm guilty of murder; that I killed Monique?' I had to give him credit for coming right to the point.

'The only thing I know is that you appear not to have

told me the truth last time I was here.' Enough of all this politeness, I thought. He hesitated for a moment, but the statement didn't faze him for long.

'Yes, it's quite clear that I have made some serious mistakes during this last week, and among the most serious was the decision to lie to the police, and to you.' Mistakes? Thundering blunders would have been putting it mildly.

'What were the lies?' Was he going to confess, I wondered.

'I'll tell you what happened.' I pulled out my notebook and when he saw it he hesitated, but only for a second. 'As you probably know, I did not take the early morning flight to London last Thursday. I came in on the ten-fifteen p.m. flight the night before which arrived at about midnight. I took a taxi from Heathrow and arrived here shortly before one a.m. I let myself in through the garage with my key.'

'Why the garage?'

'The taxi dropped me on that side of the building. I had a suitcase which I didn't feel like lugging around to the front entrance. It seemed the obvious thing to do, and I didn't think about it at the time.'

'Did anyone see you.'

'No, there was no one about at all. I took the lift straight up to the flat and let myself in.' He stopped speaking then, and flickers of emotion crossed his face. 'I came in here. The light was on. And then I noticed the light was on in the bedroom as well.' He pointed towards the bedroom. 'And the door was open.' His voice was shaking slightly now.

'When I went in, the first thing I saw were her legs. She was lying on the floor, on the far side of the bed, and all I could see were her legs. My initial assumption was that she had fainted or was ill or something, but when I went round the bed I knew it was more than that. It was like someone poured ice water down my back. When I touched her she felt cold.'

Halifax paused and swallowed. He was sitting on the white leather couch staring fixedly at the deep pile carpet, his breathing fast and shallow. 'I was on my knees next to her, and I realized quite quickly that she was dead. Her eyes were open. She was cold. She wasn't breathing. I was in shock, and I panicked.'

'Why?' I asked gently.

'I'm not sure now.' His voice was breaking. 'That's the trouble; it's easy to be logical now and consider everything calmly when it's all over. But I was in a terrible state, and I think I thought that people would automatically assume that I had killed her; perhaps because I had come home earlier than expected.' He paused until he got control again. 'If I'm honest I must admit that I also panicked about how it would look for me . . . you know, politically.'

'How did you think she had died? How did you know she had been murdered?' I asked.

'It was obvious. Her face was grimacing. Her neck was bruised and seemed to be all disjointed. And there was this terrible smell. She had . . . messed herself, you know, lost control. It was awful, and all I could think of was that I had to get her out of there; to let her be found somewhere else so that I would not be so directly involved personally. I had to distance myself from this terrible thing.'

Selfish bastard, I thought. 'What did you do?'

'Well, as you know, I made a terrible hash of the whole thing. Had I been thinking straight I wouldn't have been so stupid. Had I been thinking straight I would not have touched her and I would have called the police immediately. But I wasn't thinking straight, that's the whole point! I was in shock, and I was in a total funk. I was hyperventilating and I think I was even sort of whimpering to myself in anxiety: "Get her out! Get her out!"' I remained silent, writing down every word.

'I got some towels from the bathroom and I wrapped her up in them. Then I carried her through the flat, and down in the lift to the car park and put her in the boot. Then I came back up and grabbed her jewellery box. I suppose I thought that would make it look as if she had been killed by a burglar. No one saw me because, as you know, the lift goes directly into the garage, and in any case it was very late.

'I drove to the Heath, behind Jack Straw's hotel car park, and I put the body behind some bushes. But then I didn't know what to do with the jewellery. I couldn't leave it with the body because that would defeat the whole object of having taken the stuff, there was no point in bringing it back here, and I couldn't bring myself just to throw it away, so I stupidly hid it in the car. I put the jewel box and the towels in a rubbish bin in Hampstead, and I came back here.

'I grabbed my suitcase and walked along Prince Albert Road towards St John's Wood until I found a taxi. I went to Heathrow. I waited until I thought the flight I should originally have been on was due to arrive, and then I took another taxi. The rest you know.'

There was a long silence, during which Halifax stared fixedly at the carpet and regained control.

'Have you told the police all this?'

'Of course.'

'But they don't believe you?'

'No.'

'Do you blame them?'

He looked at me. 'No, I don't suppose so. But I'm going to have to find some way of convincing them, of proving that what I say is true.'

There was another pause, and then I said: 'Mr Halifax, supposing what you say is true—and thankfully it is not my job to decide on what is true—that still leaves us with this extraordinary mystery. How does a woman get murdered in her own home when there is no sign of forced entry, no apparent motive and a seemingly invisible murderer?' I didn't wait for him to answer. 'The last time I was here I asked you if your wife had had any enemies, and you said no. Is that still the answer?'

He stood up and paced up and down the room for about a minute while I waited patiently. Then he stopped next to the window, turned towards me and opened his mouth as if to speak. Then two things happened.

The first was that the plate glass window, and a glass-framed picture on the wall behind me, seemed to explode simultaneously, an event which was immediately followed by a flat percussive sound and the sound of glass cascading on to the floor. Halifax spun round to look out of the shattered window, and then instantly whipped around again, to look at me and the broken picture on the wall.

Then the second thing happened. Halifax seemed to jerk forward violently, and then I heard that percussive sound again. As he fell I saw that part of the front of his shirt seemed to have come away just below his right shoulder and the whole area was rapidly turning crimson.

I sat with my mouth open in astonishment, and it took me what seems now to have been an interminably long time, although it was just a second or two, to realize that Halifax had been shot.

My next thought was a surge of sheer disbelief. This sort of thing happens in films, in books and in America, not in St John's Wood, London. Not to people like Halifax; and not when people like me are around. But even as these fragments were passing through my head I was already getting up out of my seat. I ran past the shattered window, my shoes crushing glass into the thick carpet, and out through the open patio door on to the terrace and looked down. It only occurred to me later that whoever was treating Park Vistas as a shooting gallery might have been interested in more than one sitting duck, but there were no more shots. I saw PC Plod standing in front of the building, his hands on his hips, looking in the vague direction of the park. He must have heard the shooting.

'Oi!' I bellowed down at him. He looked up. 'Get up here!' Then I ran back into the flat, through the sitting-room and the dining area to the front door. I opened it so that Plod would be able to get in, and then I ran back to where Halifax was lying. Then I ran out of ideas.

He was lying face down on the carpet and I couldn't

avoid the thought that flashed through my mind that it was a shame about him bleeding into the thick white carpet. I knelt down next to him and saw that he was still breathing. It was a rasping, bubbling sound, but it was breathing. My eyes found and became riveted to the hole in his shirt at the back, just below the shoulder-blade. Then Halifax started moving, his hands and feet sort of scrabbling confusedly for purchase on the carpet and then he managed to push himself on to his side. His eyes were open and he was looking at me, a look of pale astonishment on his face.

'Hey! Take it easy,' I said. 'You're going to be OK.' But I don't think he even heard me. He was trying to speak.

It sounded like: 'Eeeee.' I reached behind me and pulled one of the cushions off the sofa and put it under his head so that he didn't have to hold it up. He was lying on his left side and now I could see the exit wound more clearly. It looked like a small crater about three inches in diameter, and there was a lot of blood welling up out of it and down the shattered shirt.

'Just try to relax, you're going to be OK,' I said.

Halifax's hand grabbed my shoulder and with strength I found surprising he pulled me towards him. 'Eeee,' he repeated, and there was a little pink froth around his lips. His eyes were burning now and he pulled me harder. I put my ear next to his lips and he spoke again. 'Key!' he said.

'Key?' He nodded feebly. 'What key?' His hand left my shoulder and flopped down on his thigh. 'In your pocket?' He nodded again, more feebly. 'You want me to take it?' His eyes glazed over and then rolled up and I could see he was unconscious. I put my hand in his pocket, met something hard which felt like a key, drew it out and put in my pocket. Then Plod came storming in. He looked at the broken window, at the glass, at Halifax lying on the carpet and me next to him and still he had to say:

'What the hell . . . !?'

'Call for an ambulance, for Christ's sake!' I shouted. 'Tell them who it is, and then call the police. Come on, move!' He moved. It took him about a minute to make the two emergency calls on his personal radio and then he joined me on the carpet next to Halifax.

'How is he? Is he dead?' he asked.

'No, he's alive and he's still breathing. As far as I can see he's been shot through the right lung.'

'We've got to stop the bleeding,' he said. I wondered why I hadn't thought of that. I didn't know what else to do, so I pulled out my handkerchief, squashed it into a ball and pushed it into the wound. Plod reached behind him, pulled an antimacassar off the sofa and pressed that down over the handkerchief. I had no idea whether that would do any good, but we couldn't think of anything else to do. There did seem to be less blood coming out now, however. On the other hand, the rasping and bubbling sound in his breathing became worse. I looked at Plod. He looked at me. We both looked at Halifax who made a gurgling and then a choking sound, followed by a feeble spasmodic tremor, and then stopped breathing.

I felt a wave of panic sweep over me, and I looked at Plod. He seemed panic-stricken, too. 'I think he's choking on the blood!' I said. 'Help me roll him on to his front.' It took a few seconds and then, praying that I wasn't doing more harm than good, I put both my hands in the middle of his back, and pushed down hard. At first nothing happened, but then a whole lot of blood rushed out of his mouth followed by some air. But when I released the pressure, nothing happened. I felt sick in my stomach, but I knew what I had to do. We rolled him over again, this time on to his right side, hoping that this way the blood would flow away from his good lung. Then I got down, held his mouth like I had once been shown a long time ago, pinched his nostrils shut, tried to forget about the blood and froth and spit, and, my own heart banging wildly in my ribcage, put my mouth on his and blew air into him. I could see the chest rise, so at least some air was going in. I started doing it rhythmically. Plod was holding Halifax's head.

'Pulse!' I gasped between breaths. 'See if he's got a pulse.' Plod felt the wrist and after what felt like an age he nodded.

'Yes! I can feel it. It's very fast and it's faint, but it's still beating.' I carried on blowing air into Halifax, letting it out, taking another deep breath and blowing it in. After a few minutes I managed to get my own panic and feelings of revulsion under control, and the process became more organized. I managed to get enough air myself to stop my own gasping for oxygen, and Plod found some paper towels in the kitchen which I used to keep Halifax's mouth clear and relatively free of blood.

I learned later that it took eight minutes for the ambulance to reach the flat from the time of Plod's call. Had I been asked how long it was, my genuine answer would have been that it was about forty minutes before those ambulance men came rushing in and took over. They quickly put a drip into his arm, and hooked him up to an oxygen ventilation system. The police arrived at around the same time, and it was only when someone had gently helped me to my feet that my own delayed reaction set in. My knees turned to jelly and my legs began to shake violently, I felt incredibly cold and I fell back on to the sofa. It was quite a few minutes before I managed to walk to the bathroom where I washed all the blood off my face and hands. Then I vomited twice, and felt much better.

I came out of the bathroom in time to see Halifax being wheeled out on a stretcher and three policemen bearing down on me. One was Theo Bernstein, one was Chief Superintendent Norman Harrison, and the third I didn't know.

'How is he?' I asked.

'He's got a collapsed lung and some broken ribs, and he's lost a lot of blood, but it looks as if he's going to be all right,' Harrison answered. 'It seems the bullet miraculously didn't hit any bones on the way in, and just passed straight through, breaking a couple of ribs on the way out. Reynolds tells me that you did well.'

'Reynolds?'

'PC Reynolds, the one who was here with you.' So that was Plod's name. Harrison continued, pointing at the third policeman: 'This is Martin Farrer; he's a firearms expert.' I nodded at him.

Theo said: 'How are you feeling, Parker?'

'A little shaky, but I'm fine.'

'Good,' said Farrer. 'We were hoping you could tell us exactly what happened.'

'Sure,' I said, but I hadn't known what I was letting myself in for. When Farrer said 'exactly' he meant 'exactly' and he took me through the minutes up to and including the shooting, demanding tiny details and forcing me to a level of precision I had never touched before. At the end we did an instant replay, with Farrer as Halifax standing at the window, and Theo taking down everything in his notebook.

They also wanted to know what I was doing there in the first place, and Harrison in particular seemed sceptical about my insistence that I had been invited by Halifax.

'Ask your PC Reynolds,' I suggested. 'He'll confirm it.'

Finally, Farrer stood with his arms crossed, thought for a few moments and then said, more to Harrison than to anyone else, 'I can't be absolutely certain exactly where the shooter was until we get some equipment up here and measure the angles exactly, but my guess is that he was in a tree over there, about two hundred yards away.

'He was obviously a professional. He didn't go for the shot on the first bullet: he used that to break the glass so there would be no chance of a deflection on the next shot. And that, ironically, was what saved Halifax's life—assuming he survives, that is.'

'Explain,' said Harrison.

'After the shot which took the glass out of the window, Halifax turned to face the park. The shooter took aim, presumably at the left side of his chest, but then Mr Parker here tells us that Halifax whirled round again to look at the broken picture, that's when the shooter pulled the trigger and the bullet went through the right side of his chest. He was lucky.'

'Can anyone be so accurate at such long range?' I asked.

'An expert marksman, with a telescopic sight mounted on a modern high-powered rifle, probably resting the barrel on the tree, would have no problem putting a bullet between three or four inches of his desired spot.'

'What about the gunman?' I asked. 'Any sign of him?'

'We would have heard something had they found anyone,' Theo answered. 'I think we can safely assume that he was on his way seconds after the shots were fired. It's getting dark now, but we've got the area cordoned off, and we'll bring in a load of police cadets tomorrow morning, and if there's anything to be found in the park, we'll find it.' I looked at my watch. It was eight o'clock.

'Can I go home?'

'Of course,' said Theo, 'but there's a minor problem.'

'What's that?'

'There's about fifty journalists waiting outside the front door.'

'Shit! How did they get here so fast?' I asked.

'You should know, Parker. Most of them listen to police frequencies on the radio all the time. It's illegal, of course, but we can't think of a way to stop them. *Ecclesiastes* tells us: "There is not a righteous man upon earth that doeth good and sinneth not".' Farrer was looking at him with a funny look on his face.

'Can you get someone to open the side garage door?' I asked Theo.

'Yes, why?'

'Because I can call a taxi,' I said, hoping that Frankie was back in the cab by now. He must have heard and seen all the commotion. I didn't think Halifax would mind me using his phone and I dialled Frankie's cab number: he was there, and I explained what he had to do.

I went down in the lift to the garage and I found PC Plod waiting for me when the door opened. Frankie was already there, the engine running. Plod put out his hand.

'You saved his life, you know, no doubt about that.' He was looking me straight in the eye. I took his hand and shook it warmly.

'You helped,' I said. 'Good night Mr Reynolds.' He grinned. I jumped into the back of the cab and down on the floor. Frankie had seen the press arrive outside, and knew instinctively what he had to do. When PC Reynolds opened the garage door, he roared out.

Only one journalist managed to jump on the running-board as we slowed down to take the turn into the road and look into the window for a few moments, and I was treated once more to the unpleasant sight of Woody Corkery's face pressed up against the window.

As he fell off, I heard him bellow: 'Parker! Stop, you bastard!' and then we were gone.

CHAPTER 12

I wanted to go home, but I knew Corkery would make a beeline for my house, so Frankie took me to Andy's flat in Kentish Town. I had forgotten that she had said she was going out, and I didn't even have the sense to telephone her from the taxi to warn her about the state I was in. She naturally got a terrible shock when she saw me on the doorstep literally covered in blood.

My explanation was as succinct as I could make it, and her shock changed quickly to concern. She ran a bath and put me in it—alone—and as I lay in the hot soapy water I began to realize how tense and knotted my body had become. She sat next to the bath, soaping my shoulders, back and neck while I went through the story again, this time in more detail. Some of the scenes were like pieces of film in my memory which I could review quickly or frame by frame in my mind, and I wondered how long that clarity would last.

I also told her about my interview with Bertrand Blake, and its abrupt ending.

After the bath I sat in her kitchen/diner, incongruous in her frilly dressing-gown which barely covered my thighs, while she served a light supper. I ate as much of it as I could, which was not a lot.

After the meal we curled up together on her couch and watched *News at Ten* which, predictably, led on the Halifax shooting. They had the story covered from every conceivable angle, including live broadcasts from Regent's Park and the Royal Free Hospital where Halifax was said to be in a 'serious but stable' condition, but it all didn't amount to much. The police had declined to release anything but the barest details, and their story was so speculative as to be absurd. There was even film of Frankie's cab disappearing, carrying what they described as a 'mystery witness' to the shooting. It wouldn't be a mystery for long, I knew. They would pour money into the pockets of the doorman and he would tell them who I was. And in any case, Corkery would plaster me all over the *Sun*.

When the news was over, Andy switched off the set and she came back to the couch. 'Didn't you say you were going out?' I asked her. It had taken a long time for it to dawn on me.

'Yes, but I cancelled my arrangement when you were in the bath.'

I looked at her. 'I'm quite fond of you, you know.'

'Yes, I know. I think I'm getting quite fond of you too.'

We enjoyed the glow of mutual fondness for a while, and then she said: 'The trouble is that you're full of mysterious bullshit at the moment. I would like to know how you can afford to keep that taxi-driver hanging around, how you can afford bottles of champagne and smoked salmon as a seemingly permanent feature of your fridge, how you can afford to order £45 bottles of wine. I could go on.'

'Are you sure you really want to know the answers?' I said.

'Yes.'

'Well then, if you're sitting comfortably, I'll begin.'

So I told her about the money. I started with Edwina and then described my various encounters with Pendleton, Douglas at Rothschilds, and the meeting earlier that day with the accountant. I happened to mention that my after-tax income, over and above what I earned at the newspaper, was in the region of forty-five thousand pounds a week. Eventually I paused.

There was a long silence, and I let her think it all out. During the silence I went to the loo, and she made some tea. It was a comfortable silence, without any pressure.

'Parker?'

'Yes?'

'This is not a joke, is it?'

'No.' There was another long silence. This time she went to the loo.

'Parker?'

'Yes?'

'This is going to take some getting used to.'

'I know.'

'And now I want to go to bed.'

We got into her big double bed with a fluffy duvet and big soft cushions and we just lay there chastely in each other's arms.

After a little while I said: 'Can I ask you something?'

'Of course.'

'This afternoon you said you had an arrangement for tonight. Then you cancelled it. Was it important?'

'Come on, Parker, you just want to know who it was with, don't you?'

'Yes.'

'My mother. I was supposed to go and visit my mother. She lives in Palmers Green.' I held her tightly.

Eventually we slept, and I had nightlong dreams in which I re-played my memory film of the breaking glass, the sound of gunshots and Halifax's bloody mouth. And then, towards dawn, I had a vivid dream about a key that burned in a trouser pocket until it was free.

CHAPTER 13

I woke up at the crack of dawn that Thursday morning, listening to the dawn chorus and watching the shapes start to take form in that strange bedroom as the sun began to come up. I lay in bed and realized that Monique Karabekian had now been dead for a week and yet I was becoming more and more involved in her life than I had ever been when she was alive.

I hadn't told anyone about the key, not even Andy. I'm not sure why. Perhaps I sensed that this was private business to do with Halifax and his wife, and I was not prepared to broadcast it until I was sure it was relevant.

There were also some immediate problems I had to sort out. Somehow I had to get some clean clothes from my home, and get there early enough to write the biggest scoop the *Hampstead Explorer* was ever likely to get. Added to the exclusive on the Karabekian diaries, my account of the shooting would be a knockout.

I lay there thinking for a while and then I must have moved, because Andy stirred. 'What's the time?' she grumbled.

I looked at the green figures on her clock radio alarm. 'Half past five.'

'Oh Lord. You can forget about spending time with me if this is the time you get up every day.'

'Sorry, it's just that I heard this body calling me.'

'What body?'

I replied by kissing her on the neck. Then I kissed her in some other places, and her arm came snaking up around my shoulders and she pulled my mouth down on to hers. We made love slowly, sleepily and gently, while the birds provided accompaniment. Afterwards we nearly fell asleep again, but I had to get moving.

'Andy.'

'Oh Lord, not again,' she whimpered. 'The man's a sex maniac!'

'Shut up. I need something to wear. The clothes I came in are caked with blood. Do you have anything?' As it happened, she did. She produced a tracksuit abandoned by a previous gentleman friend who had jogged out of her life a year or two before, and it fitted me perfectly.

'Any chance of a lift home?' I asked.

'You mean now?' she said, incredulous. I nodded. 'It's just as well you're a millionaire, otherwise I would throw you out on your arse.'

In the end she got dressed and took me home. Well, not home exactly, but dropped me in the next road from mine, which ran parallel to it. I knew a back route to my house which would avoid the reptiles I knew would be waiting out front. I kissed Andy goodbye, told her I'd see her later at the office, and then climbed over the gate between two houses whose gardens abutted mine.

I climbed over the low wall into my garden, managing to accomplish the feat without breaking a single limb, and then let myself into the back door with my key. I went through to the first-floor window and peeked carefully through the curtains. At first I couldn't see anyone, but then I saw them. Six or seven maybe, sitting in their cars, some asleep, but there was also a foursome playing cards and I could see the cigarette smoke pouring out of the window.

I had a shower and got dressed, and then made breakfast. I also had a quick look at the morning papers which had been put through the door but they had very little more information about the shooting than *News at Ten* had had the night before. By this stage it was half past seven, and I turned on my trusty Amstrad. While munching toast and sipping coffee I wrote my graphic account of the shooting of Malcolm Halifax, MP, as witnessed by the only journalist in the whole world to have been there at the time and to have participated in the saving of his life. Bloch would love it, and he would also love it that he would have it on his desk first thing. It took me an hour, and that left half an hour before Frankie was due to arrive. I decided to have some fun.

I calmly went and opened the front door. It was about a minute before anyone noticed me, and then there was instant pandemonium. Corkery was the first to reach me.

'Where the hell have you been?' he demanded. The others were sort of lined up behind him on the path.

'Why, friends and colleagues, I have been here all the time. I had no idea until a few minutes ago that you were outside. Why didn't you ring the bell?' I knew they had probably been ringing the bell all night. 'Why don't you come in, and then we'll have a brief chat. I'm sure some of you would like to use the toilet.' They all looked astonished. 'Come on, then.' They came in like a herd of goats.

Ten minutes later they had all used the loo, and they started firing questions at me and taking photographs. 'Wait, wait, wait,' I said, holding my hand up for silence. 'I have a statement.' They listened.

'I know some of you are going to find this very difficult to accept, but I believe that Mr Halifax was shot by a death ray from a Martian spaceship.' There was an appalled silence, which was broken by Corkery.

'What's this bullshit, Parker?' he snarled.

'It's not bullshit, I assure you, Woody. I was there. I saw it. This thin white light came through the window and knocked him down and when I looked out there was this huge flying saucer hovering outside—'

'What were you doing there?' one of the journalists interrupted.

'I was interviewing Mr Halifax about constituency matters, about his views on the EEC's common agricultural policy and the single transferable vote system, and he was just getting to the interesting bit about how you knock off the name of the person who came last in the first ballot when we heard this high sort of whining, shimmering noise. It was the spaceship, of course. When I looked closely at it afterwards, I saw that it had a lot of red dust on it, and that is what leads me to suspect it came from Mars.' This time there was total silence.

Then someone said: 'He's not going to tell us anything. Are you, Parker?'

'The truth is, gentlemen, that I thought you would all appreciate the opportunity to relieve your bladders. My story is something you can read about in tomorrow's *Hampstead Explorer* together with other material you don't even know about yet.'

Most of them took it well. There were some half-hearted complaints and then some jokes, perhaps because they all knew they would probably do the same thing in similar circumstances, and then they all trooped out—except for Corkery who hung behind.

'OK, Parker, name your price.'

'Level with me, Woody. What's the maximum you think your paper would pay me for my story?'

'Fifteen thousand, maybe twenty thousand.'

'I wouldn't talk to the *Sun* for a hundred times that amount.' I looked him straight in the eye. 'And in case your arithmetic is as bad as your writing, that's two million pounds. Are you beginning to get the message?'

'Fuck you, then,' he said, and he walked out.

A few minutes later, Frankie arrived and I went to work.

Arnie Bloch was a battleground of conflicting emotions when I walked in. He was furious that I had not been in contact with him, but delighted at the copy I handed him. He knew there had never been a story like this in the history of the paper, and probably wouldn't be ever again. In the end he let his delight take over and he clapped me on the back.

'Well done, boy!' he said, spraying me with crumbs and particles from his early morning chicken tikka sandwich. Even Bill Petrie, the editor, made a point of coming over to my desk to congratulate me.

'Can I have a pay rise?' I asked him.

'I do believe that may be possible, I'll speak to Mr Blackstock about it,' he replied.

I made a last-minute check with the police to make sure that nothing substantial had changed from the night before —nothing had—and the hospital told me that Halifax was 'poorly but out of danger.' He was still unconscious most of the time and was in the intensive care unit. He was certainly not receiving visitors. Then they put the paper to bed, as they say.

My colleagues were all very excited about the story, and I was forced to tell the tale again around the coffee machine.

Then Bloch, the editor and I had a conference, in which we went over everything that had happened in the last week. I brought them up to date on the interview the day before with Bertrand Blake—but I did not tell them about the key, which was safely tucked into my wallet.

'What now?' Bloch asked.

'I think we should stick with the people on that list,' I said. 'One of them has already proved difficult and shifty about it, and we need to find out what it's all about, particularly since the whole world is going to know about the diaries tomorrow and the police are going to have to issue copies since we've had one, although I'll see if I can get Theo Bernstein to stall them until Monday. It will take them a day or two, but sooner or later, some of the other sleuths are going to notice those people and come up with the same list as we've got and start looking for them. I want to be first in the queue.'

'It sounds logical,' said the editor. 'Who are you going to start with?'

'Let's go straight to the top this time. How about Adolfini?' The other two shifted nervously. Eduardo Adolfini was the owner of a chain of about 400 cinemas in this country alone, and was reputed to be one of the biggest financiers of films in the business. He was also said to be a serious crook.

'He's a very unpleasant character,' Bloch warned. 'He hates journalists, he's been known to beat up photographers, and I know people who swear he's mixed up with some very unsavoury people indeed.'

'Christ, I only want to talk to him!' I said. 'I'm not going to ask him for money or for his daughter's hand in marriage. I'll be very polite and I'll be sure to talk to him in a public place.'

'OK, who else?' said Bloch.

'How about the director, Anthony March? He's on the list, and he lives in Hampstead. I know where. That'll keep me busy for the next day or two.'

'Right, press ahead then,' Bloch said. 'But keep in touch, dammit!'

I went back to my desk and a minute later the telephone rang. It was Pendleton. 'I'm afraid I have some bad news,' he said. My heart actually stopped.

'I know, the inheritance is all a terrible mistake. She left the money to another Horatio T. Parker.' I was only half joking.

'No, no, no, no, nothing like that,' he said soothingly. My heart started again. 'It's Mr Blackstock. He turned the bid down flat.' It was bad news indeed.

'Did he give any reasons?'

'Yes, he told Morley about an hour ago that he had no intention of selling the paper to, and I quote, "a bunch of anonymous offshore hoods in dark suits who wouldn't know the difference between Hampstead and their private parts". Actually, he used another word for private parts which I don't feel like repeating. He said there was nothing wrong with the price, but that if we were serious, we should get our "boss man" to come and see him.' Dear old Mr Blackstock.

'Leave him to me,' I said. Pendleton sounded relieved. Then I telephoned a friend of mine, Hazel Cowen, who worked on the theatre magazine, *Spotlight*, and knew everything there was to know about actors, directors, producers and their private lives.

'This is a treat,' she said. 'You're quite a celebrity, you know. Your name has been in all the papers.'

'Never mind that, Hazel, I need some help.'

'What's in it for me?' she said sweetly.

'My undying love and a long boozy lunch at the restaurant of your choice. And I mean any restaurant.'

'The Riverside Inn in Bray?'

'Done.'

'Wow, you must need a lot of help. What do you want to know?'

'How do I get to talk to Eduardo Adolfini? Today?'

'Oh shit, I knew this was too good to be true. The answer is, you don't.'

'I have to, Hazel.'

'It's impossible. He won't speak to journalists and all you'll get is a rude brush-off from his office. If you try and approach him without an appointment you'll end up in the gutter, or worse—he's got two gorillas the size of oak trees looking after him, and they're nervous to boot.'

'There has to be a way. Where does he eat?'

'Hey, that's a point. Someone told me that he goes to the Bluebelle in Mayfair for lunch almost every day. I can't guarantee it, but that's what I heard.'

'That's fine, Hazel, you earned your lunch.'

'This lunch, Parker, is it just going to be you and me?'

'No, I will be bringing a person with remarkable green eyes. Her name's Andy.'

'Good. And I hope Andy's got more money than you have, because I don't want to end up having to pay.'

'Don't worry, I think I'll just manage it,' I said.

I rang the Bluebelle and booked a table for one for lunch. On the way out I stopped at Andy's desk. 'I'm going out, and I won't be back in the office today. See you at my place tonight?' A frown appeared on her face.

'Tonight's fine, but Parker, be careful. I'm beginning to worry about you blundering into all this. You could have been killed yesterday.'

'Please don't worry,' I said. 'I have a very highly developed streak of cowardice, and I have plans to live for a very long time, particularly since there's all Edwina's money to be spent.'

'Just take care. Please.'

When I got to the taxi, I handed Halifax's key to Frankie. 'What do you make of that?' I asked him.

'It's a key.'

'That part I was able to work out all by myself. What kind of a key do you think it is?' I was very patient. He examined it closely.

'I would say that it is the key to a filing cabinet or something like that. No, on second thoughts, it looks like the key to a locker, and it's got a number on it, sixty-two. I go swimming at Swiss Cottage Baths sometimes, and the keys for the changing lockers are something like this, except that they have a thick rubber band attached to them so you can slip it on your wrist or ankle while you're swimming.'

'What else?' I asked. He looked again.

'It could also be a for a left-luggage locker. You know, the sort of thing they have at railway stations.'

'My thoughts exactly, Watson. It only remains for us to find the correct bank of lockers, and this is where I could do with some more of your invaluable help.'

'What's this Watson business? I thought you were a reporter, not a detective.'

'The skills of reporting and detecting are closely allied, often to the point of indistinguishability.'

'There's no such word,' he said. 'You probably mean indistinction.'

'The grammar lesson I can do without. What I can't do without is your undisputable knowledge of places in London which have these left-luggage lockers.'

'You mean indisputable,' he said. I took a deep breath and ignored the correction.

'What I would really appreciate would be if you could make me a list of such places, so that we can arrange to pass by them now and then on our travels here and there across London.' Frankie was looking at me balefully.

'What about my studies?' he asked.

'Tell you what, you can put the meter on while you're making the list, OK?' He nodded happily. I cast my eyes upwards to heaven. I was sure that Theo Bernstein would have had an apt extract from the Talmud about man's avarice. I gave him Blackstock's address and we set off.

Arthur Ernest Blackstock came from a long line of cantankerous bastards in Hartlepool. And while he didn't have the powerful Geordie accent his father is said to have had, he was dogmatic and pugnacious and often impossible to talk to. On the other hand he had come to Hampstead in 1932 with a few thousand pounds and had started the *Hampstead Explorer* from nothing, working with a threadbare shoestring and the smell of an oil rag, fighting his way through the lean war years and into the 'fifties when the paper first started making direct profits. He wasn't even a journalist, but one of that special breed of person who want to own newspapers, and he had an unshakeable and, as it turned out, an unerring instinct about the kind of newspaper he believed would eventually flourish in the area.

He lived in a splendid big Victorian house in Templewood Avenue, just near the western part of Hampstead Heath, form where he waged furious war on property developers who were buying up similar houses in the area and turning them into shabby luxury 'apartments' for yuppies. I knew his wife had died two or three years before, that he had a married daughter living in Australia and a son who ran his own printing firm in Peterborough.

He was seventy-nine years old, and he opened the door with all the briskness and vigour of an adolescent. He peered at me in surprise. 'It's Parker, isn't it?'

'Yes, sir. Good morning.'

'My God, boy, I've been reading about this Halifax business, and my paper tells me that there was a journalist by the name of Parker actually with him when it happened. Was that you?'

'Yes, sir, I was there when he was shot. I was doing an interview.'

'Come in, come in, you must tell me all about it.' He spun on his heel and led the way into a sunny drawing-room. 'What do you want to drink? Coffee or something harder?'

'Coffee would be fine, sir.'

'Oh, for Christ's sake, stop calling me sir. This is not the army. Mr Blackstock will do. Come into the kitchen while I make the coffee. I have a housekeeper but her coffee tastes like piss. Then you can tell me all about it.'

I told him the whole story while he ground the coffee in an old hand grinder, poured boiling water on the grounds in a teapot, an then poured the aromatic brew through a tea-strainer into big blue mugs. We went back into the drawing-room, and when I had finished the tale there was a moment's silence. 'That's what they call a good story, isn't it? I presume it's all going to be in tomorrow's paper, exclusive to us?'

'It certainly is.'

'Right,' he said, banging his mug down on the table. 'What is it you want? More money? I don't believe you came here to cheer up the cranky old proprietor with a good story.'

I took a deep breath and dived straight in. 'Mr Blackstock, I am the boss man of the bunch of offshore hoods in dark suits who wouldn't know the difference between Hampstead and their private parts. I've come to see you because I want to buy the *Explorer*.'

He looked at me in astonishment for a full minute, during which I could hear the ticking of a clock somewhere in the room, and then his face softened. 'I didn't say private parts,' he said.

'I know that.'

There was another silence while he scrutinized my face, and then he cackled: 'Well, I'll be buggered! I presume you've got the money? I mean you have someone with the finance?'

'Not someone. It's me. The short version of another long and equally improbable story is that I have suddenly come into a very large amount of money. There is someone at Rothschilds who can confirm this, of course.'

'Screw Rothschilds. I leave that kind of thing to my

accountants. Just tell me, why the hell didn't you come to me with the offer in the first place?'

'I was hoping to be able to remain anonymous. It's important to me that no one, and especially not my colleagues, ever finds out—assuming you agree to sell, of course.'

'Why anonymous?'

'It's hard to say exactly what my motives are, but I think the simplest explanation is that I'm not an entrepreneur, I'm a reporter—that's what I enjoy doing. Yes, I have all kinds of ideas about what we should be doing with the paper, about hirings and firings, expansion and new departures, but I have no financial expertise, no experience of newspaper production or managing staff. I want to leave it to professionals to put my ideas into action, or tell me that they're a load of balls. But the main reason is that I want to carry on being a reporter on the *Explorer*, and if I'm known to be the boss by the people I'm working with, that would become impossible. If I can't be anonymous, I'd rather not buy the paper.'

'Who would you fire?'

'Mitchell, for a start.'

'He's that bad, is he?'

'Worse,' I said.

Blackstock sat drumming his fingers on the leather arm of the chair. 'I'm seventy-nine, and I spent most of my life building up that paper. Don't screw it up, Parker.'

'That means . . . ?' I discovered that I had been holding my breath, and my voice sounded strangled.

'I'll sell it to you for three million, lock, stock and barrel.'

'Fantastic! Can we do this quickly?'

'As quickly as you like. I'll sign any reasonable sale document as soon as your bods can come up with one, and as soon as my bods tell me you've got the cash you say you have. And I'll keep your secret.' He paused. 'Do you want to stay for lunch? We could talk about being newspaper proprietors over a chicken salad.'

'Mr Blackstock, I can think of nothing that I would

rather do. But unfortunately I have to meet a crook for lunch at the Bluebelle.'

'Good for you. I wish I was your age,' he said.

'So do I.'

'Why?'

'Because if you were, I would hire you on the spot to run the paper.'

'Cheeky bugger,' he said. We shook hands warmly when I left.

It was just past noon and I asked Frankie to head in a leisurely fashion towards Mayfair, passing on the way some of the places on his list that might have lockers. On the way I telephoned Pendleton to give him the good news about Blackstock. He promised to get Morley on to the paperwork immediately.

The first disappointment with the key was at Swiss Cottage Baths, where it was apparent immediately that it was the wrong design. Further disappointments followed at Euston Station and then at Paddington where a transport policeman watched me suspiciously as I tried in vain to get the key into the door of locker No. 62. 'Oops, wrong station!' I said with a polite smile as I withdrew. He didn't look any less suspicious.

CHAPTER 14

I was dead on time for my table at the Bluebelle, and I can't say I was impressed by the rather gloomy interior of the restaurant. On the other hand the maître d' didn't seem too impressed by the way I was dressed. Although he was smiling unctuously and rubbing his hands together I saw him looking me up and down and I just knew I was going to get the table next to the door to the kitchen at the end of the row of tables for two.

I was wearing a relatively new and, I think, very smart blue double-breasted navy blue blazer with big brass buttons which was only a couple of years old, and had on my best silver-grey trousers that I had had narrowed after flares went out of fashion. I was also wearing a pale blue shirt and a nice striped tie, and as far as I was concerned I looked classy enough for any table in the joint, so I pretended to misunderstand and on the way I plonked myself down at the table in the middle of the row, facing out into the restaurant.

'Excuse me, sir, but that table is reserved,' he said through his nose.

'Oh yes indeed, I made a reservation,' I said loudly and jovially, showing lots of teeth in my smile. I picked up the carefully folded napkin, put it on my lap, and broke open a bread roll, showering crumbs all over the table. He knew he was beaten, and he didn't bother to struggle.

'I'll have a bottle of your house champagne,' I said, also with a smile, and then I had a look at the menu. It was only after some searching that I saw, in the tiniest print, that the fixed price lunch would cost me £55. Plus fifteen per cent service charge.

The place was only about a third full, and I supposed that people rich enough to eat in this place weren't usually the kind of people who had to get back to the office by two o'clock. Adolfini was not here. The house champagne wasn't bad.

The food wasn't bad, either, but nowhere near good enough to cost that much. I poured the last glass of champagne, stirred it with my finger to get some of the fizz out, and then Eduardo Adolfini walked in accompanied by two oak trees.

My first reaction was the usual one—that he looked different in the flesh from his familiar two-dimensional image on television and in newspaper photographs. But there was absolutely no mistaking him. He was very tall, and he had those sleepy, drooping eyelids also sported by people like Salman Rushdie and Clement Freud that made him look slightly bored all the time.

He wasn't bored, of course. He had a reputation as a

merciless corporate raider and, it was said, any sign of apparent inactivity on his part was usually the precursor to a ruthless pounce on some unsuspecting company in the film or entertainment business that he didn't already own.

The press loved him because he was excellent copy. Whatever he did made news because he always did things dramatically and decisively, more often than not emerging from some wild mêlée of commercial fisticuffs with a substantially larger bank balance, and with an even more vice-like grip on the entertainment world than he had had before.

His name had also been mentioned in a host of criminal cases, everything from simple embezzlement to major stock exchange frauds, violence and extortion, but the allegations about him had always been sufficiently peripheral to the central issue to allow him to escape real scrutiny.

Only once had he been alleged to have been directly involved, in a case of GBH. A young Italian immigrant, accused of a horrific attack on the owner of a small chain of cinemas in Nottingham, and having been expertly sweated by the police, implicated Adolfini in the plot.

He claimed he had been hired by Adolfini and paid two thousand pounds to break the legs of the man who had refused to sell his cinemas. This allegation only emerged half way through the trial and although the defence moved quickly to have Adolfini subpœnaed as a witness, he was tipped off and managed to leave the country minutes ahead of the warrant. He arrived back long after the trial had ended, angrily denying through his lawyers that he had ever even met the young Italian. That same young Italian started an eight-year prison sentence, but never finished it. He was killed during a disturbance in the prison in circumstances that were never satisfactorily explained, despite an official Home Office inquiry.

Adolfini was treated with enormous reverence by the maître d'. Although he was on his own—apart from the two oak trees, that is—he was put at a large table directly across the restaurant from mine, and the trees got the small table next to the kitchen entrance that had so nearly been mine. They didn't seem to mind. Until his food arrived, Adolfini read from a slim file of papers.

I watched him for a few minutes while I sipped my coffee, then summoned up my courage. I pulled out my notebook, tore out a clean page and wrote: 'Mr Adolfini, I don't wish to disturb your meal, but I am anxious to speak to you for a few minutes about Monique Karabekian. May I join you?' Then I asked a waiter to deliver the note.

The waiter did so, pointing to me as he offered the folded piece of paper to Adolfini on his tray. Before he even touched the note, Adolfini gazed languidly over the restaurant at me, those lazy eyes boring into mine and almost turning my resolve into a discreet withdrawal. Almost.

Then he dropped his eyes, picked up the note, read it quickly, and my heart missed a beat as he flashed a quick look at his two oak trees next to the kitchen. I flashed a quick look at them too—and was disconcerted to find that they had stopped sipping their glasses of Perrier, and were looking at me with flat, unwavering stares. Then Adolfini looked back at me, paused, and nodded once. I swallowed.

I felt very self-conscious walking across the restaurant, but I doubt if many people even noticed, apart from the two minders and the maître d'. As soon as I sat down, the latter hurried up to the table, a new respect in his eyes, and asked if I wanted more coffee. I said yes.

'Who are you and what do you want?' my host said in an unexpectedly precise and well modulated public school voice. It cut through the air between us like an ice pick.

'My name is Horatio Parker and I wanted to ask you something about Miss Karabekian.' I had the feeling that there were to be no polite formalities. Not even any chit-chat about the weather.

'What do you want to ask?'

'I know you had lunch with her on October the fourth, two years ago. Can you tell me if there was anything special about that meeting?' I was looking at him intently and nothing changed in his face. But his eyes, without moving off me, seemed to lose their focus and glazed over with the chilling, milky blindness of a shark.

'Are you trying to blackmail me?'

The words exploded in my mind with a flash of enlightenment, sending messages along pathways in a host of directions at once.

'Is that what Monique Karabekian was doing: blackmailing you?' I asked quickly.

Now his eyes were scanning me, reading me and seeming to find messages in my face as precise as the words on the papers he had been reading earlier. Then he seemed to relax slightly. 'You haven't the faintest idea what you're talking about, have you?' he said softly.

'Quite frankly, I haven't. If I had, I wouldn't have felt the need to disturb your meal.'

'Exactly what do you know?'

'She noted the fact of her lunch with you in her diary, but wrote nothing about it. It is, however, one of a number of entries in her diary which is distinguished from others by a small symbol, the letter "T" with a circle around it.'

'How did you come by her d—Ah, now I know who you are. You are the newspaper reporter who was with Malcolm Halifax last night.' He looked away from me, for the fist time since we started speaking, and he deftly speared a medallion of beef. It was if the fork had gone through my heart. He put it in his mouth, chewed, swallowed, and then spoke again: 'You should know than I do not, in any circumstances, speak to journalists. I cannot help you further about Monique Karabekian or anyone else, and now you must leave my table immediately or I will have you removed.' He went back to his medallions.

'Thank you for your time,' I said politely as I got up, nearly colliding with the waiter just arriving with my coffee. 'I'll have it at my table,' I told him, 'and please bring me my bill.'

The house champagne cost more than forty pounds and that, together with the service charge, took the total to well over a hundred pounds. But it was money well spent. I handed the waiter my credit card, and I sat back, trying to hide the excitement that was coursing through me.

A few minutes later the maître d' arrived back at my table. He was accompanied by another man in a smart dark suit who was probably the manager, and he had a new expression on his face that I did not recognize. He leaned over and, speaking clearly but discreetly, he said: 'I regret that your credit card company has informed us that you are at your credit limit, and they cannot cover this bill.' My mouth dropped open in astonishment. And then closed in dismay, since I had neither cash nor cheque-book on me. I was distinctly flustered and was just about to ask if I could use the telephone when I looked up and saw Adolfini standing at the table.

I can only assume he had seen the tense little tableau, noted my dismay and put two and two together. 'He can't pay?' The maître d' did not reply, but the answer was obvious. 'Let him go, I'll cover it.'

'I assure you . . .' I began, but Adolfini had turned on his heel and was already half way back to his own table.

'Look here,' I protested, 'it's not necessary. All I need to do—'

I was interrupted. 'Monsieur may leave the restaurant, and I would appreciate it if you would do so quickly and quietly,' the manager said, 'and do not come back.'

I left the restaurant quickly, and quietly, and with about as much dignity as if I had been thrown out physically. I don't think any of the other guests had really known what had transpired, but the humiliation left me seething.

In the taxi I telephoned Douglas at Rothschilds and told him what had happened. He was horrified. Less than fifteen minutes later he called me back: 'You now have no credit limit on that card,' he informed me. I thanked him, but it made me feel only slightly better.

I telephoned Pendleton. 'Please ask Mr Morley to investigate the ownership of the Bluebelle Restaurant in Mayfair. When he finds the owner I want him to make a reasonable offer to buy it for Parker, Inc.' That made me feel a lot better.

On the way back to Hampstead we made a detour via Liverpool Street, Kings Cross and St Pancras stations to investigate left-luggage lockers, but I had no luck with the key.

It was shortly before three o'clock and I decided to see whether Anthony March, the film director, was at home. He was. The door to his large Victorian gothic house in Cannon Lane was opened by a young Filipino woman who asked me who I was and what I wanted. She disappeared for a moment and then returned to show me into March's study at the back of the house on the ground floor.

It was a wonderfully large room, with elegant French doors leading to the garden and walls that were covered with framed movie posters, photographs of film stars, certificates and autographs of the rich and famous. On one side of the room there was a plush sofa, a few armchairs and a coffee table strewn with books, magazines and what looked like a pile of scripts. Near the window there was an enormous desk, similarly covered with piles of paper, from which March rose to meet me. He waved me to an armchair.

'What can I do for the *Hampstead Explorer*?' he asked in friendly fashion.

'I was hoping I could talk to you about Monique Karabekian.'

'Yes, so Maria said. Tragic business, that. Horrifying. We are all terribly shocked and upset.' He didn't look shocked or upset. 'But how can I help you?'

'How well did you know her?'

'About as well as any director knows any of his leading ladies. She was in a few films of mine, you know.' I nodded. 'But I didn't really know her personally or socially at all. I don't think I could have got on with her husband, although I never met him. Different politics, you see.' He sounded relaxed, but I was watching him carefully, and it was my impression that he was choosing his words very carefully.

'What did you think of her acting abilities?' There was a silence.

'Are we off the record here?'

'If you like.'

'In that case, I can say "not much", but that's only between you and me. And of course your next question will be why I cast her in my films.'

I smiled, and he continued: 'And the answer is not a simple one. Monique was not a great actress, but she could hold her own and she was a powerful presence on screen. Her brilliance was in her beauty and her sexuality—she oozed a sort of visual musk that caught the eye and held it. But, in a way more important, was the fact that she brought out special performances from the male actors she worked with. They all appeared to be temporarily besotted by the woman and put great intensity into their work with her.'

I was not convinced. In fact it sounded to me like a load of crap. I might have believed him had be said he had used Monique as a certain box office draw—but there were other, much more talented, actresses who could be just as sexy as Monique, and who could have made much more of the roles. I decided to take a flyer.

'I heard a rumour once that she had blackmailed a director into giving her a role. Did you ever hear that.'

'No.' His answer was too quick, too pat. There was no surprise, or even the curiosity one would have expected him to express. Then he must have realized that his manner had been too fast, and he tried to cover his tracks. 'That's the first time I ever heard that one!' He laughed. 'Was it someone I know?'

'I've no idea,' I said, 'I never heard any names, just the rumour. But do you think she was the kind of person who could do that?'

'I really don't know. As I said, I didn't know her personally all that well. I don't think I can help you much more.' The warmth had gone out of the interview. 'Just what sort of a piece are you writing?'

'I'm not even sure I am writing a piece. I'm just trying to find out more about her.'

'There must be other people you could talk to who knew her better than I did.' He looked at his watch, pointedly. 'The trouble is I'm rather busy at the moment. Perhaps we could talk again another time?' But I had to ask one more question.

'You had lunch with her on the third of May, three years ago. Can you tell me if anything significant happened that day?'

'Nothing whatever. Now you really must excuse me.' That answer was also wrong. If nothing had happened, he would not have been able even to remember the occasion. And he didn't even ask me how I knew. But I could take a hint, and I left while the atmosphere was still relatively cordial.

During the short taxi ride home I tried to stop myself from jumping to conclusions too quickly. I told myself that I had only spoken to three people on the list, that I had no evidence, and that there were probably other explanations. But I jumped anyway.

CHAPTER 15

'All of them? She was blackmailing sixteen people?' Andy was incredulous.

'It looks like it. I've only spoken to three of them and already the picture is clear when you put it all together. First we have the dashing and outspoken Bertrand Blake who tears a strip off her every chance he gets until, miraculously, he has lunch with Monique, and suddenly she turns into the most neglected actress on the face of the earth. When I asked him about this sudden transformation, and about the lunch, he gets shirty in the extreme and threatens me with a libel writ.

'Then I track down the panther, Adolfini, while he is

eating, and after one simple question about his lunch with her, he asks me if I'm trying to blackmail him! Where else would he get that idea from? He realizes too late that I know nothing, but by then the damage is done.

'Number three is Anthony March who may be a hot-shot director, but is a terrible actor. He starts off admitting that he didn't think much of Monique as an actress and then comes up with a load of bullshit to explain why he gave her leading roles in his films. When I mention the word blackmail, he makes a cock-up of the answers and then gets unfriendly.

'And besides,' I added, 'I think I have the key to the whole problem.'

'And what's that?'

I held up the key Halifax had given me.

'What's that?' she asked.

'It's a key.'

'Even I, silly mere woman that I am, can see that! Explain, Parker, before I give you a smack!' There was a distinct warning tone in her voice. I explained, and showed her Frankie's list of possible places with lockers. There were still a handful of main line stations, a host of suburban stations, air and coach terminals and a few other places such as other municipal swimming pools and the YMCA.

'Frankie and I will cover most of them tomorrow, and if there are any left over perhaps you and I can chase them up on Saturday, assuming you're prepared to drive me around.'

'Perhaps.'

We had had a quiet dinner in my kitchen, during which I described the details of my activity-packed day, from the success with Blackstock through my humiliation at the Bluebelle (she loved that) and the meeting with March.

'So, it looks as if you are going to be my boss as well as my lover,' she said.

'Yes, but I'm going to rule with such a light touch that you'll hardly feel it.'

'I know all about your touch.'

We watched a little television together, and later she asked me: 'Shouldn't we tell all this to the police and let them handle it?'

'No fear, there's just no evidence yet. Anything these people told me is merely hearsay, and they are hardly likely to admit anything directly to the police—particularly when their blackmailer is dead and presumably no longer a threat to them. No, I'm going to give it a few more days, and then I'll talk to Theo Bernstein and Harrison about it.

'But in any case,' I added, 'this is my story. I'm not going to pack it in and hand it all over to the cops just when it's getting interesting.'

'But what worries me,' she said, 'is that our theory suggests that there are at least sixteen people out there who could have had a very powerful motive for murdering Monique. The police should know that at least.'

'The police had exactly the same information we had from the diary, together with all the resources for following it up, but they still don't seem to have done anything about it. This is because they are convinced Halifax did it. I have my doubts about that, but the point is that the other sixteen possible suspects aren't going anywhere. If there is a guilty person among them, he's languishing in the belief that Halifax is going to be tried for the murder, and that the police are not even looking for another possibility.'

'So who shot Halifax, then, and why?' she asked.

'I've been thinking about that. It could well have been one of the sixteen, worried perhaps that Halifax would continue to blackmail them with whatever Monique had over them. We just don't know.'

'Don't you think you might be in danger?'

'No, because it must be obvious to anyone who might be interested, that we don't know what it's all about. As I said to you this morning, if and when we find out anything, that is when we become a threat, that's when it could get dangerous, and that's when we'll give it all to the cops.'

'But what worries me, Parker, is that he may think you know something, even if you don't, or may fear that you will find out something that will make you dangerous to him. I'm worried about you.'

'I know, and I'm sorry. Flippancy is my defence. The point is that we could go on second-guessing and theorizing all night and still not come up with anything concrete. The way I feel is that I have gone so far, and I have to see it through. Apart from anything else, it's the story of a lifetime. There may even be a book in it.'

'Let's just hope it doesn't have to be published posthumously.'

CHAPTER 16

That Friday morning I opened my eyes to find them looking directly into Andy's, and she smiled at me. I needed no further encouragement and one thing led to another.

Minutes later the telephone rang. It was the BBC's *Today* programme, apologizing for ringing so early, and wanting to record an interview with me over the telephone. They had got hold of the *Hampstead Explorer* at the crack of dawn and seen my piece on the shooting of Halifax. I gave them what they wanted: lots of crisp action, briefly told, and the smooth-voiced interviewer was delighted.

We had another exquisitely silent breakfast while we read the newspapers. Ours had a one-line banner headline across the top of the page: EYE WITNESS! and then the strap underneath: THE EXPLORER'S OWN HORATIO PARKER REPORTS ON THE SHOOTING OF MURDER SUSPECT MP. And across the bottom of the page: *Exclusive in your Explorer: Monique Karabekian's diaries! See Page Three*. It was a great read. And a full-blooded, old-fashioned scoop!

Andy had grabbed *The Times*, so I decided to have a look at what Corkery had written in the *Sun*. I had expected him to have a go at me, even to smear me a little, but what he actually wrote left me unsure whether to roar with rage or collapse with laughter.

He went into a lot of background stuff, describing me as the 'childhood sweetheart' of Monique Karabekian, and said that we had remained 'good friends' although I had been 'devastated by her marriage to Halifax'. Then he got on to the shooting, describing my presence there as 'a sinister mystery now being investigated by the police'.

I showed Andy. She laughed, so I decided to as well.

After Andy left for work, I did a few things. First I wrote out a cheque for the amount of my Bluebelle restaurant bill and sent it to Adolfini care of his company headquarters in Bayswater, in an envelope marked *Personal and Confidential.* (It was never presented for payment.)

Secondly, I asked Pendleton how the negotiations with Blackstock were going on the sale of the newspaper.

He replied, 'Morley is seeing Mr Blackstock and his lawyers this afternoon to look at the final draft of the agreement drawn up. If all is agreed, the document will be signed, Rothschilds will issue the cheque, and the newspaper will be yours as soon as Blackstock's solicitor deposits it at his City bank first thing on Monday morning, in other words, shortly after nine-thirty a.m.'

'Excellent! Did you manage to contact Bob Price and offer him the job of general manager?' I asked.

'Indeed I did. He was delighted, and agreed immediately.'

'When can he start?'

'Virtually any time, he said.'

'OK, let's ask him to report for work at ten a.m. on Monday morning—and his first task will be to fire Mitchell. If Mitchell wants confirmation he can telephone Blackstock, and perhaps we can ask Blackstock to be available for that call.' I was warming to this kind of executive action.

I continued: 'Tell Price that he will also receive a letter from you beforehand, setting out basic priorities and ideas that he might want to start working on, but that in all other respects and particularly in terms of day-to-day decisions, he is to use his own discretion.

'That letter will also contain a statement which he is to

read to the entire staff at a meeting to be called later that morning. These letters will, of course, be written by me, although I will put your name at the bottom of them.'

My next call was to Arnie Bloch, who sounded positively jovial.

'It's only ten o'clock and we've sold out!' he chortled. 'We added fifteen thousand to the print run, and gave every newsagent thirty per cent more than they ordered, and we've got calls stacking up on the switchboard asking for more.' Happiness is a massive scoop.

'We've also got calls stacking up from national newspapers wanting to use the story, and we're selling it to them at a thousand quid a time. There's an ITN crew here looking for you and offering bags of gold for an interview, and there's even a guy from the Health Education Council who wants to use you on a video they're making on mouth to mouth resuscitation. Oh, and Chief Superintendent Harrison at Hampstead nick called. He wants to speak to you.'

I told Bloch about my interviews the day before, and about my theory that Monique had been blackmailing all the sixteen people on the list.

'What for, money?'

'No, work. She forced them to put her into their films, in the case of producers and directors. She forced the actors to stand down in her favour and/or recommend her for parts, and she clearly had a powerful hold over Bertrand Blake—and that didn't do her career any harm at all.'

'I hope you can prove all this, Parker, because without black and white proof, and without affidavits signed to the last dot and comma, we're not going to run a bleddy word of it. The last thing we need is sixteen libel writs landing on our doorstep, man.'

'Don't worry,' I said. 'I'm working on it.'

'Oh, and by the way, Parker, the editor had a word with Blackstock this morning about the salary increase you asked for.'

'What did he say?' I asked, intrigued.

'Well, apparently Blackstock said, and I quote: "Don't give the lazy bastard another penny. He already gets too much, and tell him I said so."

'Wow,' I said.

'You must have upset him or something. Have you been rude to him or anything like that?'

'No, but we all know he's a difficult bugger, so don't worry about it, Arnie.'

'I'm not worrying about it,' he said, and hung up.

Then I telephoned Theo Bernstein, and when he came on the line I said, 'Good morning, this is your international media superstar speaking. Did you want to interview me?'

'He who is proud in heart is an abomination to the Lord,' Theo replied wearily.

'Is that from the Talmud?'

'No, *Proverbs*, chapter sixteen, verse five.'

'What does the Talmud say about pride?' I asked.

'It says that man should reflect on three things—where he has come from, where he is going, and before whom he will have to make his final account and reckoning. You came from a putrefying drop, are heading for a place of dust, maggots and worms, and it is to the Lord himself that you will have to submit your final piece of copy. Some humility is called for.'

'I'll bear that in mind. In the meantime, what does Harrison want me for?'

'He wants to know what you're up to.'

'Ah, I understand. You crimebusters are getting nowhere and you want to know if I've found anything out.'

'I suppose that's one way of putting it, although I would have expressed it differently.'

'Well, as a matter of fact, I have found something and I'll tell you about it on condition that you never refer to that little Harlesden/Neasden error again.'

'It wasn't Harlesden/Neasden, it was Willesden/Harlesden, and it wasn't a little error, it was a gigantic fucking cock-up!' he protested.

'Goodbye, Theo—'

'Wait! It's forgotten. I promise. Never to be referred to again. What have you got?'

'If only you can bear to wade through the Karabekian diaries again—' he groaned loudly—'you will notice that sixteen of the entries are distinguished by a little symbol at the end, a letter "T" with a circle around it.'

'What's the significance of it?' he asked.

'You will also find that in each entry she has had lunch with some famous person in the film world, all men, and on each occasion her husband was out of the country.'

'Interesting, but what's it all about?'

'One of the men was Eduardo Adolfini.'

'Was he now?' Theo paused for a moment. 'And do you have some theory about all this?' I told him about the three interviews and my blackmail theory, and suggested that a more formal approach, from the cops, to the others on the list might yield more information than I had managed to get.

'I think you may have something here, Parker. We'll look into it. Anything else?'

'No,' I lied. I wasn't going to tell him about the key. 'But you do realize that if it turns out that Monique Karabekian was blackmailing these people, you have another sixteen people with quite a strong motive for murder, and you may find yourself having to look at Halifax's protestations of innocence in a new light.'

'That thought had occurred to me,' he said patiently.

My left ear was still all hot and red from having a telephone pressed against it for so long that it was a pleasure to get out of the house. The sky was crisp and blue after some overnight rain, and everything had a brilliant clarity. The radio had reported that this was the sunniest May for forty years. It was an excellent day for a funeral.

There was a very large crowd at Highgate Cemetery where they put Monique in the ground within sight of the famous bust of Karl Marx. There were many minor celebrities from the world of show business present—far more than might have been expected to have turned up to anything to do with Monique Karabekian when she had been alive.

There was also a group of people who were obviously from the Karabekian clan, the women weeping copiously and without shame and the men all dark and taciturn, casting smouldering glances about as if searching for someone on whom terrible vengeance could be wreaked.

I stood about a hundred yards away, too far away to hear what was being said at the graveside, but then I didn't want to hear.

I was much more interested in seeing who was there and, perhaps more significant, who was not there. No one really important had come. None of the top directors or producers, none of the really famous stars, and certainly no interesting politicians. I noticed something else. Eduardo Adolfini was not there. Nor was Bertrand Blake, Anthony March, or any of the other names on my 'T' list.

I sat against a gravestone in the sun until it all ended, thinking and daydreaming and doing my own spot of mourning for Monique. It is possible that I even dozed for a few minutes, for the next thing I knew the graveside was deserted. No, not quite deserted. There was a solitary figure there, standing with his back to me, his hands in his pockets and his head bowed forwards in a posture of such abject misery that I knew it couldn't be one of the actors. A little while later he turned and came walking up the path towards me. I kept very still in my little patch of undergrowth and he didn't see me, but I could see who it was, with tear stains glistening on his black cheeks. Nathaniel Jackson.

I got back to the cab feeling depressed. I needed a walk, so I invited Frankie to join me for a ramble on Hampstead Heath.

It was an absolutely perfect day, yet all I could think of was Monique decomposing in her grave, unable to tell anyone which of the sixteen men had put their hands around her beautiful throat and closed off the air. Well, possibly seventeen, if you included Halifax.

Then we resumed our search for lockers in central London. The Friday traffic was heavy and as the sun got hotter and the key refused resolutely to fit any lock, I began to feel more and more despondent. Even the lunch with Pendleton didn't cheer me up.

I signed all the necessary documents for the takeover of the *Hampstead Explorer*, and Pendleton had two pieces of news for me. The first was that Bob Price had declared himself satisfied with the arrangements, confirmed his arrival time on Monday, and looked forward to his first task —sacking Mitchell. The second was that Bill Petrie, the editor, had decided to retire. Apparently Blackstock had felt constrained to inform him of the impending sale, as a matter of courtesy. Petrie, who was 62, decided that he didn't have the energy to take on a new set of owners, and had asked for early retirement, which Blackstock had granted instantly.

I thought about that for a few minutes, had a brainwave, and gave Pendleton some more instructions for Price.

After lunch Frankie and I worked our way down the list of left-luggage lockers in south London and had no luck at all. We had decided to call it a day at about four o'clock, and we were driving up Tottenham Court Road when Frankie slid back his communication window and said: 'How worried are you that we're being followed?'

Christ, that's all I needed. Murder, burglaries, shootings and now I was being followed. Someone must think I live in a bloody novel, I thought to myself. 'Who's following us?' I said, looking out the back window.

'He's about four or five cars back at the moment, a grey Toyota. He's very good, and keeps well back, but I've been catching sight of him every now and then since we left Hampstead Heath this morning. He's following us, OK.'

'Can you lose him?' I don't know why I asked that, since we were only going home, but I think it was the sheer effrontery of it that annoyed me.

'I can try, but this is not something I have a great deal of expertise in,' Frankie said.

He swung the cab into a left turn, going through a yellow light as he did so. We were half way down the block when

I saw the grey car jump the red light and turn in after us. Now that he saw that we were on to him, that I was looking out the back window, and that we were trying to lose him, he stuck close and there wasn't much Frankie could do about it. I couldn't see the driver properly through the reflections in the windscreen, but it was clear that he didn't intend to lose sight of us. I memorized the index number. We played a silly game of going around a lot of corners for about ten minutes, but he was still there.

We were stopped at a red light when Frankie said: 'Hang on, there is a way of getting rid of this guy, but it'll cost you, because I'll have to recruit a few more taxi-drivers.'

'Do it, whatever it costs,' I said. He pulled off when the lights changed and then parked on a yellow line. The grey car pulled in behind us. It was an eerie feeling having someone so overtly hostile so close. Now I could see the driver—a dark-haired man I didn't recognize who sat impassively, gazing back at me. Frankie got on to his radio and spent about five minutes having complicated discussions with a number of other drivers. Then we appeared to drive around aimlessly in the Fitzroy Square area for a few minutes, until I noticed that there were now three or four taxis driving around with us.

The trap was sprung in Charlotte Street when we all stopped for a red light. I noticed that the grey car was surrounded by taxis, and when the light turned green we pulled off and they all just sat there, boxing him in completely and not moving. I heard his hooter blast angrily, but he must have realized fairly quickly what was happening, because the last thing I saw before we turned a corner was him out of the car remonstrating with the other drivers.

A few minutes later Frankie got some calls on his radio and reported to me. 'Looks like he's gone home now. The drivers say he drove off finally in the direction of Marble Arch. They each want twenty quid—me too.'

'No problem,' I said. 'I'll give you the money and you can pass it on.'

Then I phoned Theo Bernstein and gave him the number

of the car. 'Can you find out from your computer who that is?' I asked him.

'No. Apart from the fact that we are not your private investigation agency, it is against the law to give confidential information to members of the public, and all information held on the computer comes under that heading.'

I sighed patiently, and explained that the guy had been following me around all day.

'There's no law against following people, unless he made any threats or intimidating gestures—'

'Theo,' I interrupted, but, remaining patient, I added: 'It occurs to me that this person might have been, or might have been working on behalf of, one of the sixteen people on that list who, knowing or suspecting that I was on the trail of more information, decided to keep tabs on me.' It was a long and pedantic sentence but grammatically correct. 'I think it might be worthwhile finding out who it was.'

'I will make inquiries, but I'm not sure if I will be in a position to let you have any of the information,' he said.

'Let's face that problem when we come to it. In the meantime, I'm going home.'

Frankie dropped me off at a specialist car-hire place in Marylebone, and I drove home in an unusual surprise for Andy.

CHAPTER 17

When I asked Andy whether she would like to spend the weekend with a millionaire at a quaint little seventeenth-century hotel in the Cotswolds whose restaurant just happened to have three Michelin rosettes, she said she would have to think about it.

About three or four seconds later she remarked that the suggestion had some positive attractions, but then she added: 'Oy, I don't feel like driving hundreds of miles on motorways in my little car.'

'That will not be necessary,' I assured her.

'Don't tell me that Frankie Freud is going to take us in the taxi!'

'No, that is also not on the agenda.'

'How, then, are we going to get there, Parker?' she said, beginning to sound a little impatient. 'Are we going to fly?'

'Something like that.' I took her to the window and pointed at the gleaming red Porsche 924 parked in the street.

'Wow! Did you buy that?'

'No, just rented for the weekend.'

'I've never been in one of those!'

'Nor had I until yesterday evening.'

Despite my unfamiliarity with the car, which seemed to be able to do things a split second before I realized that they needed doing, we arrived safely at the hotel a few hours later. We spent the time walking in the delightful countryside, eating a great deal and returning frequently to the bedroom for bouts of recuperation following our touristic exertions.

The room we slept in was the size of a football field, and the bathroom boasted an Olympic-sized tub with massive claw feet and pipes that must have been nearly two inches in diameter. The bed was a four-poster, firm and sturdy, and well it needed to be.

The restaurant, we decided, richly deserved its Michelin rating, but we both actually preferred the breakfast, which was one of those country house affairs that one reads about in Edwardian novels, with guests coming down at a terribly reasonable hour to be faced with a ridiculously long sideboard crammed with food.

I mention all this only because of what happened that afternoon on the way back to London, cruising eastwards on the M40 in the Porsche and marvelling at how effortlessly the needle on the speedometer passed the part where all the noughts lined up, and then how slow seventy miles an hour felt after that.

If I hadn't been so anxious about lurking police cars with speed trap radar gadgets I wouldn't have been checking the rear view mirror with such diligence, and I would never have noticed the olive green Jaguar that was following us.

At first I accused myself of being paranoid following the incident on Friday afternoon. After all, fast cars often behaved this way on motorways, tucking themselves in behind another fast car exceeding the speed limit in the hope that if there was a speed trap, the car in front would get caught. But this car was too far back for that and was staying, where possible, in the slow lane.

Without telling Andy, I slowed the Porsche down gradually to sixty-five miles an hour without touching the brake, and kept watch in the mirror. The Jaguar at first gained a hundred yards or so before the driver realized that I had slowed down, and then slowed down himself until the same five or six hundred yards was between us again. Just as gradually I took the car up to ninety-five, and at first the Jaguar fell back. But within a few minutes, there he was again, hiding behind other cars whenever he could, but essentially matching my speed mile for mile.

When I told her, Andy was scornful at first, asking why on earth anyone would want to follow us around on a dirty weekend, but when I went through the experiments again she saw for herself.

'It's weird,' she said.

'I know. When it happened for the first time on Friday I had this feeling that I was in some kind of crime novel or in a detective series on TV where this kind of thing happens all the time. I haven't the faintest idea what to do about it,' I said.

'Do you think we're in any danger?' she asked.

'I don't know. I mean, all the guy is doing is following us, like the one on Friday too. There's no one trying to force us off the road, and there are no hoods with thin moustaches wearing white spats standing on the running-board and shooting at us with revolvers. He's probably just following us to see where we go and, presumably, to find out what we do when we get there.'

'Did he follow us from London yesterday?'

'I didn't notice him, but I presume he did since he is now behind us on the way back.'

'I don't like it, it's really creepy. Can't we go very fast and leave him behind?'

'Well, I think this car is probably faster than his, but that would require a kind of driving I know nothing about. I would say that trying to outdrive him would be a good deal more dangerous than just letting him follow us. When he realizes we're not doing anything, maybe he'll get bored and go home.'

'If he's not bored already, he'll never be,' Andy said.

We drove in silence for a minute or two, and then she said: 'Does this car have an immobilizer? You know, one of those switches that cuts off the ignition system and makes it impossible to steal the car?'

'Yes, it does,' I said, 'it's a little switch hidden under a flap of the carpet where it comes down off the gearbox mound to the floor. It's the first thing they showed me at the car hire place. Why?'

She leaned over and felt around until she found it, and didn't answer the question.

'OK, Parker, I've got a plan. Make like you're having engine trouble, and then pull up on to the hard shoulder with the hazard warning lights on.'

I looked at Andy, and she wasn't joking. My eyebrows went up, and it took her about twenty seconds to tell me what she had in mind. Simple and ingenious, and probably not very dangerous. Something even a coward like me could go along with.

I lifted my foot off the accelerator and then put it back on a few times, making the car surge and bounce noticeably as I moved into the slow lane, then I just put the car in neutral and let it slow to a stop on the hard shoulder, the hazard lights winking.

Andy was looking intently out of the back window as I reached down and activated the immobilizing switch. My heart was beating furiously, and I could see a vein in Andy's neck pulsating fast.

'Here he comes, he's stopping,' she said breathlessly. In the mirror I saw the Jaguar slide smoothly on to the hard shoulder and draw up behind the Porsche. I was pretending to be trying to start the car, the starter motor pushing the engine around and around without a hint of a spark from any cylinder.

A man got out of the Jaguar and walked over to my side of the car. There was nothing odd about him at all, nothing distinctive, and if we were expecting a hood with a black silk shirt, white tie, pencil moustache and ominous bulge under his armpit, we couldn't have been more wrong. He was about five feet ten, of normal build, and with a rather bland face that would be impossible to describe because it was so utterly without distinctive features. Just an ordinary face; you know, two eyes, one nose, mouth, two ears, that sort of thing. But he could speak.

'Having trouble? Can I help?' There was a slight accent which I couldn't place, but the demeanour was of the perfect good Samaritan. 'I saw your hazard lights go on, and I know a bit about cars, so I thought I'd stop. It's a bummer to get stuck on a motorway . . .'

Both Andy and I got out of the car. I was looking—and feeling—flustered.

'Well, thanks very much,' I said. 'I don't know what's wrong with it. It's a hired car. It just sort of cut out, and it won't start now.'

'You've checked the obvious things like petrol, oil warning light, generator light, that sort of thing?' he asked.

'It's none of those,' I said.

'Well, let's have a look at the engine, then. Release the bonnet catch, and I'll see if I can see anything wrong.'

I leaned in and pulled the bonnet release lever as he went round to the back of the car where the engine was and opened the lid. I stood with him as he bent down and fiddled with things. He checked the distributor leads and a few other things I didn't understand.

'Try turning the engine over again,' he suggested.

I got into the driver's seat, and turned the key. The starter motor droned into life with its rhythmical pulse, but of course nothing else happened.

'Hang on,' he called. I waited a few seconds, and he called again. 'Try her now.' The starter motor droned again for about ten seconds. Then Andy got into the car, pale and her breath coming in quick gasps.

'I've done it, let's go!' she hissed.

I reached down to the immobilizing switch, turned it back off, and then hit the starter again. The engine roared into life, and I slammed the automatic gear lever into Drive and put my foot down. Rubber burned and the car swayed slightly from side to side as the powerful engine did what it was designed to do. I glanced in the mirror and saw our good Samaritan sprawled on the hard shoulder, but then I had to concentrate on my driving and get the car back into the traffic on the motorway in one piece.

'What's he doing?' I gasped.

Andy was kneeling backwards on the seat, looking out of the back window. 'I can't see! The engine cover is still up, and it's blocking the view!'

'Look out of your window!' I yelled.

She pressed the electric window switch and stuck her head out. 'He's getting into his car!' she shouted. A moment later she shouted again: 'Now he's getting out again, and he's pounding on the roof!'

Andy was looking at me, with tears running down her face—either from the release of tension or from the wind on her face, or exultation. Maybe all three. There was also a triumphant grin on her face as she dangled a set of keys from her index finger.

'He didn't notice a thing. He was so busy with his head stuck into the engine that he didn't even hear me open the door of the Jaguar,' she whooped.

'Do you thing he might have spare keys?' I asked.

'No! There's two of everything on this bunch. He's screwed. He's not going anywhere for a while.'

After about two miles I pulled the car off the road again, on to the hard shoulder.

'Why are you stopping?' she asked.

'I have to close that engine cover before we get stopped by the cops.'

When I got back in the car Andy was looking thoughtful.

'A guy like that; won't he have some other way of starting the car? Putting the wires together or something like that, in the same way that car thieves do it?'

'I suppose he would.'

'So maybe we should get the hell out of here before he gets going?'

I pulled out into the traffic again. 'I agree, so we're going to take a detour.'

I drove as fast as I dared until we reached the intersection with the M25 motorway that runs right around London, and then took the exit which led on to the southbound section of the anti-clockwise carriageway. For once it wasn't completely choked with traffic and we covered the few miles to the junction with the M4 motorway in good time. Then we turned east again, towards London, in even heavier Sunday afternoon traffic than before.

It was as we were approaching London Airport in a slow-moving queue of cars that wheels began grinding in my brain and thoughts began to mesh, and suddenly Andy and I were looking at each other and we shouted in unison: 'HEATHROW!'

'Have you got that key with you?' she asked.

'Of course,' I said, as I cut across two lanes of traffic like a lunatic to get to the airport exit in time. Behind me dozens of cars hooted and at least fifty people renewed their instinctive hatred for Porsches and those who drive them.

I managed somehow to get on to the Heathrow spur of the motorway in one piece, and Andy said: 'Which terminal, do you think?'

'Terminal Three,' I replied confidently. 'Theo Bernstein

said that the taxi-driver who brought Halifax to London for the second time that night picked him up at Terminal Three. That was one of the mistakes he made, you see. Had he come straight off the Lufthansa flight he would have been at Terminal Two. We're a couple of prize idiots, though, that we never thought of the left-luggage lockers at the airport.'

'Speak for yourself, Parker, I've only been on this job with you for a couple of days.'

I drove into the car park, found a parking place, and we walked over to the terminal.

'Let's try the Arrivals section first,' Andy suggested.

It took us a few minutes to find them, a bank of lockers tucked away behind the bookshop at the end of the concourse. My hand was shaking slightly when we found No.65 and I put the key into the lock. It went in smoothly, and turned like a greased ball-bearing. The door swung open without the slightest protest.

But the locker was quite empty. The interior gleamed with shiny walls. Its emptiness yawned.

CHAPTER 18

The busiest airport in the world swirled around us with a roar of arrivals and departures and constant streams of humanity flowing in every direction. But Andy and I were immobile, transfixed by the sight of that empty locker. It was not possible that it was empty. It was not feasible. Worse than that, it was not fair.

'I don't understand,' Andy said. 'Could he have come back to collect whatever it is that he put here?'

'No, that doesn't make sense. If he collected whatever it was, he wouldn't still have had the key with him when he got shot. No, Halifax expected whatever it was to be here. We have to work out where it's gone.'

'Have you lost anything, sir?' We had been so intent on

that mockingly empty space that we had not noticed the approach of a large policeman. We must have been radiating consternation.

'As a matter of fact, yes,' I said. 'We had something in this locker, and now it's gone.'

'When did you put it there?'

'Ah . . . about a week ago.'

'Well, that explains it, then,' he said, with the air of one who has just solved a difficult and complex crime. He pointed to a large yellow notice on the wall behind the lockers. Whoever had put it there must have been convinced that no one could possibly miss it. We sleuths had missed it thoroughly. It read:

PLEASE NOTE: ALL LOCKERS
ARE CLEARED FOR SECURITY
REASONS EVERY 24 HOURS.

'Your goods will have been removed the next day,' the policeman explained.

'Removed to where?'

'Airport luggage office, administration building, third floor, room 206,' he intoned. 'You'll have to produce your key and describe the goods, but they'll have it all there all right.'

We thanked the helpful lawman and set off, hand in hand.

'How are you going to describe the goods?' Andy asked helpfully. 'We don't even know what it is he left there.'

'I don't know, we'll just have to play it by ear.'

Finding the administration building at Heathrow was the first hurdle. Various airport workers gave varied, and different, vague directions about how to get there, and after trudging for what felt like miles along underground corridors which led nowhere, and above-ground corridors which led back to the underground ones, we finally walked across three open-air car parks and one elevated walkway and found it.

It looked deserted and it was with a sinking feeling in my stomach that I wondered whether the office would be open late on a Sunday afternoon. We took the lift to the third floor, and found Room 206 which had a notice on the door: LEFT LUGGAGE CLEARANCE. I turned the handle. The door opened. We went in.

The room was divided in half, with a counter running across. Behind the counter was a wall of metal shelving holding an array of suitcases and packages of all descriptions. On our side there was a bench along one wall, a low table with a dying pot plant on it, and two soft chairs that had been pulled together by the man who was lying fast asleep on them, a Sunday newspaper partly covering his face. On the counter there was a button and a notice which read:

Please ring ONCE for service.

Andy's hand was moving towards the bell when I clamped my own around her wrist, putting my other finger on my lips for silence. We stood at the counter for a few minutes, listening to the faint snoring of the man behind us, while I scanned the contents of the shelves on the other side of the counter. I didn't know what I was looking for, but I hoped I would recognize it when I saw it. In the end it stood out like a beacon on a dark night. I pointed to the bell button, and nodded to Andy. She gave it a good long push, and it rang loudly.

The man under the newspaper snorted with surprise, dropping the paper on the floor as he swung his feet to the ground and tried to stand up before we could notice that he had been asleep. Then, as if he had just walked into the room, he gave us a broad smile, let himself through a flap in the counter and, for all the world like one who has been keenly on duty all afternoon, he said: 'How may I help you?'

I showed him the key, told him that the article had been left in the Terminal Three lockers early in the morning of the second Thursday previous, and apologized for not seeing the notice about the contents being cleared daily.

'No need to apologize. Without people like you I wouldn't have a job,' he said, grinning. 'Thursday two weeks ago . . . uhmmm . . . that would have been the eighteenth, wouldn't it?' I nodded. He began filling out a form. 'Can you describe the article?'

'It's a brown leather attaché case with gold-plated clasps, and the initials M.K. in gold letters,' I said easily. Andy looked at me with delicious admiration in her gorgeous eyes.

The clerk wrote it all down. 'You do understand that we had to open the article when it was brought here, for security reasons, you understand, and if it was locked we will have had to break it open.'

'Of course,' I said, as if I was used to having my attaché cases broken open by security staff with sniffer dogs.

'Your name, please, sir?' That caught me off guard, and I resorted to a coughing fit until I could think of a suitable name.

'Kahn, Mike Kahn,' I said, 'with an "h" before the "n" .' He wrote it down.

'Address?' This one I was ready for.

'42, High Street, London N16,' I answered casually. He wrote that down too. Then he turned the book around and pushed it towards me.

'Please sign here,' he said, pointing with a dirty fingernail. I signed 'Mike Khan' like I had been doing it all my life, and a few seconds later the attaché case I had seen on the shelf was in my hands. Both catches were broken open, but the case was secured by a tough, heat-sealed nylon tape.

'Thank you,' I said. He yawned, and I thought he glanced quickly at the chairs on which we had found him asleep. No doubt he would be asleep again in a matter of minutes.

We only got about half way along the corridor towards the lift when Andy grabbed my arm. 'I can't stand this, what's inside the case for Chrissake?'

'Wait until we get to the car, we can't start tearing it apart here in the corridor. Besides, we need something to cut through this nylon band.'

We hurried back to the car park and, sitting breathlessly in the Porsche, we managed to cut through the nylon with a nail file from Andy's handbag. I threw open the lid of the case.

Video films. That's what was in the case. *The Sound of Music. Annie. Mary Poppins. Showboat. Guys and Dolls. Oklahoma. Singing in the Rain. South Pacific. The Wizard of Oz. Seven Brides for Seven Brothers. Half a Sixpence. West Side Story.*

Andy frowned at me in consternation. I frowned back. I opened the outer cases of the cassettes, thinking that this was perhaps merely camouflage, but each contained the correct film cassette. I took them out in turn, shook them and held them up to the light, but they were just video films. No drugs, no photographs, no files, no incriminating letters, no money. Just musical schmaltz.

'We'll need to put them on the video machine,' Andy said, 'to see if they are what they seem to be.'

'I have a dreary feeling that they are exactly what they appear to be, and we are going to have to sit through all of them to make sure.'

'It won't be so bad—I quite like *Guys and Dolls.*'

'So do I. But *Mary Poppins* . . .' I groaned.

We got back into the London-bound traffic on the M4 again, the mood of anti-climax hanging heavily in the air.

And it started raining as we got into the Cromwell Road. Thick early-summer sheets of rain that swept under skirts and umbrellas like billowing curtains, sending unprotected pedestrians scurrying into doorways, and giving drivers momentary impressionistic glimpses of their surroundings as windscreen wipers beat gamely backwards and forwards against the cascades of water.

The rain was just letting up as we arrived home. There were no journalists outside, and no burglars had been inside. Andy went up to run a bath, and I made a light meal.

It was about half past ten when we arranged ourselves on the couch and I slipped *Guys and Dolls* into the video machine. There was a moment of tension as we wondered what was going to appear on the screen, but it turned out to be Frank Sinatra, Marlon Brando and the rest, going through their paces exactly according to the script.

It's a great film, full of classic lines and golden tunes, but it had also been a long day and a tiring one. After half an hour or so Andy went to bed. And fifteen minutes after my eyelids were drooping and I also gave up on Nathan Detroit, Sky Masterson, Nicely-Nicely Johnston and the boys and, without bothering to rewind the tape, I took the cassette out of the machine.

I was just putting it back in the box when I noticed something that snapped my eyelids open and started my heart beating quickly. There was a stickiness on the front edge of the tape cassette that bellowed at me. I looked more closely, and it was perfectly clear where the sticky tape had been placed across the square indentation in the cassette which was designed to prevent accidental recording over a pre-recorded tape.

Blank video cassettes intended for constant recording and re-recording come with the indentation already closed by a piece of plastic. Pre-recorded tapes come with it open so you can't inadvertently lose what you've bought unless you deliberately cover it—with a piece of sticky tape, say—in order to record it.

My hands were shaking slightly and my fingers were tingling as I put the cassette back in the machine, and turned it on. This time I put it on fast forward and sat in the silence as the characters whizzed on and off the screen, and frantically went through their song and dance numbers at nine times their usual speed.

And then suddenly I was looking at the face of Eduardo Adolfini. And not just his face, but his whole body. All of it. Naked.

I lunged for the remote control and brought the tape back to normal speed. The sound came on and the room was filled with heavy breathing, the creaking of a mattress and the rustle of bed linen.

I was watching a film of Eduardo Adolfini, nude, on a very large and ornate brass bed, lying on his side and propped up on one elbow, gazing with some fascination at something off-screen. It was more than fascination; it was quite impressive arousal. There was no doubt about it.

The angle of view was high, as if the camera were mounted high up on a wall, and the clarity of the sound effects suggested a hidden microphone somewhere in the region of the many pillows or on the headboard. It was all in sharp focus, and in glorious colour.

Any absurd doubts about what it was that I was seeing were dispelled a second or two later when Monique Karabekian came into the picture, also naked, moving with all the sensuous grace and beauty that had persuaded millions of men to part with good money to see her strip in films. But none of the millions had ever seen her in a film quite like this.

She didn't lie down on the bed, but sat on the edge, in profile to the camera, and ran her right hand down Adolfini's body, starting at his shoulder and ending at his knees, having made all the required detours on the way. There were no words, just sharp intakes of breath, and a low moan from Adolfini when cool fingers met hot flesh. He reached out for her to bring her down to the bed with him but she caught his wrists gently but insistently in her hands. She leaned forward and whispered in his ear with all the sexy huskiness of her voice, 'Indulge me, Eddie.' Her voice was recorded perfectly.

'Eddie's' breathing was a bit ragged, a wholly understandable state in the circumstances. My own breathing was a bit ragged—and I was only watching the video. This was not the poised and powerful man who moved in the highest circles with authority and fabled menace. This was a lump of male putty in expert hands. His reply was acquiescence when she pushed him gently back on to the bed so that he was lying on his back.

She took one of his hands and moved it gently across her right breast, just brushing the fingers across the nipple and exerting firm pressure to stop the hand closing over the breast, or from making its own movements.

'Let me do it,' she whispered, and again he acquiesced.

During the next few minutes she continued to tease him mercilessly. There is no other way to describe it. She caressed him briefly here and there, placed his hands on different parts of her own body, but whenever he tried to respond or participate in anything but the most passive way she would respond with a hint of withdrawal, a flash of coldness, a little frown of disapproval on her beautiful face, which would then disappear before another soft caress when he relaxed again.

'I can see that I am going to have to restrain you,' she whispered.

'What?' His confusion was tinged with surprise.

'I want to make love to you—' she spoke softly in that throaty voice of hers, but also slowly and clearly, so that every word was picked up breathily on the tape—'I want to do extraordinary things with you, but I want to do it my own special way.' Her hand went to his penis and stroked it softly. 'Will you let me restrain you . . . ?' The words tailed off as he arched his back involuntarily with the sensations in his groin, and then the hand left him, and he was stranded in the vacuum which followed her question. His breathing was quick now.

'Restrain me? How?' he said, having to clear his throat first.

'With handcuffs, on the bed,' she said simply. His eyes darted around momentarily, and a frown appeared on his face, but she reacted immediately, as a mother might placate a worried infant. She leaned over and began to kiss his mouth and face tenderly, her hands massaging his neck and shoulders, and she lowered her body so that her breasts brushed his chest. His arms came up almost instinctively to embrace her—but again she caught his wrists and twisted away from him.

'You see? You can't be trusted.' And without waiting for a response, she slipped off the bed and disappeared from the screen. But only for a few moments. There was the sound of a drawer being opened swiftly and then closed, and a second later she was back. With handcuffs. 'Don't worry, I'm not going to hurt you,' she said as she got to work. 'No whips or anything like that. Just me.'

It wasn't that Adolfini had lost the initiative; he had never had it from the first moment of the encounter, and by the time she had handcuffed one wrist to a brass bedpost, the opportunity for protest had long passed. Adolfini may not have been happy with the idea, but the choice was now a simple one: go along with this and get your rocks off in a new and, who knows, possibly even exciting way, or exert yourself and bring the whole scene to a messy, rather embarrassing, and certainly unrequited, end. The task was accomplished expertly in less than a minute, and Adolfini was spreadeagled on his back, now helpless.

Then she went to work in earnest. It was an exhibition of calculated cruelty that had me breathless and shaking, remembering my own tingling encounter with her in that dark hallway in her parents' house so many years ago. Remembering the passion of her body and hands, my own swelling response, and the suddenness and completeness of her withdrawal. Seventeen years later, I was watching her doing the same thing to Eduardo Adolfini. But on a much grander scale. It was more explicitly sexual now, more subtle and much more developed, and it was nothing less than the utter demolition and deliberate humiliation of a man.

Her sexual caresses became no more than fingering of his body and genitals. Her kisses became sloppy and crude as she put her tongue noisily in his ear, and then she fiddled flippantly with his penis and testicles, moving them this way and that, almost as a child might experiment with something new and unfamiliar, seeing how far it would lie in each particular direction. And yet it was done amid a stream of spoken endearments which clearly took the sting of the treatment out of the experience for Adolfini. Now and then he would frown slightly, or grunt with disappointment, as if some inkling of what was happening had begun to penetrate his understanding—and when this happened she was careful to mollify him with a more genuine caress, a more pleasing sexual touch, a more sensual kiss on the mouth, an even more complimentary murmur about the joys of touching his body, and he would be carried along again without protest by the impetus of events.

This was not a blue movie or a piece of pornography, and certainly not borne out of any desire on the part of a lover to record the delights of an encounter. It was an object lesson in degradation, carried out by an expert who never lost concentration for a moment, and never once obscured some little touch of contempt or flick of flippancy from the unblinking eye of the video camera.

There were times when her treatment of him was so bizarre and offhand that he lost his erection, and when this happened she would squeal with disappointment and concentrate her efforts on the flagging member until it stood proud again. Then she would abandon it once more.

The climax to the whole process followed one of these cycles when, bringing him back to erection, she continued to rub and stroke his penis but this time with abandon. Adolfini's eyes bulged, and although he croaked 'Wait!' she disregarded the warning signs and his orgasm began—at which stage she withdrew her hand quickly, leaving him to ejaculate convulsively, but utterly alone and exposed, on to his stomach and chest.

There followed a moment of utter silence. Adolfini's eyes were tightly shut, probably with a mixture of frustration and embarrassment, and his limbs were rigid. Monique had a surprised look on her face as she stroked his cheek.

'I'm sorry! I didn't realize!' she said softly. 'Hang on, I'll get something.' She disappeared again from the screen, leaving the stretched out torso of Adolfini, with the ejaculate now beginning to run down the side of his body, to the callous lens of the camera.

She returned to dab ineffectually at him with a handful of tissues, as if this was something she had never had to do before, and was not quite certain what to do. Adolfini looked stricken.

And it was then that Monique chose to twist the knife, and to begin to display passion. She moved into position over Adolfini, her breathing becoming faster, and she began to press her body to his for the first time. As she undulated against him he tried to respond—but it was, of course, much too soon for him, and the stricken look on his face increased in intensity when it became obvious that she was trying to get him to enter her.

'Now, darling! Now! Do it now!' she was croaking desperately in his ear as her pelvis ground against his. When there was, predictably, no response, she stopped moving abruptly and rolled off him. His humiliation and destruction was complete. You could see it in his face.

'It's OK, really. Don't worry about it,' she cooed. 'Honestly, it's not that important to me.' Her words came soothingly as she unlocked the handcuffs. Adolfini, by now totally off balance on unsure ground, said nothing at all. He allowed himself to be cradled briefly in her arms as she murmured: 'You were wonderful! I loved touching your body. Really. It was beautiful.' And then she moved off the bed. A few moments later Adolfini sat up and swung his feet over the side of the bed. He sat there, dazed, for a few moments, and then he too walked off the set. *Guys and Dolls* came back on, with the famous scene of the crap game in the sewers.

I turned off the video machine. I could feel tears running down my cheeks.

'Monique,' I said aloud, 'why do you hate us? What did we do to you?'

CHAPTER 19

There were sixteen video films, and it took me just over two hours to establish that they were depressingly similar. Hidden in the middle of each musical was an almost identical scene to the one I had just watched. Sixteen men drawn to the lower depths of subjugation and impotence, some more willingly than others, and others caught more by surprise and who, as a result, were more shocked by the experience. Sixteen faces that changed from confident leers of conquest to masks of grey embarrassment as Monique Karabekian reduced them all, in slightly different ways, to flaccid husks.

I knew some of them to be creative and fiercely independent men who had clawed their way through the entertainment jungle with talent and accomplishment. Some of them were household names, enormously powerful money-men, and actors whose faces were known to millions.

I didn't watch them all. I sat through the show with Bertrand Blake, and Anthony March and one or two others. But generally I re-wound the tape as soon as I had established the identity of the victim. And of course the list of names matched exactly the list we had extracted from the diaries.

When I went upstairs, Andy was fast asleep. I got into bed as quietly as I could but she sensed my arrival and curled up against me without waking. I put my arms around her and held her in the gentlest embrace, feeling her soft breath on my shoulder. As sleep crept up on me I wondered if Monique Karabekian had ever been held softly and tenderly like this, whether she had ever held anyone close to her, whether she had ever taken delight in anyone else's physical presence. Had she ever been touched with genuine affection and then allowed herself to return it? On the evidence I had, the answer was no in every case.

I told Andy about the tapes during breakfast, and she stopped chewing on her toast. She even put down the newspaper. 'Do you want to see any of them?' I asked.

'No fear, it sounds as if it could put me off sex for ever.' She paused. 'So what's next? What do we do with the tapes, and what are their implications?'

'The implications appear to me to be crystal clear. We have here sixteen very humiliated men who, as if their treatment at Monique's hands wasn't enough, also find that she is blackmailing them,' I replied.

'Not for money, of course, but for favours. For scripts, for parts, for better parts, for more exposure for the films, for better reviews. It's all quite obvious now. Any one of these men could have become enraged enough to have killed her regardless of the consequences, and for the time being, my money's on Adolfini. I think Halifax is telling the truth, that he came home to find her dead and simply panicked.

'But as for what we do next, that's simple. The tapes are going straight to the police, first thing this morning, before anyone can accuse us of withholding evidence.'

I put the video films back in the broken suitcase, tied it up securely with string, and we dropped it off at the police station as Frankie drove us to work. It was addressed to Theo Bernstein, marked URGENT! and CONFIDENTIAL!, and I attached a note which read: 'Theo, these are musicals with a difference. When you've watched them, ring me. Parker.'

Then we headed for the *Explorer* where, I reminded Andy, we had a very exciting morning ahead of us.

CHAPTER 20

The half-hour between nine-thirty and ten on Monday morning at the *Hampstead Explorer* is a period of intense concentration. The ticking of the office clock is distantly audible as the staff sit quietly at their desks, brows furrowed, chewing the ends of their pencils. Incoming telephone calls are answered sharply and queries are dealt with briskly. There is little conversation other than hushed conferences about weighty details, and the air is filled with the silent hum of creative minds at the peak of their capacity. Now and then there is the tap tap tap of fingers on pocket calculators. Journalists are filling out their expenses forms.

If Andy and I weren't giving the matter our full attention for once, it was because we alone knew that an event was about to take place that would change for ever the nature of the newspaper and the working lives of our colleagues, and I admit that as the clock moved towards ten a.m., my heart was thumping painfully in my chest.

It was in fact at about five to ten that Bob Price appeared quietly at the door of the large newsroom, wearing a light grey suit, and carrying a briefcase. The look on his face was what I can only describe as a mask of contentment, the expression a messenger might wear when about to deliver a summary deportation order to a universally hated despot —which was, of course, exactly what he was about to do.

Having entered the room, he stood silently just inside the door and for a few moments no one (apart from me, that is) noticed him. The first to see him was Arnie Bloch, whose beady eyes seldom ceased roaming around his domain, and he moved swiftly across the room.

'Hell man, Bob, it's good to see you!' and the smile was even genuine. 'But what the hell are you doing here?' Bloch demanded, with all the delicacy, subtlety and tact at his command.

This alerted others to his presence and Bob Price was soon surrounded by a quietly welcoming throng of reporters and sub-editors. He fended off the questions and, after a glance at his watch, he held up his hands for silence.

'I have something to do, but I'll be back in a few minutes. Don't go away,' he grinned. Then he picked up his briefcase, and with a purposeful stride he set off across the long newsroom towards the two partitioned offices at the end.

One housed the editor, when he was there, and the other was Mitchell's. Bob Price was clearly heading for the latter, and everyone watched, transfixed.

Bob strode up to the door, opened it abruptly without knocking, went in and then positively slammed the door shut behind him. For a few moments there was total silence, and then we began to hear voices which quickly rose to a crescendo of shouting. Then, quite abruptly there was silence again. Andy and I knew why: Mitchell was telephoning old Mr Blackstock for confirmation of his marching orders. Two minutes passed, and the tableau of journalists did not move. All eyes were riveted on that closed door.

Then, at last, the door opened and Bob Price stood in the doorway, his cheeks pink, but his eyes blazing with triumph and the fire of sweet revenge, and he spoke loudly into the room: 'Mr Mitchell is just leaving the building, and he needs someone to help him take his possessions out to the pavement. Anyone care to volunteer to assist?'

No one volunteered.

Mitchell, trembling and as white as a sheet, started walking, and as he did so a corridor opened before him through the silent throng of employees. He made his way unsteadily through the hostile ranks, and I realized that there was not a person in the room who felt a shred of sympathy for him. We had all seen members of staff victimized, humiliated, disciplined, exploited, and demoted and dismissed by this arrogant and vindictive little snot, and there was no one inclined to make this moment of retribution any easier for him.

It was only when he was actually at the door, his hand on the handle, that someone spoke. It was 'Junior' Gerry Walker, one of the two indentured trainee reporters, who had gone through a period of merciless hounding at Mitchell's hands.

He said, in a quiet, mocking voice: 'Dear me, Mr Mitchell, are you going home early today? Thanks for dropping in.' And then everyone cackled and whooped for joy as we saw his back disappear through the door.

It wasn't long before the merriment died down, however, and the throng again turned its attention to Bob Price, this time with collective eyebrows definitely raised and with a clear expectation of an explanation. He did not disappoint them.

'As you may have gathered, the previous general manager appears to have resigned suddenly and, for my sins, I appear to have been appointed in his place. As you might expect, I have some important announcements to make and some information to impart, so I would be very much obliged if someone would pop upstairs and ask the entire advertising department to join us down here, since what I have to say applies equally to them. Gerry, would you mind?' Junior was out of the door in a flash.

It took a few minutes before the surprised and expectant members of the advertising department, secretaries and accounts staff began to troop in. By now they'd all heard the incredible news about Mitchell, and no one at all was weeping. Bob Price perched himself on the edge of a desk and addressed them all.

'Good morning, ladies and gentlemen. Most of you know who I am, and the rest will find out soon enough. The most important piece of information I have for you is that as of ten a.m. this morning, the *Hampstead Explorer* has new owners—who have appointed me to run the company.' There was a buzz of excitement and speculation, and at least three or four questions were voiced simultaneously.

'Hang on! Give me a chance and I'll tell you everything I can.' He waited for the buzz to die down, and then continued: 'Heathlands, Limited, which is the company that owns the paper, was sold this morning by Ernest Blackstock for an undisclosed sum and is now owned by a company called Golden Daffodils Holdings Limited.

'And, before you ask, I have to say that I do not know who or what Golden Daffodils is, other than that it is a company registered in Jersey—and that means, given the business secrecy legislation in Jersey, that it is not possible to find out any more about it.

'All I know is that it has a managing director, a charming elderly London solicitor by the name of Pendleton, who approached me for the first time only a few days ago with an offer I did not hesitate to accept. I have no idea who actually owns the company, Pendleton is most definitely not forthcoming with the information, and so your guess is as good as mine.' Now there was silence.

'However,' he continued, loudly, 'from what I have seen and heard so far, I don't think you should all be unduly worried by the mystery of ownership—there are other matters which I suspect you will find rather more interesting. I think the best thing I can do is read out the list of instructions I received through Mr Pendleton from our new employers. You will see that, whoever they are, the new owners are both eccentric and very progressive.' He extracted a piece of paper from his jacket pocket and unfolded it.

'It reads: "Dear Mr Price, we are your new employers. We regret that we cannot make ourselves known to you. You have been hired because we believe you have the ability to run the *Hampstead Explorer*, in partnership with the staff, without constant reference to any higher authority. You are empowered, therefore, to take all day-to-day decisions that you feel are necessary for the continuation, expansion and improvement of the newspaper. We have confidence in you, so get on with it as you see fit.

'"We are attaching to this letter a short list of instructions and announcements that are to be made to staff."' Bob Price pulled out another piece of paper, and started reading:

'"Firstly, Peter Mitchell is to be dismissed as soon after ten a.m. as is practicable. We ask you then to hold a staff meeting at which you will explain the situation as you understand it. We would wish it to be known that we regard the staff as the most valuable asset of the company and, in recognition of this fact, we are taking certain steps to improve remuneration and working conditions in the company. In the first instance there will be an immediate fifteen per cent increase in pay across the board.

'"The staff may also be interested to know that we have decided to allocate fifty per cent of the annual profits of the company to a special bonus payment to staff, so that all employees will now have a direct stake in the success of the newspaper.

'"There will be no dramatic changes in staffing, other than those necessitated by the retirement of the editor, Bill Petrie, who, it will be understood, is an old friend of Ernest Blackstock and who expressed the wish to take early retirement. This wish has been granted and Mr Petrie will not be returning to this office. In his place, Mr Arnold Bloch is to be offered the appointment of editor as of this morning, on a contract to be negotiated with Mr Price, and the post of news editor is to be offered to Ms Andy Ferris."'

I sneaked a quick look at Andy, who was sitting thunderstruck at her desk. Arnie looked equally gobsmacked, and was gazing at Price with a totally dazed look on his face.

Price stopped reading and put the papers back in his pocket. It was so quiet you could hear jaws still dropping all over the office.

'So, what it amounts to, colleagues, is that while you may have been sold down the river, the first port of call seems to have been a five-star marina with all the luxuries you could desire. I confess that I feel a little uneasy not knowing who I am working for, and many of you may feel the same, but on the evidence we have so far, I think we are going to learn to live with that unease very easily.

'Let's all think about things for a day or two, and I will be happy to listen to everyone's thoughts and ideas. Thank you, and now let's get back to work. Perhaps Mr Bloch and Ms Ferris would care to come and talk to me in a few minutes.' People began wandering out, slightly dazed. Then Bob Price called out:

'Wait! I nearly forgot. Everyone is invited to the Holly Bush tonight where Mr Blackstock will be picking up the tab for a farewell party for both himself and Bill Petrie. We hope to see you all there.' Not even I knew about that one.

Price, Bloch and Andy disappeared into one of the offices, and I went back to my desk where, a minute later, the telephone rang. It was Theo Bernstein. An irritable Theo Bernstein.

'What the hell is all this, Parker?'

'What is all what, Theo?' I asked infuriatingly.

'This bloody suitcase full of musicals and a cryptic note from you. I don't have time to sit and watch television; I'm not some lazy journalist—'

I interrupted sweetly: 'Theo, cast your eye at the initials on the suitcase, and see if you can think of a recent murder victim that might fit them.' There was a long silence. 'I assure you that it is necessary for both you and Inspector Harrison to see those films, although you may find that it will save some time if you fast forward them until you come upon items of interest. But you'll have to stick with it, Theo. Just remember, it was only by perseverance that the snails managed to get on to Noah's ark.'

'What?' he snapped.

'That's from the Talmud,' I said.

'No it's bloody not!'

'Well, it should be,' I retorted. 'How else would the snails have got on the ark?' And I put the phone down. When I looked up I found I had a visitor at my desk, a very beautiful visitor who was glaring at me angrily through slitted eyelids.

'Oi,' she said, 'why didn't you warn me?'

'This was irresistible,' I protested.

'Why?'

'Because Arnie was the obvious person to replace Bill Petrie and he deserved it. And you were the obvious person to replace Arnie. Anyone in their right mind would have given the job to you.'

'But why didn't you tell me?' she hissed.

'Because if I had you wouldn't have had that necessary look of total astonishment on your face when Price made the announcement, and someone might have wondered why.

Besides,' I continued, 'I can't think of a better arrangement than having you as my news editor.'

'I think I might have you fired,' she said.

Arnie Bloch, still looking a little shell-shocked, was busy moving his stuff into the editor's office, and Andy was moving to his desk. Around me my employees were happy and hard at work, and I felt contentment creeping upon me.

CHAPTER 21

An enormous amount of work was done at the *Hampstead Explorer* that morning, little of it connected with journalism. The calculators came out again as people worked out the effect of their pay increases, and then again as they searched their desks for the company's last annual financial statement to see what half the annual profits might amount to in the current year, and how that might be divided up among them. And however they did their sums, it became clear to everyone that it meant a further three or four thousand pounds each, possibly more, from the bonus scheme alone.

From time to time knots of people gathered together around the tea-and-coffee-making area, and at random around individuals' desks, to discuss the momentous news, debate furiously about the figures and speculate about the identity of the new owner. Even Arnie Bloch put down his slave driver's whip for a while.

'John Paul Getty. That's who it must be,' said Mike Graham with a certainty which, for a while at any rate, gave his theory pole position.

'No,' said Arnie, with an unusually thoughtful look on his face. 'It's obviously someone who knows the paper and knows us all. No faceless businessman or remote philanthropist would have gone about it this way, or made the changes in that way. I have a feeling we already know him.'

'Anyone recently won the pools?' asked Junior Walker.

'Parker must have,' said Amanda Popplewell. 'He rides around in his own private taxi nowadays.' All eyes looked at me.

'My Aunt Lily,' I explained. 'She died a few months ago, and left me a few thousand pounds.'

'No, it's not someone who won the pools,' Arnie said. 'It's someone with a good deal more money than that, millions more.' And then, as an afterthought, he added: 'And it couldn't be Parker, even if his Aunt Lily was a bloody billionaire. The new boss is subtle, man.'

It irked me a little that everyone seemed to accept that without comment, and no one even thought to remark that perhaps Arnie Bloch was the last person who should be talking of subtlety—especially since he had pronounced the word 'subtil'.

Eventually all the talk and speculation died away, and by the time they all came back from lunch, some of them even got back to doing some work. Even me. I had a pile of mail and a sheaf of telephone messages, most of which I threw away immediately. But two caught my eye: from Nathaniel Jackson, the porter in Halifax's block of flats. The number was a Kentish Town one, but as I picked up the telephone to dial, two large blue shadows fell across my desk.

Well, the shadows weren't really blue, perhaps, but the two men in dark blue uniforms and helmets were certainly large. And they were unsmiling.

One said: 'Mr Parker?' I nodded, and he continued: 'We would like you to accompany us to Hampstead police station.'

'I beg your pardon?' I think it's almost compulsory to say that to policemen who ask you to accompany them to police stations. But this one knew I had heard him perfectly well, so he did not repeat his invitation and he just looked at me patiently. I conceded the point.

'Am I being arrested?' I asked. Already there was a semi-circle of journalists formed up behind them and I could see Arnie Bloch pushing his way through the crowd.

'What's going on here?' he demanded. (It sounded like: 'Wot's goin' on hya?') But the policeman kept his cool.

'No, sir, you are not being arrested. We are merely requesting that you accompany us. We have reason to believe that you may have information relevant to an on-going police investigation in progress.' It was the usual pompous constable-ese, but he was being polite.

'Did Theo Bernstein have anything to do with this?' I asked.

'It was Chief Superintendent Harrison, I believe, who issued the request that you should be invited to the station.' He was choosing his words very carefully. Then he added: 'But Sergeant Bernstein was there at the time.'

I saw no reason to prolong the conversation. 'It's OK, Arnie, I know what they want to talk to me about.' I went quietly.

When we arrived at Hampstead police station, I was ushered into a small interview room with bottle-green walls and the usual worn table and chairs. 'Wait here, please,' said one of my entourage.

'Any chances of some coffee? Black, no sugar, filter preferably, but instant will do.'

The gaoler lifted one eyebrow sarcastically. 'Would that be all, sir?'

'A couple of choccie biccies would be nice,' I replied. He slammed the door. Perhaps they only served tea.

For a few minutes I studied the wanted posters on the wall, the crime prevention information, the appeals for assistance, and the notices about police doctors, use of the telephone, neighbourhood watch schemes and the availability of legal advice. Some wag, probably also left alone in here, had written on the wall a list of 'Rules for the Fabrication of Evidence'.

I only got time to read the first one ('In no circumstances allow your prisoner to make any telephone calls!') when the door flew open so violently that the ceramic door knob on the inside shattered against the wall, and pieces of porcelain skidded across the floor.

Norman Harrison didn't seem to notice what had happened to the door knob, and he too slammed the door shut. Maybe slamming the door was obligatory. But maybe it also had something to with the fact that his face was bright red, there was an expression of thunder on his features, and veins were pulsing on his temples. He was carrying a brown cardboard file which he slapped down on the table, creating a minor dust storm as he did so. He didn't sit down but bent towards me over the table, leaning on his knuckles rather how one might imagine an aggressive gorilla might stand.

'I've had you, Parker, right up to here!' he shouted, his right hand moving to indicate a position just underneath his nose. 'Everywhere I look in this goddam investigation I find a bloody Horatio Parker with his big flat feet muddying the water, and I've had enough!'

'You seem a little upset, Chief Superintendent,' I ventured to comment.

He took a short breath, as if to explode, but then thought better of it and took a few deep breaths. Perhaps he was counting to ten. Then he pointed a stubby finger at me. 'You are walking on very thin ice, my lad. You have on two occasions been found to be in possession of material pieces of evidence in this case.

'You are that far—' he showed me a one-millimetre gap between thumb and forefinger—'away from a charge of withholding evidence, or even for conspiracy to pervert the course of justice!'

'OK, where's Mr Nice-guy?' I asked.

'What?' His eyes bulged a little.

'You know, the pleasant one. Isn't that how it works? First they send in the aggressive one to soften up the prisoner and terrify him. Then they send in Mr Nice-guy who lets the prisoner confide in him. Who is it? Theo?'

A look of true perplexity crossed his face. 'You think this is some sort of game, don't you? We have had one murder, one attempted murder, two burglaries apparently related to the former and in which you were obviously connected, and you carry on as if it's all a big joke. I don't understand it.'

'No, it's not a joke,' I said seriously. 'It is very far from being funny. You forget that I knew Monique Karabekian, that it was my house that was ransacked, and that I was present when Malcolm Halifax was hit by a bullet, and that was in no way an amusing episode, I assure you.' He was listening, so I continued.

'But what is a joke is the way you people keep reacting when I hand you, promptly and properly, important pieces of evidence lawfully obtained by me in the diligent pursuit of my occupation—which, you may have forgotten, is concerned with the gathering of facts.' I was in my righteous stride now.

'But, instead of saying, "Gosh, Mr Parker, what a help you've been to us," you send policemen to my office to embarrass me, you bring me here and start shouting and banging doors.

'That's the joke, and it's not even a funny one, because even when I give you these important items of evidence you have failed to grasp their significance. It was I who had to point out to you that there were sixteen significant entries in the Karabekian diaries. It was I, again, who had to point out that the bag of video films of Hollywood musicals contained material which put beyond any question the significance of those diary entries.

'It was my deductions, based on my investigations, which led to the inescapable conclusion that Monique Karabekian was blackmailing a long list of important people in the film industry, and that this suggested that there were a number of other people in London with powerful motives to see Monique dead. And where were the highly trained and highly paid professional police investigators all this time? You tell me that.' It was a good speech. I was enjoying myself, and Harrison was looking decidedly subdued.

'Can you tell me how you came to be in possession of those films?' he asked.

'Certainly. Malcolm Halifax gave me a key to a left-luggage locker at Heathrow Airport and intimated to me that he would like me to retrieve its contents.'

'Intimated?'

'Yes, well, he wasn't speaking very clearly with a bullet through the lung.' Harrison sighed deeply and shook his head. I continued: 'Look, there's no way I could have known that it had anything to do with Monique. And as soon as I discovered what they were, I took immediate steps to hand them over to you. They were delivered by me, first thing this morning, as you well know, only a matter of hours after I saw them.'

'We could split hairs about this for ever, Parker. The fact is that you must have been in possession of that key for days—presumably while you drove around looking for the correct locker, right?' I nodded. 'OK, so there have been some failures on both sides. So where do we go from here?'

'Well, for a start I could do with a bit more police assistance in protecting my own safety,' I said.

'What are you talking about now?' he said, clearly puzzled.

'I was followed around London all day on Friday by some kind of hood in a grey Toyota. I gave the registration number to Theo Bernstein and I'd like to know what he has managed to find out. I've never been followed before, and it has to have something to do with all this.'

'I'll go and ask him.' He turned towards the door.

'You're going to have a spot of bother, doing that,' I remarked.

'Now what are you on about?'

'Look, there's no door handle.'

Harrison went red again, but he kept his temper, even when he had to shout through the keyhole and kick at the door for a few minutes before anyone noticed anything out of the ordinary and came running. My suggestion, that it was because they were all used to the sound of kicking and shouting coming from the interview rooms, was not appreciated as great humour.

While he was gone I read a few more of the Rules for the Fabrication of Evidence, such as, 'Always tell the suspect that there is a police car on its way to arrest his mother,' and 'As far as possible, do not let the prisoner see the statement he is signing, and ensure there are gaps in the writing,' and, 'Always leave a few pages blank in the statement; you never know when they'll come in handy.'

After a minute or two, Harrison came back into the room, this time with Theo in tow, both of them looking thoughtful. Theo nodded at me pleasantly. He was carrying a video camera which I could see was an expensive item, and not just the kind one would use to take videos of the kiddies' parties.

'Monique's?' I ventured.

'Yes,' Theo said. 'We found it mounted at the top of a cupboard in their bedroom, right opposite the foot of the bed. It was on the top shelf, screwed on to a bracket which enabled it to film through the little glass windows in the cupboard door.' He shook his head as if such iniquity was quite beyond his understanding.

He continued: 'It was wired to a switch at the side of the bed, next to the switch for the bedside lamp, and the microphone, they tell me, is concealed in the upholstered headboard.'

'So she could turn it on and start recording whatever was happening on the bed while pretending to switch on the light?' I suggested.

'It looks that way.'

'Would Halifax have known it was there?'

'Perhaps, perhaps not. She may have had the work done while he was out or abroad or something, and it's possible that he never ever looked in her side of the cupboard.'

Harrison chipped in: 'Of course he bloody knew. I suspect lots of couples have some sort of similar arrangement for filming their sexual activities. The question is: Did Halifax know she was filming her adventures with other men?'

'Was there a tape in the camera?' I asked.

'No.'

There didn't seem to be much more to be said about the camera, so I asked: 'What have we got on the car which was following me?'

'The grey Toyota is registered to a company by the name of Screenbrite Limited, which leases lighting equipment to film companies. It's a subsidiary of Adolfini Holdings plc,' Theo said. A cold chill went down my back; I distinctly didn't like the concept of being followed by anyone connected to that hooded-eyed snake—especially now that I knew how desperate he would be if he thought anyone had got hold of the video film he knew to exist. So I told them about the green Jaguar on the motorway the day before.

'Did you get its registration number?' Theo asked.

'No, he was too far back, and when he was close enough, we were too busy giving him the slip.'

'A bit less of the James Bond stuff and a little more writing down of index numbers would have been a great help,' he responded.

'Hang on.' I had an idea. 'Surely the DVLC computer in Swansea can work backwards?'

'What do you mean, backwards?'

'I mean if it can tell you what company owns a car, can't it tell you whether that company has any other cars registered in its name—including, perhaps, a late model green Jaguar?' Harrison looked meaningfully at Theo, and the latter went to find out.

Harrison remained in the room, so I didn't feel free to read any more items of advice on creative evidence gathering. Instead I asked him whether the charges against Halifax were going to be dropped.

'Not quite yet. I agree that we were misled by what now appear to have been a string of circumstantial factors which pointed to the MP. There are clearly a number of other avenues of investigation that need to be carried out, but I don't think we'll withdraw the charges just yet. It's not as if he's rotting in prison; he's in hospital, and he's on bail.

And anyway, if someone else is responsible for the murder, I'd much rather he thought we were still convinced it was Halifax.'

There was a certain logic in what he said, although I wasn't quite sure how one would 'carry out an avenue of investigation'.

'How is Halifax?' I asked.

'He's well off the danger list, and mending fast, but he's under armed guard and no one is being allowed to visit him.'

'Not even the person who saved his life?'

'Watch my lips, Parker: no one.'

Then Theo came back, with a significant glint in his eye, and I felt that sinking feeling again. 'Screenbrite Limited does have a Jaguar registered—but of course we have no way of knowing whether that was in fact the car that followed you yesterday,' he added quickly.

'Well, all I can say is that I would feel somewhat more secure if I knew that valiant and intelligent policemen were looking a little more deeply into the Adolfini connection,' I suggested.

'So far we have no evidence at all that he is connected with the murder other than the fact that he was one of Monique Karabekian's sorry victims,' Theo said. 'If someone connected with him was following you, and so far we have only your say-so that this was the case, then it could also have something to do with the fact that you were pestering him the day before.

'At the moment he is just one of a number of new suspects who will have to be interrogated with some delicacy. We can't go jumping in on someone like Adolfini with hobnail boots.'

Theo then escorted me back through the police station towards the car park. We were going down a particularly dark corridor when he said: 'You know, Parker, my instinct tells me there is something you are holding back.'

'No doubt the Talmud has something to say about that,' I ventured.

'Of course: Take care not to pervert justice, for by so doing you shake the world.'

'What, little old me shake the world? Never.' But he was giving me a steely look.

I arrived home ravenous and found Andy there.

'What's for dinner?' I asked.

'Curried goat,' she said.

I shuddered. 'Explain, please.'

'Someone by the name of Nathaniel Jackson telephoned and invited us to join him for dinner tonight at a West Indian club in Finchley Road.'

'You accepted?'

'I accepted. We're going there after the staff farewell party for Bill Petrie and old Mr Blackstock at the pub. I love curried goat.'

'You love curried goat?'

'Yep.'

It proved that you can be someone's lover for days and days and still have no idea what they're really like.

CHAPTER 22

The farewell party for Bill Petrie at the Holly Bush pub, hosted by Ernest Blackstock, was a lavish affair in which reporters more used to warm beer and gin put back Veuve Clicquot 1982 Gold Label like it was Perrier water. Blackstock could afford it, though—Rothschilds had paid him three million of my pounds that morning.

Both men made moving speeches of farewell, punctuated only by the sound of corks popping and journalists falling to the floor. Bill Petrie reminded everyone that he had been only the second editor in the newspaper's 58-year history, and he wished Arnie Bloch a long and distinguished sojourn in the editor's chair.

Old man Blackstock didn't even look in my direction the whole evening. It was only when Andy and I left, and I went to say goodbye to him, that he gripped my hand with fierce strength and looked me straight in the eye. 'They tell me you've been doing a great job over the last few weeks. Keep it up!' he said, and he kissed Andy for a shade longer than I thought was strictly necessary. Dirty old bugger.

We got a taxi down to Finchley Road and, after some searching, we found the dimly lit entrance which led down an even more dimly lit staircase to the Calabash Club, whence drifted an array of enticing aromas, not least among them the tang of curried goat and the sweet promise of marijuana.

We paid ten pounds each to get in, plus five pounds each temporary membership fee and then, without anything further being said we were shown to a table for four by a waitress whose short skirt seemed to have been shrink-wrapped around her.

'Nat Jackson booked the table,' she explained in a broad West Indian accent. 'He's late, of course, but you can order any time you want,' she added, slapping two menus on the table.

We ordered curried goat, of course, and I was delighted to discover that it was both tasty and hot without being stringy and fiery as I had feared, and we were on our third beers when Nathaniel arrived with a most exquisite woman on his arm who he introduced to us as Tina. He was wearing a maroon silk shirt with the buttons undone right down to his navel, and she had on a black cross-over dress with a neckline that plunged almost as far. They must have started drinking elsewhere because both were well oiled and in high humour.

'Parker, you came, mon!' And you must be Andy that I spoke to on the 'phone. That calls for a drink,' and he waved frantically at the waitress. When she came she was carrying four glasses and a bottle of Johnnie Walker Black Label. Ignoring our half-finished beers, he poured out four heavy tots.

'To Andy,' he said, and an inch of whisky disappeared in one swallow. I knew then that it would be a very long, or perhaps a very short, evening. Everyone else had sipped, so he refilled only his own glass, and raised it again. 'And to my frien' Parker, the newsman.' And another inch of scotch disappeared.

That's when the band started playing, a loud combo of guitars, saxophones, drums, double bass and a strange percussion instrument which looked like two hollow sticks being smacked together. It set up an insistent, pulsing rhythm which made conversation impossible. They played without a break for nearly forty minutes, and there was nothing else to do but join the surge of movement to the dance floor. When it finally stopped and the musicians headed for the bar, we were flushed and breathing heavily but elated too.

The Johnnie Walker bottle came around again, but this time I topped up our glasses to the brim with ice and Perrier and it went down very easily.

'So, Parker mon, tell us about the murder investigation,' Jackson said, stretching out the vowel sounds in investigeeeeshaaan almost into a parody of the West Indian accent. His face was glistening with sweat, and his eyes were bright, but in among the animation of his features I saw a shadow of anxiety, and there was a tightness in his voice which transmitted more than the casual concern of his words. But it was Tina who spoke next.

'Why are you so interested in that, Nat?' she said.

'Hell mon, I'm involved. I mean I feel involved. The thing happened in the building where I work, and I knew that Monique Karabekian—she got me that job, remember.'

What he said was perfectly true and his concern was quite plausible. The porter in a block of flats where one murder had taken place and another attempted might reasonably be expected to be interested in what was going on. But there was also an element of desperation trying to break through the studied detachment he affected. I might have expected him to ring me at the office and ask questions, but it was now becoming obvious that the invitation to the Calabash Club had a more serious intent than we had first realized.

My answer was accurate, if incomplete. 'The police have what looks like a powerful case against Halifax,' I said. 'But the trouble is that all the evidence they have against him is circumstantial, and no one has yet been able to suggest a motive on his part. Halifax claims he found the body when he came home and just panicked. What the police don't know is who shot him and why he—'

'He killed her,' Jackson interrupted tersely. 'That bastard killed her.' There was a silence at the table accentuated by the boisterous noise around us.

'How do you know that?' I asked with a studied mildness. Andy and Tina were sitting very still, looking at him, but he was focused only on his thoughts.

'I just know he did it. I feel it, mon.' His eyes were boring into the tablecloth.

'You just feel it? Or do you know something?' My question was delivered quietly, and deliberately without accusation. His eyes flicked up and caught mine, and for the most fleeting instant I saw the conviction about that statement in his soul, but then it was gone and his face broke into a smile. He banged his hand down on the table.

'Let's have another drink!' he said, and the whisky bottle did another pass over the glasses. The subject was closed and remained closed for the rest of the evening or, rather, the rest of the morning, because by this stage it was something like 1.30 a.m., and the party in the Calabash Club still resembled something that was just getting started.

My memories of the rest of the party are more hazy. At some stage the whisky bottle was replaced by a full one, and significant inroads were made into its contents. Also, a joint was passed around. Then the band started playing again, and Andy and I got up again to weave our magic on the dance floor.

When we made our farewells about an hour later, Nathaniel beamed at us and although he didn't say anything I suspected that he was thinking that white people just didn't have the staying power really to enjoy themselves. No one else was even showing signs of leaving when we climbed the poorly lit stairs to the outside world and the hope of finding a taxi in Finchley Road.

In bed I had expected to sleep immediately, but I found myself lying awake in the dark and aware, from the sound of her breathing, that Andy too was not asleep.

'What are you thinking about?' I asked into the blackness around us.

'Nat Jackson, and the way he said "I'm involved".'

It's what I was thinking about too.

CHAPTER 23

That Tuesday dawned with a vengeance. The early summer weather had been replaced by pouring rain, driven almost horizontal by powerful gusts of wind that rattled Victorian window frames and threw the water in fury against the glass. It was the sort of sound that depresses the spirit and, having had less than four hours' sleep to dissipate the effects of gallons of beer and whisky, Andy and I both whimpered in sleepy despair when the clock radio chirruped into life at half past seven with a breezy news headline about a passenger ferry disaster in the South China Sea.

When we left the house after a subdued breakfast of black coffee and dry toast, the rain was still coming in horizontal bursts and vertical fusillades and although Frankie was parked only a few yards up the road we were thoroughly wet by the time we got into the taxi.

The weather had even dampened the high-spirited mood that had prevailed at the office the day before. Or perhaps the mood had something to do with the amount of alcohol consumed the previous night at Bill Petrie's farewell. Either way, the journalists were in more sombre mood, and one or two of them were actually pecking away at their keyboards and blinking weakly at their computer screens.

I was just realizing that I did not have a lot of work to do when I was saved by the bell. The telephone bell. Or rather the telephone warble. It was Theo Bernstein.

'We need you here at eleven o'clock.' Then there was a pause, before he added: 'Please, Parker.' There was an intriguing suppressed excitement in his voice.

'What's up, Theo? You've never said please to me in all the years that I've known you.'

'We want to see if you can identify anyone in a line-up we've arranged.'

'Who is it?' I asked.

'If I told you that there wouldn't be much point in the line-up, would there?' That was more like the acerbic Theo I knew.

'OK, I'll be there.' I left my desk like a bullet.

When I got to Hampstead police station both Theo and Norman Harrison were looking pleased with themselves, and there was a general air of expectancy around. It was the way police got when they expected a major collar to be felt. Harrison carefully described the procedure to me.

'We are going to take you into a room in which you will find a line of men. You will say nothing to any of them or to us. You will walk along the line of men, twice, and when you have done so, and if there is anyone in the line whom you recognize, you will not say anything but you will walk up to him and briefly put your hand on his shoulder. Again, you will say nothing until you have been taken out of the room. Is all that clear?' I nodded.

It was a big room that looked like it might be some sort of meeting room because there was a lectern at one end, together with a blackboard on the wall and one of those wooden easels that hold large paper flip charts. All the chairs had been gathered together and stacked against one wall, and against the opposite wall there was a line of nine or ten men, all approximately the same height—around five foot ten or eleven—but of varying builds, complexion and modes of dress. Apart from Theo and Harrison, there were three uniformed policemen in the room, standing to one side with a sharp-looking man in an even sharper dark suit. The suspect's brief, I suspected.

I didn't have to walk up and down, because there was a man in the line-up I recognized instantly. But I did what I was told and I walked slowly up and down, looking dutifully and carefully at the various faces on view. Then, without hurrying, but also without hesitating, I walked up to one of them and touched him on the shoulder. His eyes bored coldly into mine. The last time I had seen those eyes was on Sunday when he had tried to help me get the Porsche started on the M4. I was then led out of the room immediately.

Back in Harrison's office he and Theo were like two soccer fans who had just seen England beat Brazil six nil. They were grinning and slapping their fists into their palms with glee. 'Got the bastard!' Harrison said.

'I'm impressed,' I said. 'I didn't think you would take my complaint about being followed and harassed by him so seriously.'

They both looked at me in astonishment. 'We haven't arrested him for following you or harassing you, you pillock! That's not an offence.' Theo gave me a look which suggested that I had disappointed him yet again.

'Then perhaps you'll let me into the secret, then. Why have you arrested him?'

Harrison looked at me. 'Off the record?' he asked.

'Sure, although it makes no difference, since if you're going to charge him with something I can't report on any matters of evidence until the trial anyway. What's he done?'

'First, he is to be charged with the unauthorized possession of a firearm, the gun being an Italian-made sniper's rifle fitted with a telescopic sight.' My eyebrows went up.

'Secondly, he is to be charged with the attempted murder of Malcolm Halifax, MP.' My eyebrows went so far up they almost merged with my hairline.

'Thirdly, he is to be charged with the premeditated murder of one Oscar Gladstone, formerly known to one and all as Bagman Gladstone, whose shot to death body was discovered two years ago by picnickers near a beauty spot in the Wye Valley.' I had forgotten about my eyebrows altogether. I was at a loss for words. Almost.

'Where did you find him?'

'He was arrested shortly after half past six this morning. He was sitting behind the wheel of a green Jaguar parked in Estelle Road—about thirty metres from your front door.' Harrison was clearly enjoying himself.

I wasn't enjoying myself. I think I was partly in shock. I was also getting pissed off by this particular style of delivery of the facts. 'Do me a favour, cut the clever stuff and just tell me what's going on.'

Harrison looked at Theo and nodded. 'Despite what you think of us, we are not a bunch of bumbling PC Plods,' Theo said. 'After what you told us about this man following you, and when we discovered the possible link with Adolfini, we put our thick heads together and surmised that since he was following you, he must have known who you were. And since he knew who you were he must have known where you lived. So even a probationer constable would have known that the next step would be to keep an eye on you to see if he made another appearance.'

'You've been following me?'

'Not exactly. We've been keeping an eye on you. We had someone outside your house yesterday morning, outside your office during the day yesterday, and from early this morning. And it was then that our plain clothes officer radioed in that a green Jaguar had just arrived and parked nearby. We put the registration number through the computer, confirmed that the car belonged to Screenbrite Limited—Adolfini's company—and sent some of the boys round to see what he was up to.

'Police cars quietly sealed off the road at each end, and a few officers went to have a word with him. It was all done discreetly and, what with all the rain and everything, without any disturbance, and he was back here within ten minutes. You didn't hear anything, did you?'

I shook my head. The way I was sleeping at half past six

that morning, I wouldn't have heard a steamroller going over a Scottish bagpiper in the street outside.

Theo continued: 'The fact that chummy was probably the one who had been following you, and that he was sitting suspiciously in his car early in the morning, gave us more than enough due cause to search the car when we got it back to the station—and the rifle was found in the boot.'

'Just like that? A rifle sitting in the boot of the car?'

'Not exactly. It had been dismantled into quite a few parts and secreted in various places around the boot, including the tool kit under the spare wheel. We also found sixteen rounds of ammunition taped behind a panel in one of the rear doors.

'The rifle was sent down to the Yard's forensic laboratory pronto, and within an hour they had produced a preliminary report clearly identifying it as the weapon used to deliver the bullets that were fired into Halifax's flat. Furthermore, chummy's dabs were all over the rifle.

'The news about Bagman Gladstone was an unexpected bonus and a total surprise to us as well. They put one of their juniors on to looking through a few unsolved shootings involving bullets of the same type and calibre, and through a stroke of luck he happened to start in the right place at the right time. They're doing a more detailed trawl through the forensic records right now, so who knows, perhaps we'll clear up a few more murders before the end of the day.'

'What's chummy's name?' I asked.

'We don't know,' Harrison said, with an edge of irritation in his voice. 'When he was arrested all he would say was that his name was Benito Mussolini and that he believed he was being kidnapped by people impersonating police officers. We think perhaps that that may not be his real name. Nevertheless, once he was in custody he refused to say a word before his brief arrived. Perhaps he'll talk to us now when he hears what we've got on him.'

A few minutes later Harrison went out, leaving me alone with Theo.

'Nathaniel Jackson,' I said.

'What?'

'Nathaniel Jackson, it's a name. Does it ring any bells?'

He thought for a minute. 'Yes, it does ring bells, but I can't remember who he is.'

'He's one of the porters at Park Vistas, and he was on duty the night Monique was killed.'

'Ah yes, he didn't see anything or hear anything or know anything and he didn't much like us asking him anything. What about him?'

'He's not a great fan of the people's police force,' I explained. 'He was also the guy some of your compatriots beat up in Finchley Road in the mistaken belief that he had perpetrated a misdemeanour on the nose of a WPC. Remember that incident?'

He remembered, although, like most Hampstead police, he didn't like having to do so. 'Yes, I remember now. What about him?'

'Does he have a police record?'

'I can't remember, and even if I did it's confidential information and I couldn't tell you.'

'Yes, you could.'

Theo put on his patient look. 'Oh yes? Why could I?'

'Because I have been a major informant on this case, and on various occasions I have been of significant help to the boys in blue. My hunches have nearly all paid off, and furthermore you owe me one. Come to think of it, you owe me two or three. Favours, that is.'

'What's your hunch this time?'

'I can't tell you—yet.'

Theo had his expressionless face fixed on, the one which wouldn't reveal whether he thought you were an idiot, or just plain mad. But he didn't say no, so I persevered. 'Come on, Theo. It may be nothing, but it may also be something, and I give you my word that nothing will get published without your agreement. It may also be of help in this investigation, I don't know.'

He made his decision. 'Wait here,' he said and went out.

I resisted the temptation to see if there was anything

interesting on Harrison's desk. Instead I sat there wondering why Adolfini—for he must have been behind it all—wanted Halifax dead, and why he was having me followed around by a hood with a rifle. Did he want me dead as well? I found the answer to none of these questions.

Theo came back after about ten minutes holding a computer print-out in his hands. 'Some of these convictions are spent. You know what that means?' I nodded. Theo sat down. 'The first offence was when he was fifteen. Shoplifting at Marks and Spencer. No charge because of his age, just a formal police warning. Then he's eighteen, suspended three-month sentence for taking and driving away a motor vehicle. Another TDA charge a year later—found not guilty. Then there's another TDA, age twenty-one, except that this time stolen goods were also found in the car—one-year sentence, suspended, probation and community service order imposed. I'm beginning to see why he doesn't like the police.'

'Don't be simplistic. What's next?'

'Six-month prison sentence, four months suspended, when he's twenty-three. Stolen cheque-book and credit cards found on him when he's trying to buy shoes on someone else's American Express account. Then, eighteen months later, he's found not guilty of breaking and entering with intent to steal. After that his luck runs out—three burglary convictions in five years with prison sentences ranging from three months to one year served.'

'Then?'

'Nothing.'

'Nothing at all?'

'Not even a speeding fine.'

'How long ago was the last prison sentence?'

Theo calculated. 'Just over eight years ago.'

'Maybe he's given up crime?' I suggested.

'Or he's just got better at it.'

'I doubt it,' I said. 'The record doesn't exactly portray a successful criminal. He seems to have got caught every time he walked on the grass in contravention of local bye-laws.'

'Well, there it is,' Theo said. 'Does it take your hunch anywhere?'

'Perhaps.'

'Enigmatic as ever, right?'

'Right,' I said, and I took my leave. 'I'll speak to you later.'

'Yes? About what?'

'About what chummy in there tells you, of course.'

'What makes you think we'll tell you anything?'

I sighed. 'Goodbye, Theo.'

It was still raining heavily outside and Frankie scowled at me when I got into the cab. He had exams coming up, and he didn't like to be disturbed while he was studying. He also didn't like people draining water all over his cab, but we managed to drive back to the office without too many scowls and muttered complaints. When he switched off the engine I asked him: 'Can criminals give up crime?'

'You mean, are they addicted to crime?' He didn't wait for an answer. 'No, I think it's more of a habit than an addiction—although often there's not much difference between the two.' He thought for a few seconds.

'People give up all kinds of habits and addictions, for various reasons and with varying degrees of difficulty and success. But even if you've managed to break a habit or an addiction, it doesn't mean you are free of the problem. Look at smokers and alcoholics, for example. They become free of the craving for tobacco or alcohol—but they could start smoking or drinking again very easily. They end up as non-smoking smokers and non-drinking drinkers.'

'So someone could be a law-abiding criminal?' I suggested.

'I suppose so. Do I get paid for these consultations?'

'Put it on the bill,' I sighed.

CHAPTER 24

By the time I got back to the office, Andy had gone home. I wasn't too disappointed because a quiet evening at home alone felt quite attractive.

Later, I sat around thinking about things and watching television, until I suddenly realized that I was hungry, and that I could hear a pizza calling me all the way from South End Green. I set off on foot.

After the rain it was cool without being cold, and there was a clarity and crispness in the air that made being outside very pleasant indeed. I ate the pizza sitting on a bench near the water fountain watching the traffic and the people queuing for a late film at the cinema.

I tried to concentrate on all these things, but my mind kept returning to what might be happening at Hampstead police station. Was chummy talking? And if so, what extraordinary and bizarre tale might be be telling? Would it provide answers to the puzzles of the previous weeks and even give a clue to the identity of Monique's murderer?

I walked up Pond Street past the hospital and then up Haverstock Hill to the police station where I found, by sheer coincidence, that the officer on duty behind the front desk was PC Mark Turner.

'Hello, Parker, want another trip down through the cells?' he grinned.

'Another time, maybe. Is Theo around?'

'He's here, but he's with the Chief Superintendent interrogating that geezer you identified. It's an all-night job, I gather, and they don't want to be disturbed.'

'Of course.' I had no intention of disturbing them and I was about to go when Turner spoke again.

'What about those videos, eh?'

'What?' A shock wave went through me and I was rooted to the spot.

'You know, those videos Monique Karabekian took of her men friends. Strong stuff eh?' There was an awful locker-room grin on his face, and I couldn't believe my ears.

'I owe you a favour, Turner, and I'm returning it right now.' My voice was seething with anger. 'I won't tell anyone what you just said. And I suggest you don't say it to anyone else, either. OK?'

It took him a few seconds to realize that I was serious, and the leer disappeared slowly. He said nothing and I left.

I walked home with furious thoughts of Monique Karabekian filling my head. I wanted to give her a lecture, push her down in a chair and force her to listen while I explained that whatever it was that she had in mind when she made those films, their existence now served only to distort and vilify her life. Whatever motive she had was now lost for ever—all that remained was pornography.

The frustration I felt kept me sleepless, and the sleepless night made me grumpy and irritable when I woke up that Wednesday morning—just the mood I wanted to be in when I next saw Theo and Harrison. I got Frankie to take me straight to the police station, before my bad mood could wear off.

I asked for Theo and he appeared unshaven, with red eyes, and a dangerous warning expression on his face. That was OK, I was ready for him with my own dangerous look.

'I want to speak to you,' I said, 'and Harrison.'

'Not now, Parker.'

'Right now!' I snapped and, ignoring the astonished gaze of the desk officers, I added, 'And in private.'

I could see that he considered getting tough with me for a moment, but he must also have seen the determination on my face and decided that it would be easier in the long run to humour me. He lifted the flap on the counter, waved me through and then led the way to Harrison's office. He was also red-eyed and dishevelled, sitting at his desk sorting through a pile of papers that looked to me like witness statements. He looked up irritably as we came in.

'Parker has demanded to speak with us, despite my

suggestion that this was not a convenient moment,' Theo said, clearly hoping that Harrison would lose his temper and blast me out of the water.

'I want to know,' I began before Harrison could say anything, 'why every Tom, Dick and bobby in this building seems to have seen the Karabekian videos. What did you do, screen them on the telly in the canteen?'

There was a long and deep silence. Theo looked astonished, but Harrison looked shifty, and I knew who was responsible.

'How do you know they have seen the videos?' Theo asked softly.

'That doesn't matter. The point is they have, haven't they, Superintendent?' Both of us were looking at him now. He was uncomfortable, but not apologetic.

'It is true that some of the officers have seen some of this material. I gave instructions that the relevant sections of each film should be copied in sequence on to a new video tape, so they could be viewed without the films they were hidden in. That meant we had to get hold of another video recorder and connect it to the one in the staff recreation room. While the recording was being made, I was aware that there were a number of officers in the room, but I saw no harm in that. I consider it to be important for them to see what goes on in the real world.'

'A number of officers!' I said sarcastically. 'I can just imagine the scene—the entire off duty contingent trying to get in through the door to see Monique Karabekian getting bonked! Is that how you protect the confidentiality of evidence—not to mention the rights to privacy and protection of blackmail victims?'

'I am not going to argue with you about this, Parker. Is that what you wanted to speak to us about, or is there something else?' He was even more uncomfortable now, but still unapologetic.

'Yes, there is something else. I want to know who chummy is and what he told you.'

Harrison sighed and picked up a piece of paper. 'All I

can tell you is that his name is Charles Pavey, although he was born Cesare Pavese in Milan. He's forty-nine years old, is employed by Screenbrite Limited as a chauffeur, and lives in Chiswick. He's a British subject and he's been charged with the three offences I outlined to you yesterday. Other charges may follow. This information will be released through Scotland Yard's press bureau this afternoon. Anything else you will hear along with everyone else at the eventual trial.'

'That's not good enough. I want to know what happened.' I kept my voice sharp.

'And I'm refusing to release any further information.'

'In that case,' I said, standing up, 'I am going back to my office where I am going to write an exposé about how sensitive evidence and confidential material regarding blackmail victims is handled in this police station, giving details about the nature of the evidence and the way it was allowed to be shown to a large number of officers who were not in any way connected with the investigation of the case.'

'You do that and I'll have you arrested for contempt of court.' Harrison was blustering now.

'Go ahead. By then the story will be published, and what I will have to say in court in my defence will make further interesting reading.'

'I'll get a High Court injunction to stop you publishing!'

'Try it! I'll contest it vigorously and I'll say everything in open court at the injunction hearing, and I'll also issue a press release that'll make your hair curl. You'll have to get an injunction against every newspaper in the country, and by the time you've finished doing that, you will be so exposed that every one of your bosses from the Metropolitan Commissioner to the Home Secretary himself are going to be lusting for a taste of your blood.'

There was another deep silence, but I swear I saw a smile flicker across Theo's face. He cleared his throat discreetly.

'Sir, if Parker gives us his word that he won't use any information in any way before the appropriate time, I see no reason why he shouldn't hear what Pavese told us.'

From the length of time it took Harrison to answer, I knew that I had won. 'You tell him,' he said to Theo. 'But don't take too long. I'm going to organize our little raiding party.' And he went out of the room. A second later he popped his head back around the door: 'If you publish a word of all this before the proper time, I'll prosecute you, so help me. I don't care what happens, I'll have your guts for a washing line.' I smiled sweetly at him.

'What raiding party?' I asked Theo immediately Harrison had gone.

'All in good time, Parker. I presume you want this from the beginning?'

'Carry on,' I said, whipping out my reporter's notebook.

'It didn't start too well. His brief, a slimy little turd by the name of Jerome Gates, had seen him and was hanging around outside demanding that we charge or release his client and, apart from finally giving us his name, address and occupation, Pavese was exercising his right not to say anything which might be used against him in a court. In fact he was refusing to say anything at all, and we were getting nowhere.

'Then we had a bit of luck. An alert desk sergeant put Gates's name through the computer, and discovered that there was a warrant out for his arrest in Glasgow on charges of smuggling narcotics to prisoners. Gates wasn't even aware of the warrant, and he was well surprised when we nicked him and put him on a very slow train to Scotland.

'After that, Pavese felt more exposed, and it was just a matter of time. We just piled on the evidence we had on him and made it clear that as a convicted contract killer not only was he going away for a very long time, but that unless he cooperated he was also likely to get the kind of sentence in which the judge recommends no release before thirty years.

'We got the confessions at around four o'clock in the morning, and Harrison was brilliant. There was lots of praise for the prisoner, lots of respect, pats on the back, encouragement, sympathy, a cup of tea, corned beef sandwiches, cigarettes, the lot. Then we packed him off to the cells to sleep.

'Half an hour later Harrison has him frogmarched up here again, and we sit him down in the chair again, while he's still half asleep, totally confused and blinking against the light. "OK, sonny Jim," Harrison tells him, "you've gone half way towards cooperating. Now we want to know who put out the contract on Halifax!"—as if we didn't already know.

'He's stunned, the poor bugger, but he's also terrified of what Adolfini will have done to him if he talks, so he says nothing. Then we had another stroke of luck—there's stuff on the teleprinter from the Yard about there being an Interpol international arrest warrant out on Pavese from Spain, on cocaine smuggling charges.

'Harrison hits him with that right between the eyes, and tells him that unless he improves his cooperation, we might waive our own charges against him and send him off to rot in a Spanish prison for the next twenty-five years. It's total nonsense, of course, but Pavese is so confused by this time that the thought of spending any time at all in a Spanish prison is more frightening even than anything Adolfini could do to him, and he cracks right down the middle. We watch a grown man cry, and it's not a happy sight I can tell you, Parker. They all cry the same way, the hit-men, the con-men and the child abusers.

'Anyway, he tells us that Adolfini ordered the hit on Bagman Gladstone. He gives us times and dates and details about the way he was paid.

'And then he tells us that Adolfini personally ordered the hit on Halifax last week because Halifax was trying to blackmail him.'

I was confounded. 'Halifax was blackmailing Adolfini? Not Monique?'

Theo continued: 'Well, that's what he says. He says Adolfini got a letter from Halifax demanding fifty thousand pounds in cash, to be delivered to Park Vistas.'

'Or else what?' I asked, still totally puzzled.

'He didn't know. That's all Adolfini told him. He was given ten grand upfront for the hit, and a promise of another ten afterwards. But he's no genius, our Cesare. If he was he would have got rid of that rifle years ago, and certainly wouldn't have been riding around with it in his car.'

'So what happens now?' I asked.

'Pavese appears in court tomorrow morning for his first remand, and we arrest Adolfini, of course. That's the raiding party Harrison was talking about.'

'But Adolfini will be long gone by now. He'll be out of the country and thumbing his nose at you from Brazil or somewhere equally safe,' I said.

'No, he won't—he has no idea that Pavese has even been arrested. Because he refused to give his name at first, Gates had no idea who he was coming to represent when he was called to the station. Gates made no telephone calls from here, and he certainly won't be making any while he's handcuffed to two constables on his slow train to Glasgow.'

I looked at my watch, and found that it was just after twelve. 'Where are you going to arrest him?'

'We'll send two squads—one to his office and one to his home.'

'If I tell you where to find him at lunch-time, will you let me witness the arrest?' I found that my heart was pounding in anticipation of a sweet revenge. Theo was giving me his hard look again.

'Out with it, Parker. If it's good I'll put your request to Harrison, but I'm not making promises.' I told him where Adolfini would be, and ten minutes later Harrison reluctantly agreed to my suggestion. The trouble was, there wasn't much he could do about it.

I ran out to the cab and put a call through to Andy. 'Drop everything, we're going to have lunch at the Bluebelle,' I said breathlessly.

'Don't be ridiculous, Parker, it's Wednesday and I'm much too busy,' she said, but she changed her mind quickly when I told her what was going to happen.

'Book a table for three,' I said.

'Why three?'

'You, me and a photographer. And make the reservation in your name—they probably wouldn't accept it in mine. I'm on my way to collect you now.'

We three arrived at the Bluebelle just after one o'clock, and the maître d' was not pleased to see me back again. Andy flashed one of her brilliant smiles at him, however, shot him through the heart with her green lasers, and he was all smiles and ooze when he led us to a very nice table, not too far from the one Adolfini always used, although there was no sign of him yet.

But he did come, around one forty-five. He sauntered in without a care in the world, and again his two gorillas were seated separately at a table near the kitchen. He noticed me after about five minutes, and although I got a long and languid gaze from those heavy-lidded eyes that turned my spine to ice, he then obviously decided to ignore me.

It all happened about fifteen minutes later, and I hardly tasted my profiteroles in my excitement. It was as smooth and without fuss as the movement of a digital watch. First two large men in plain clothes sauntered inconspicuously through the restaurant, stopping finally at the table occupied by the bodyguards, as if to have a chat. I nudged the photographer, John Pickles, to make him abandon his dessert and get his camera ready.

Then Harrison, Theo and four other uniformed police came through the door and, without hesitation or fuss, strode to where Adolfini was sitting. So quickly did it happen that he was not aware of their presence until he looked up in astonishment. There was an expression of surprise, anger and even a little fear on his face that John Pickles was to capture for ever on film. There was not much talking. Handcuffs went on in the practised, fluid way that the police have, and there was a lovely touch of class when one of the policemen leaned over, removed Adolfini's serviette from his lap and folded it neatly on the table. And all the while—much to the horror and consternation of the maître d', although much to the utter fascination of the other guests—Pickles was taking photographs as fast as his flashgun would re-cycle.

I did and said nothing at all until Adolfini was actually being led out of the restaurant, past our table.

'Don't worry,' I said very loudly, to him and the maître d', 'I'll cover your bill.' Pure deadly venom spat at me from those eyes, and then he was whisked out the door.

CHAPTER 25

The arrests of Adolfini and Pavese made a big splash in the evening papers and on the television news. Adolfini was charged with two counts of conspiracy to murder, and Pavese with murder, attempted murder, and various firearms charges. There was pandemonium again when they were remanded in custody at Hampstead Court on the Thursday morning—and further consternation on Friday morning when the nation's press discovered it had been scooped yet again by the *Hampstead Explorer*, which carried an enormous colour picture on its front page of Adolfini, with a look of demonic hatred on his face, being arrested at the Bluebelle. It must have been the moment when I offered to pay his bill.

Arnie Bloch was delighted by it all. He called me into his office and told me that although he thought I was a lazy bastard most of the time, I had done bloody well ('bleddy well'), and he had decided to give me an increase in salary. I was stunned, and didn't know what to say.

Arnie said, furthermore, that he was taking me off diary work, and would allow me to find my own stories, seeing as I had been doing that so well in the last few weeks. That idea I liked, and I wondered why I hadn't thought of that myself.

I sauntered over to Andy's desk and said: 'In no circumstances should you laugh at what I am about to tell you.'

'What is it?'

'Arnie gave me a rise.'

She laughed.

By about eleven o'clock I had run out of things to do at the office and I knew the time had come to pay a visit to Nat Jackson. Frankie drove me down to Park Vistas and, since Halifax was still in hospital, there was no policeman guarding the door. It was another warm day, and the front door was wedged open with a piece of wood, so I walked straight into the plush foyer.

Nat Jackson was on duty at his desk. Well, sort of on duty. He had his feet up on the desk, and his chair tipped back so that his head was resting on the fancy wood panelling near the lift shaft. He was wearing large wraparound mirrored sunglasses and there was a funny grin on his face, with lots of teeth showing.

It took me a few seconds to realize that he was fast asleep —which accounted for the open mouth and the fact that he had not reacted to my appearance in any way. So that's how he coped with drinking and boogying and heaven knows what else all night. He slept all day.

I walked quietly across the deep pile carpet and seated myself equally quietly on the chair on the other side of his reception desk. Then I slammed the palm of my hand down on the desk with a bang like a gunshot. Nat Jackson appeared to rise three or four inches straight up into the air before his feet hit the floor, his sunglasses flew off and he looked at me in total shock and confusion.

'Jeeeezuss . . . !' he began.

'You burgled my place, man,' I said softly. 'Why did you do that?'

Maybe, if he had had any warning at all, he might have been able to carry it off. He could have laughed at me or asked, angrily or otherwise, what the hell I was talking about, and I would have been out of ammunition because all I had was a growing hunch, and no evidence. But it had all come too quickly for him. I saw him look down in confusion and shake his head as if to clear his mind. Now I had no doubt.

'Why, Nat?' I repeated. 'Was it the diaries?'

Finally he lifted his head and looked at me with weary, bloodshot and defeated eyes. 'Yeah,' he said.

'Why?'

'Me had to know what was in dem, maan.'

'Why didn't you just ask me?' Still speaking softly. No need to spook him.

'Me couldn't.' There was no defensiveness in his voice, just shame, which I expected. But then I noticed that there had been something else in his voice that I hadn't expected. Anguish. And were those the beginnings of tears in his eyes?

We sat in silence, looking at each other. I was puzzled by the stricken look on his face and then, agonizingly slowly, like a worm emerging from a rotten apple, the truth began to dawn on me.

'You thought you might be in the diaries?' He didn't have to answer; his eyes and face said yes. 'You and Monique . . . ?' I didn't have to finish the question.

'You thought that if you were mentioned in the diaries you might be seen as a suspect? And you didn't want to be involved?' Again the eyes answered.

'And you couldn't ask me because I would have suspected that you were having an affair with Monique?' Yes, said his face.

About a minute passed, and neither of us spoke. I was looking at him, and he was looking down at the desk. Then I said: 'Tell me about it.'

It was an effort. He had to gather shreds of himself together. Then he took a deep breath: 'I loved her,' he said in a voice mangled by emotion.

'You and about ten million other men.' I deliberately put scorn in my voice.

'No.' He spoke quietly and he looked me straight in the eye. 'I loved her.' There it was again. Another simple statement, delivered deadpan. He meant it, and I felt it.

'And she . . . ?'

'She loved me.'

A lot of things passed through my head at that moment.

I remembered my own distant romantic encounter with Monique. I though of Monique the ruthless blackmailer. I thought of the woman who made those videos. The woman who hated men with such a passion that she could hardly contain it.

'Nat, what would you say if I told you that Monique had had at least sixteen lovers just in the four and a half years since she married Halifax? And that's sixteen that I know about, it could have been much more. I don't mean to deridc you, but what makes you think she loved you?'

If I was expecting him to get angry, I was wrong. He remained quietly composed and, I suddenly noticed, his strong Jamaican accent had completely evaporated. 'You don't understand, man. I knew about those guys, and I knew they didn't matter to her. I tell you that Monique loved me.'

I said nothing. An old reporter's trick; the silence becomes unbearable and the interviewee goes on talking. 'She got me this job, you know. Halifax let off a lot of hot air about the whole business, but she was the only one who did anything about it. I was still in plaster and I couldn't go back to my old job.' Then he paused. 'You don't even know what my old job was, do you? You never even asked me at the time. No one did.'

'What was it?' I asked.

'I worked on freelance contracts for British Telecom. I'm a fully qualified electrician.' There was bitterness in his voice, and no deception.

'But I thought you'd been in prison!' I said the words before I realized I shouldn't have had that information.

'So, you knew that, did you? And I suppose you know all about the other arrests and convictions?' I nodded. 'It's funny how everyone knows about that. But what you don't know is that the last time I was in prison one of the adult education people took an interest in me. I discovered I could actually do things, and when I got out I did the whole thing, apprenticeship, City and Guilds qualification, the lot. It was bloody tough, but there were people who helped me, and I did it.'

He went on: 'But for most people that didn't change anything. All they saw, all they wanted to see, was just another black man who everyone assumed was some sort of unskilled labourer, habitual criminal or just a social security scrounger.

'Except Monique. She came to see me in hospital, and that first time I didn't even know who she was. I'd never heard of her. That first time she came because Halifax asked her to, I think, but I don't think he even knew she came the other times.

'I wasn't employed by BT, so there was no sick pay, and I needed some light work until I recovered properly, so when I came out of the Royal Free she spoke to the owners of this building and that was it.' I still said nothing.

'Who knows, maybe she fucked the owners of the building to get me the job, I don't know.' He spat the hard words out. 'But she did it. She did it for me. And she did it because she liked me. We used to talk a lot. She used to come down here and sit where you're sitting, and we'd talk. And when Halifax was away she would invite me to come up when I was off duty, and we would talk and listen to music.' He stopped speaking.

'And you became lovers?'

'Not for a long time!' he said sharply. 'I was still in plaster, for Christ's sake. But it wasn't that either. We just enjoyed each other. We did ordinary things. We used to watch television and discuss the programmes, we used to argue about politics, about books, films, music, whatever. Sometimes she would cook a meal. Once or twice I cooked her West Indian food. We became very close, and I discovered that she was a very unhappy lady.'

'In what way?'

'Well, for a start she really hated Halifax. She couldn't bear his presence. I asked her why she married him and she said she felt she had to marry someone eventually, and she chose someone she thought was quite glamorous and wouldn't be too bad. Someone rich enough and busy enough to let her get on with her career and important enough to stop people making passes at her.

'But she knew it was a mistake pretty early on, she said, and the only reason the marriage didn't collapse years ago was the amount of time Halifax spent away from home. That gave her room to breathe and time to be on her own a lot.'

He was talking fluently now, and I let him get on with it.

'It was about eight months before we became lovers. I think we were both surprised, because neither of us thought it would happen. I was there one night when he was in Kuwait or somewhere equally far away, and she was upset about something. I tried to comfort her and the next thing we knew we were in bed.'

'What would you say,' I ventured carefully, 'if I said there was a lot of evidence that Monique's relationships with men were . . . well, not very satisfactory?' He looked at me blankly, but without hostility. I continued: 'What I mean is that far as I can see she didn't like men, and tended to try to humiliate her lovers.'

He listened carefully to what I said and thought about it. 'I would say there was probably something in that,' he answered. 'I know that these other guys she brought home now and then were all creeps, and none of them ever put in a second appearance either. A lot of men have given her a rough time. Did you know she was raped by an uncle in Armenia when she was ten years old?'

I felt the ground shift sharply under my feet. 'She told you that?'

'Yes, a few months ago. Apparently there was a big family rift after that, and that's why they came to live in England. But with me . . . with us, there was nothing of what you said. I'm not going into details for you, Parker, but we were . . . gentle together. She cried a lot and laughed a lot.'

I believed him. And I was finally beginning to understand the tortured core of that terrified, beautiful little girl I can still see arriving for her first day at our English school.

The confusion and guilt is overwhelming, but not as strong as the fear, and then hatred, of men. Paradoxically, her beauty draws men closer to her, and she learns how to use it as a weapon, razor sharp and deadly, to keep them away and, later, to torment them. The sexually abused child turns into the avenging adult, wielding and exploiting the very instrument of her own abuse.

And then, when she least expects it, and possibly because she does not expect it, Monique finds a soul-mate. The bruised immigrant girl, the victim finds another victim! Another outsider.

They have much in common, not least a contempt for English men and Monique finds she is establishing real contact with a man. The relationship flourishes unconsciously and when it finally breaks the surface, Monique, for the very first time in her life, finds herself actually rewarded by her own sexuality.

We had been sitting in total silence for a few minutes. 'These other men Monique had affairs with, did you recognize any of them?' I asked.

'No.' But the answer came much too quickly, and I could almost see the veil of mendacity that came down again between us. What intrigued me was why he should deny having recognized the men, some of whom—including the film critic Bertrand Blake, the actors and Adolfini—were household faces.

'Don't bullshit me, Nat. I know all the names, and I know what dates they were here. Some of them are famous people. Why tell me you didn't recognize them?'

But even as I asked the question, and looked at Nathaniel Jackson's ungiving face, I began to know the answer. I wasn't the only one who knew their names and the dates of their adultery with Monique. He also had that information, not only because he had seen some of them coming and going, but because he had obtained for himself my copy of Monique's diary, and the significance of the marked entries would not have escaped him.

But then another small suspicion germinated and started growing in my mind. It grew very fast, and the elegant way it fitted into the circumstances of recent weeks almost made me smile.

'Hey, you haven't been indulging in a spot of amateur blackmail, have you?'

'What do you mean?' he said defensively. But I knew I had scored a hit. Now I had to laugh.

'Oh shit, Nat!' I giggled, much to his consternation. 'Do you have any idea what you've done?'

'What the fuck are you talking about?'

'I'm talking about Malcolm Halifax getting shot, and I'm talking about people following me about with felonious intent!' He looked at me in astonishment.

'It was you that wrote to Adolfini demanding fifty thousand pounds, wasn't it?' I didn't wait for the answer. 'You told him something to the effect that if he didn't come up with the cash you would reveal his misdemeanours—meaning his visit to Monique—to all and sundry, and you told him to have the money delivered here, so that you could intercept it and disappear.

'But what you didn't know was that Monique was already blackmailing him. And since Monique was dead, Adolfini assumed that it was Halifax who had found the incriminating material. That was just too much, particularly in view of the nature of the material Monique had over him, and Adolfini ordered the hit in a fit of rage.'

Nat was looking . . . well, gobsmacked.

'And then, because I started turning up like a bad penny all over the place, and even asking him questions, Adolfini began to wonder whether perhaps I had something to do with the blackmail as well. And so he had me followed. Who knows how close I came to getting shot at!'

For a moment we just looked at each other. Then he said: 'I didn't know she was blackmailing him.'

'She was blackmailing all of them! Not for money, but

for parts in films and, in the case of Blake, for good reviews.'

He dropped all pretence. 'I needed the money. I can't stay working here any more, now that Monique's gone. I wanted to get set up somewhere else. And I wanted Adolfini to think it was Halifax, so if the money was delivered here I could take it. I figured Halifax wouldn't miss it, since he didn't know anything about it in the first place, and I hoped Adolfini would think he had bought Halifax's silence once he didn't receive any more demands. I didn't know anything about the other stuff.' All this came out in a rush.

'What did you think when Halifax got shot, for Chrissake?!'

'I suppose I suspected it might be Adolfini behind it, but I didn't care, really. I hate that bastard Halifax.'

'Why?' I asked.

'Because he killed Monique.'

'You said that before, but you don't have any proof, do you?'

'No.'

'Do you know anything that might be relevant?'

'No.'

'So how do you know that he killed her?' There was, I admit, an edge of frustration in my voice.

'I just feel it.'

There wasn't really anything I could say to that. We were still sitting at his desk in the foyer, with the afternoon sun streaming through the glass doors. It was quiet and warm, and I wondered how long he would remain working there.

'So what happens now, Parker? Are you going to the police with all this?' He didn't look too concerned either way.

'I'm not sure, but in any case it's more a question of whether you're going to the police with all this,' I said.

'But what do you think?' he asked.

I didn't think anything, so I thought for a while. Then I answered: 'It seems to me that it doesn't matter either way. The fact that you were having a relationship with Monique is a private matter which has nothing to do with the police, unless they regard you as a suspect, which they don't.

'The fact that it was you who burgled my house is relevant only to me, and I am not interested in pressing charges. Apart from the damage to the door, some of the furniture and the appalling mess you made—' this was said with a thunderous glower in his direction—'you didn't actually take anything except the diaries at the office, and the damage has already been covered by my insurance company. The same applies to the *Hampstead Explorer* burglary. Something tells me that the punishment you would get, with your record, just wouldn't fit the crime, so I'm inclined to let it remain a mystery.

'Now we get to your amateur blackmail activities. Would it make any difference to the police, or the nature of their evidence against Adolfini and his hit man, if the blackmail letter turns out to have come from you? My feeling is no. The police will still be able to produce a motive for the shooting, and it's probably better in the long run that Adolfini never finds out that it came from you. Who knows what he would still be able to arrange from behind bars. And Halifax will, of course, deny it all, and will be believed because he's stinking rich and doesn't need fifty thousand pounds.

'So, all in all, if you're asking me, my answer is: I'm not going to the police.'

'What's the time,' he asked me.

'Four fifty-five,' I said.

'I'm off duty in five minutes.' Then he sighed very deeply. 'Can you give me a lift to the police station?'

'I'll come with you,' I said.

Nathaniel Jackson spent a very difficult three hours at Hampstead police station with Theo Bernstein and Chief Superintendent Harrison. Jackson, they decided at first, was nothing less than a major irritant who could jeopardize their cases against Halifax and Adolfini.

But Nat played his part carefully and coolly. He dropped

all remnants of the uppity West Indian character, feigned a good deal of respect and politeness, and told his story as clearly and concisely as he could, leaving out some of the more personal details he had told me.

It took an hour before the two policemen began to accept that his disclosures had no effect whatsoever on their case against Halifax, such as it was. They were also relieved to find that their case against Adolfini and his hit man remained watertight, even though the blackmail letter may have been sent by Nat. Then they began to relax.

'There are at least three or four charges which we could bring against you, including burglary, blackmail and impeding the course of justice,' Harrison warned. 'But in the light of the special circumstances appertaining to this case, together with the fact that Mr Parker here is not pressing charges, and the fact that you came in voluntarily to make a statement, we are inclined not to pursue these matters further.'

It was half past eight when we finally emerged from the police station, and I gave Nat a lift back to his building. On the way there, I told him about the Edwina Llewellyn Memorial Trust which, I had heard, had funds specifically set aside for people wanting to change towns and make a new start in life. I gave him Pendleton's telephone number, and he said he would make an application first thing in the morning.

Then I asked Frankie, who had had the meter running since exactly six o'clock, to take me home.

CHAPTER 26

The promising spring turned into a typically disappointing summer with lots of rain, but life at the *Hampstead Explorer* remained satisfyingly hectic. There was also a better atmosphere as Bob Price's influence and reforms streamlined operations and production and continued to raise morale.

Even Arnie Bloch seemed to have mellowed in the security of the editor's chair and he became more like the experienced and respected captain of the ship than the slave-driver below decks beating the drum for the hapless oarsmen.

I found myself particularly busy at work. The publicity given to my own exploits in connection with the Karabekian murder case and the attempt on Halifax's life had given our readers a name to latch on to. So now when people rang in with tales of drama, injustice, corruption, scandal and disaster, it was me they asked for.

It was a busy time for both of us, both at work and in our new life together, and we were rather oblivious of anything else. There were weeks on end when we didn't give a thought to poor Monique Karabekian.

I didn't even know Malcolm Halifax had been discharged from hospital until I received a telephone call on a Wednesday afternoon towards the end of June. Wednesday afternoons are always a busy time as deadlines approach, and I was in a tetchy mood after a string of interruptions by public relations consultants, novelists looking for free publicity, estate agents and the like, and my telephone manner had become somewhat abrupt.

'Yes?' I barked into the receiver when it rang for the umpteenth time.

'Who is that speaking?' a vaguely familiar man's voice asked politely.

'Parker!' I snapped. And then I added savagely: 'Shit!' It was not directed at the caller but at the fact that the call had distracted me to the extent that I had pressed the wrong key on my keyboard, and had inadvertently erased the story I had been working on for the past two hours.

'This is Malcolm Halifax.'

Luckily we all have a facility within ourselves which, given suitable stimulation, can summon hitherto unfathomable reserves of recovery power. I took a quick breath, shut my eyes tightly for a moment, and I was instantly in a different mood.

'Well, goodness me, what a surprise! Are you calling from the hospital?' I asked cheerily.

'No, I'm at home. They finally let me out this morning.'

'How are you?' I asked. 'I mean, have you recovered fully? They kept telling me you were too ill to have visitors.'

'Oh yes,' he said apologetically. 'I only found out what was going on yesterday. Apparently after I was first admitted the police told the hospital that I was to have no visits from the press, and although I was out of intensive care within four or five days, no one at the police station had thought to reverse that instruction, and no one in administration had thought of questioning it. I was rather critical of them about it, I assure you.'

I could imagine. If there was one thing Halifax thrived on it was attention from the press, and it must have been hell for him lying there for five weeks thinking that journalists had forgotten all about him.

'But I'm fine really. I've been exercising in the hospital gymnasium and swimming every day. I've lost some weight, but they tell me that I am perfectly all right and that I should experience no ill-effects whatsoever . . .' He hesitated, and then added: 'Thanks, of course, entirely to you.'

'Well . . .' I began modestly.

'I am aware of precisely what you did, Parker. The events have since been recounted to me in great detail by Constable Reynolds and there is no doubt whatsoever that I owe my life to your knowledge of first aid.'

'I acted instinctively and I did what anyone would have done in my position,' I said quietly.

'You say that, but I wonder how many people would have been able to do anything effective when it came down to it.'

'I was only pleased to have been able to help,' I said.

'Nevertheless, I owe you my thanks at the very least. Why don't you come for dinner?' That last bit threw me off balance completely.

'Me? You mean tonight?'

'Yes, tonight. Bring your wife. I have a housekeeper who says she's a terrific cook.'

'My wife, a good cook?'

'No, my housekeeper.'

'I'm afraid I don't have a wife, but there is someone else whom I've been seeing.' I was desperately looking for a definitive excuse to refuse the invitation but failing miserably.

'Bring her, by all means. I've been talking only to doctors, nurses and policemen for weeks on end—it'll be good to talk to someone who knows what's going on in the real world for a change. You can also bring me up to date on what has being going on in Hampstead recently. I'll have to resume my Parliamentary work at some stage, and I feel rather out of touch. Please come.' His manner was casual, even jovial, but there was also an edge of urgency in it that he was narrowly failing to conceal.

'Of course. We'd be delighted. What time do you want us?'

'Eight o'clock?'

'Fine,' I said. Then I went to break the news to Andy.

We drove to Park Vistas in Andy's nifty new red Volvo sports car (was I paying her too much?) and found there was no policemen on duty outside the block. Nathaniel Jackson wasn't on duty either, of course. He had received a five thousand pound grant from the Edwina Llewellyn Memorial Trust to help with his relocation expenses to Bristol, where he was now living at an address in St Paul's and, we understood, working for British Telecom again.

There was a new porter on duty whom I'd never seen before, but he was expecting us, and we were sent straight up to Halifax's flat.

The MP was looking thinner than when I had last seen him, but the loss of weight hadn't done his looks any harm. If anything it made him even more attractive, with that sort of gaunt appearance that some women find irresistible. He may have been in hospital for five weeks, but he clearly hadn't been without his sun lamp, for he was looking as bronzed as ever, and his perfect white teeth were flashed to maximum effect at Andy when I introduced her to him, and explained that she was my boss.

He said something sexist but gallant about how pleased he was to meet someone so attractive who clearly had a great deal of power over his future career as MP for Hampstead, and for a moment I thought he was going to kiss her hand. But instead he took her arm and ushered us into the splendid living-room overlooking the park.

It was a weird feeling walking back into that room. The last time I had been in it, it had been full of broken glass, blood and heart-pounding drama, but now, of course, the window glass had all been replaced and everything was in perfect order. When Halifax disappeared to fetch us something to drink, I couldn't help moving quickly to the patch of carpet where he had lain bleeding and I had performed mouth to mouth resuscitation. My pulse quickened slightly as I stood looking down at the spot where it had all taken place. The thick white carpet had either been cleaned by an expert or else replaced altogether, but there was no trace of the blood which had poured out of him. For all the evidence remaining here, the whole event could have been taken place in another flat entirely.

Halifax returned with a bottle of Dom Perignon in a silver ice bucket and three glasses on a tray which also contained an enticing selection of canapés. The centrepiece was a plate of freshly grilled prawns impaled on cocktail sticks, each one with a little mound of real caviar heaped on it.

'You've gone to a lot of trouble. It really wasn't necessary,' I said.

'Nonsense! It's not every night that I get released from hospital and have the opportunity of thanking the person who made sure that I got there in the first place, if you know what I mean.' He was beaming benignly.

From the way the table was set, it was clear that we were the only guests expected for dinner and the food, when it started arriving, proved that the housekeeper had been telling the truth. She was indeed an excellent cook.

During the meal Halifax served three different and highly appropriate wines, poured from dusty bottles that had obviously come out of storage from somewhere dark and cool. He also led the way in drinking them, consuming a lot more than Andy and I between us.

And he was as smooth and agreeable as his wines. Any fears we may have had about spending a difficult and embarrassing evening with a man facing a murder charge who might have been expected to be defensive and at bay against the world, were disseminated before a wave of charm. This was Malcolm Halifax as he must have been when he was selected as their candidate by the Hampstead Conservative Association; as he was when he faced his voters; when he spoke in Parliament and when he dealt so effectively with foreign heads of state, ambassadors and anyone else with enough clout to beat their way to the door.

It was also the Malcolm Halifax, it occurred to me, who had wooed and won Monique Karabekian.

He worked hard at it. He was amusing and urbane, but constantly sensitive to the drift of the conversation, steering it past potholes and minefields alike, so that we never found ourselves discussing anything on which we could totally disagree.

And, unlike many politicians, he demonstrated an ability to listen and to hear what people said to him. He turned the full force of his approach on Andy and I was astonished to see that although she easily dismissed the flirting in his manner, she nevertheless responded with a torrent of opinion and conversation that I had not witnessed before. He had an ability to seem interested and fascinated by the slenderest thought, cocking his head intelligently when one spoke, and throwing his head back in amusement at the slightest hint of humour.

He was also entertaining, with a store of intriguing, if harmless, indiscretions to recount about life as a junior minister, and all kinds of gossipy revelations to make about other politicians, both major and minor. We were, we found to our surprise, enjoying ourselves immensely.

After the meal we went back into the living-room where we found the housekeeper had left a tray with a cafetière jug of coffee and a small bowl of Belgian chocolates. A few minutes later she put her head around the door to say she was leaving, and we all responded with profuse thanks and compliments about the food. She blushed happily and waddled off, and a minute later we heard the flat door close behind her.

'Cognac?' Halifax offered. Andy, who knew she would be driving home, declined but I was definitely in the market. He walked over to one of the low cabinets against the wall and started pouring what looked like an interesting Marc into two large brandy balloons. And, while his back was still to us, he said: 'OK, Parker, you must have some questions for me about this distressing court case. Fire away.'

I looked at Andy quickly, and she shrugged as if to say: This is the one subject all of us have been avoiding all evening at all cost, but if he wants to talk about it, why not? When he handed me my brandy, there was a tightness in his smile that wasn't there a few minutes before, but at least he was still smiling. And he broke the short silence himself.

'Did you know, for example, that the police are likely to drop the charges against me in the next few days?' Now I understood why he was so keen to raise the subject.

'No, I didn't,' I said.

'Well, that's what my lawyer tells me, based on what the police have told him. Apparently they would have withdrawn the charges before but reasoned that since I was in hospital it wouldn't make much difference to me one way or another, and they were hoping that other avenues of investigation would prove fruitful in the meantime.' Now that I thought about it, that did fit in with what Theo and Harrison had told me the last time I had spoken to them. They had been hoping to flush a new subject out of the woodwork while pretending that Halifax was still their prime suspect. They had begun a series of tough interviews with all sixteen of Monique's video co-stars.

'There may still be some charges arising out of my stupidity in not immediately calling the police and the idiotic things I did that morning, but they appear to be accepting that I was terribly shocked by what I had discovered, and that my bizarre behaviour was due to that. The rest of the case against me was pretty circumstantial and, really, unsustainable in the absence of any witnesses or corroboration of any kind.' He was standing in front of us, his eyes blazing his innocence. He was holding the brandy glass, but he hadn't yet taken a sip. Neither Andy nor I knew what to say, so we didn't say anything.

'I mean, they didn't even have a motive!' His voice had risen a pitch. 'At no stage could any of them come up with any reason why I would have wanted to murder my wife. The whole thing was just too absurd for words!'

But now I did have something to say. 'What about jealousy?' I tried to put it conversationally, as merely an item for debate, but it stopped him in his tracks.

I continued: 'You had seen Monique's video tapes, obviously, because you took them to the airport. And you were very concerned about them, because you insisted on giving me the key for that locker—even though you had just been shot. Did you find them that morning, or had you known for some time what she'd been up to?'

I think we were all a little alarmed at the turn the conversation had taken, but now that the cosy dinner-party chat had been ended at Halifax's own insistence, there was no going back. He'd gone a little pale, but there was no sign that he resented my question.

'The police have asked me that question too.' He paused and took a sip of cognac. 'And my answer is that I did know what she was doing; that she was having affairs with these people . . . and blackmailing them. I was horrified when I found out, and I begged her and pleaded with her to stop it!' He was very agitated now.

'But she wouldn't. Or couldn't. I'm not sure which, and

I just couldn't force her. And when I came home that night and found her dead, I knew it had to have something to do with those tapes. I knew one of those bastards must have killed her to shut her up. To stop the blackmailing. The police now think that it was probably Eduardo Adolfini, although I don't know how much evidence they've got.

'Among the other stupid things I did that night was to take that suitcase to the airport. I wasn't thinking straight, and I suppose my motive was somehow to protect her. I didn't want anyone to see those films.'

'And you wanted to protect yourself from scandal,' Andy said quietly.

'Yes. That too. Of course I didn't want anyone to know what a fool she'd made of me. Can anyone blame me? I was a member of the Government, for God's sake. Think what the papers would have made out of it!' We all thought for a second, and it was not a pretty picture that we all painted in our minds.

'I was going to destroy them, but I couldn't think how to do it, and I didn't have time to do anything, so I left them in that locker for the time being.'

'Why did you give me the key?' I asked.

'I thought I was dying. I was lying there and I couldn't breathe and I was in shock and there was blood everywhere, and all I could think about was that everyone would think that I had killed her. It sounds ridiculous now, I know, but that's all that was in my mind. I wanted you to get the films and give them to the police so that they would know that I hadn't committed murder; that one of those bastards had killed her.'

'You're a fucking liar, Halifax!' That was a fourth voice, which came from the doorway behind us, and we whirled round in shock.

Nathaniel Jackson was standing there.

CHAPTER 27

The moment was so suffused with shock that I have no recollection of my thoughts when I saw him standing there, if I had any thoughts at all. The three of us sat transfixed and open-mouthed as Nathaniel walked into the room. I noticed that he was carrying something in his left hand, but it was his right hand that our eyes followed with stunned intensity. It held a large revolver.

'What the hell are you—' Halifax had leaped to his feet, but his blustered words were cut short.

'Shut up!' Nat barked loudly. He levelled the revolver at Halifax and for an instant I thought he was going to pull the trigger. I closed my eyes in horror. 'Sit down!' he spat. 'And stay sitting! If you get up or try to do anything stupid, I swear I'll shoot you.' Halifax, having already been shot once that year, fell back on to the couch as if he'd been pushed.

Then Nathaniel looked at Andy and me, although the gun remained pointed at Halifax. I saw that his eyes were rimmed with red, and he was swaying slightly as if he were drunk or on drugs. 'What the fuck are you two doing here?' he asked.

My heart was pounding and my mouth was dry, but I could still speak, just. 'We could ask you the same question,' I said, but it was as if I hadn't spoken.

'It doesn't matter,' he muttered, and it was as if he was looking through us and not seeing us at all. But then he focused on me, and he spoke again. 'Yes, it does matter. It's good that you're here, you'll be witnesses!'

'Witnesses to what, Nat?' I asked, but he ignored the question. He turned to Halifax.

'Did you think I wouldn't know? Did you think I would just go away and let you get away with it? What did you think I was? Just some stupid porter who would be happy to escape without getting involved because he's just some coloured man who knows his place? Jeeesus!'

Halifax was as white as a sheet, and trembling under the unwavering stare of the gun. But he showed no sign of moving or of even considering trying to do anything brave and foolish. 'How did you get in here?' His voice was very shaky indeed.

'I had my keys copied before I left,' Nat said. 'And how did I know you were out of hospital? Because I have friends there who promised to tell me; people you wouldn't see or take notice of because they're black!

'And you—' he turned to me—'I TOLD you that he killed Monique, but you weren't interested, were you?'

'I asked you for evidence, Nat. I'm still asking.'

'I've got evidence!' he said, his eyes gleaming triumphantly, and he held up what he was carrying in his left hand. It was a video tape. I shuddered.

'OK, let's phone Theo Bernstein and he'll—'

'NO!' he shouted. There was no doubt in my mind now that he was on something, either very drunk or very high, and that rational argument was not going to get us far. And since he was the one with the gun, we were going to do it his way.

'We're going to watch a movie! Here, Andy, put that in the video.' He held the tape out towards Andy, who was also as white as a sheet and had not moved a muscle since he entered the room.

'What is it?' Halifax said, and I heard a note of horror in his voice.

'You'll see soon enough. You just sit there and shut up. Come on, girl,' he said to Andy, who still hadn't moved, 'I'm not going to hurt you. I promise.'

'Give it to me, I'll do it,' I said. He hesitated for a moment and then handed me the tape. I went over to the television set and turned it on. I switched it to the video channel, and put the tape in the machine. Then I pressed the play button.

'OK, come back and sit down,' Nathaniel said to me. I

did what he said, bringing the remote control keypad with me.

We were watching TV snow and listening to the high pitched 'white' sound that you see and hear when a channel has gone off the air. Or when a video tape has been wiped clean.

'What is this?' I asked.

'Fast forward it,' he commanded. He had moved around behind us so that he could watch us and the television screen, and the gun was now pointing at the back of Halifax's head. I pressed the fast forward button and the sound cut out but there was still nothing on the tape. I looked at Nathaniel's face and realized that he knew there was nothing on this part of the tape.

A minute passed, and then another, and another, and still there was nothing on the screen. And slowly I began to understand what it was that we were watching, or rather, not watching.

'You erased this part, didn't you?' I said. There was no answer, but I knew. 'This was a film of you and Monique, wasn't it?' Andy gave a gasp of understanding, and reached out to grip my hand.

'She just couldn't resist it, could she? She filmed everyone else, so why not you? And you didn't know it was happening, did you?' Nathaniel was looking at me balefully with his red-rimmed eyes, and he shook his head.

'Just watch, Parker. You don't understand yet.'

We sat in silence watching the flickering screen and listening to the whine of the video recorder. Halifax was staring at it in a fixed, unfocused way, as if looking past the TV set into another time altogether. Andy had moved closer to me on the couch and was resting her head on my shoulder. We were like that for another four or five minutes, and then suddenly we had a picture.

'Slow it down!' Nathaniel snapped, and I pressed the play button again and the picture steadied. It was a film of Monique asleep in bed.

The camera was in the same position as it had been for

the other films I had watched, giving a perfect view of the big double bed. The only difference was that she was alone, and the room was fairly dark, although there was a bedside lamp on which gave enough light to see that it was Monique lying quietly asleep under a duvet, her dark hair falling slightly over her face, and her body moving rhythmically with her breathing. Minutes passed, and nothing happened.

'What now?' I said.

'You'll see.'

But as we sat watching the sleeping woman, I had another flash of understanding. 'She left the camera running!' I exclaimed. 'She forgot, and she left it running after you left her!'

This time Nathaniel said nothing, but as the idea permeated into Halifax's brain an expression of unspeakable anguish took over his face. He drew his knees up on to the couch until his position was almost foetal and be began to whimper, 'Oh my God, oh my dear God, oh God, oh God . . .'

'Shut up, you bastard!' Nathaniel ground the barrel of the revolver into the back of Halifax's neck and the whimpering became only just audible.

On the screen a light suddenly snapped on in the bedroom, and Malcolm Halifax was standing there, with his back to the camera, wearing a raincoat and looking down at Monique. He took off his coat and her eyes opened.

'You're early. I wasn't expecting you until tomorrow,' she said in a flat, sleepy voice, picked up clearly by the microphone which had captured the voices of all her victims.

'Well, thanks for the enthusiastic welcome,' said Halifax's voice. 'You make it a real pleasure to come home.' There was no mistaking the sarcasm. She didn't reply, and he moved towards the bathroom and disappeared. She waited unmoving in the bed until the toilet flushed and he came back into the room.

'What have you been doing?' he asked. But she didn't

reply. 'Seen any of your fellas lately?' At this she flopped over in the bed, turning her back on him.

''Course you have! You've had someone here tonight, haven't you? God! I can smell the aftershave and the stink of sex!' He reached down and snatched the duvet off her, throwing it down at the right-hand side of the bed. She didn't move, and her very passivity seemed to inflame him.

'Look at you!' he said, looking down at her nakedness. 'You're still wet, for Christ sake!' He was angry, but he was also aroused. He leaned down and did something which the camera could not see. Perhaps he tried to touch her or fondle her, or maybe he hurt her, but Monique moved suddenly, like a cat spitting and squalling, flailing her arms at him until he stepped back.

'Get away!' she rasped.

'Why?' he challenged.

'Because you disgust me!'

We were watching a row which anyone could see had been well rehearsed and played out a number of times before. Two unhappy people goading each other and knowing exactly where to stick the pins to create maximum pain.

'How do you know I disgust you? You never let me get close enough to find out!' he said.

'You have bad breath, and you couldn't even get your dick up!' There was a moment of stillness in the room, but the fury was palpable.

'Yeah, you know all about that, don't you. That's your little party trick, isn't it? I've seen you do that to your little boyfriends in your video album. The only time in your life that you ever enjoyed sex was with those actresses in that film you made in Sweden about lesbians.' His voice was grating.

'You're the homo.' Said quietly, tauntingly.

'You know that's not true.' Menacingly.

'Yes, it is, you only ever wanted to stick it up my bum.'

He whirled round on her, we saw his right arm go up and down, and there was the sound of a stinging slap.

'You bastard!'

'Cunt!'

'I want a divorce.' Then there was a real silence.

'What?'

'I want a divorce.' Bolder.

'What are you talking about?' Now there was alarm in his voice.

'You heard! I want a divorce!'

'That's bullshit. It's impossible and you know it. It's out of the question. You agreed, no divorce for ten years. I can't get divorced now.'

'Well, I don't care what the fucking Prime Minister or the fucking cabinet think. I want a divorce, and I'm going to leave.'

'No you're not!'

'I bloody well am. Tomorrow.'

Halifax was raging now, but he checked himself. 'Monique, what is this? What are you doing?' The words hissed out.

'I hate you!'

'So what's new?'

'I love somebody else.' Defiant.

'Ha! One of your dyke friends! How pathetic!'

'It's a man, you bastard.'

'A man? A man. You "love" a man? Don't make me laugh! He must be gay; or else he hasn't got a prick for you to tease.'

'He's not gay. He's the only real man I ever met!' she shouted at him. 'In my whole goddam life!' She was kneeling on the bed now, facing him, holding the duvet around her, and he still had his back to the camera.

'Who is this superstud you think you're going off with?' He leaned forward, took a handful of her hair and twisted it so that she winced with pain.

'Nathaniel.'

'Who? Who the fuck is Nathaniel?' He sounded genuinely confused.

'You know, Nat. Nat Jackson, the guy who works downstairs.' It was as if Halifax turned to stone, so still did he become. There was a thunderstruck silence for four or five seconds, and when he spoke there was something icy and dangerous in his voice, and he no longer shouted.

'Oh no. Oh no. No way. There is no way on this earth that you are going to walk out on me and go off with a penniless black porter.' He spoke the words through gritted teeth in short bursts, quietly and with a rhythm in which he twisted the handful of hair with each emphasis. 'It would be the end. It's just not going to happen. It would be the end of my public life. That is just not going to happen. Is that clear? Do you understand? It's not going to happen.' He took a step back from her.

'Tomorrow. I'm going tomorrow.'

'NO!' he roared, twisting round and delivering a vicious backhand blow which sent her flying off the bed, out of the view of the camera.

'Tomorrow!' The small voice came from off screen.

Halifax leaped across the bed, scrabbled off the right-hand side and then we heard him start to kill her off screen. She made no sound. How could she with his hands around her throat? But he grunted with the effort of holding her down, and within five seconds I couldn't stand it any longer and I switched off the TV set.

Andy was with me on the couch, her face buried deep in my shoulder, and she was crying. Halifax was curled up on the couch a few feet away, his expression vacant, and his lips making what looked like involuntary movements, as if he was whispering to himself. And Nathaniel stood behind us with tears pouring down his black face.

'That's it, Nat, we're not watching any more,' I said firmly, but I needn't have bothered. We had clearly seen enough for his purposes.

'It wasn't true! We never spoke about going off together. We knew that was impossible. I don't know why she said that to him,' Nathaniel said. He was shaking his head from side to side.

'It sounds to me like she was at the end,' I said. 'It was the thing she knew would hurt him most; the most damaging scandal he could even conceive of. Top politician's sexy film-star wife runs off with black janitor. No one could ride that story and stay in politics. They both knew that.' I saw that he was listening to me.

'So, while she loved you, she was also using you, Nat. Do you see that? She used everyone. Even the people she really loved. And she destroyed everything she touched.' He was nodding.

'Sit down and tell me the rest of the story.' He looked quite calm now, and Halifax seemed as if he was asleep. 'You were down in the foyer, on duty and, contrary to your statement to the police, you must have been aware of the movements of the lifts. I noticed them when I was in the foyer with you a few weeks ago.'

'Yes. I had been with Monique earlier and, as you saw, she filmed us without telling me. I wiped that off.' I nodded. 'And she left the camera on.

'About half an hour later I saw the lift go up from the car park to their floor, and I assumed it was Halifax arriving home. I didn't think much about it until half an hour later the lift gets called to the same floor and then goes down to the car park. I thought that was very suspicious, so I went down the stairs to see what was going on. I saw Halifax carrying something heavy, wrapped up in what looked like a duvet, which he put in the boot of his car and drove off.

'I was worried, although I think I already knew what he'd done. I went back up to the flat and let myself in. There was no one there, of course, but there was a mess in the bedroom, and I knew he'd killed her. I was standing there next to the cupboard, in shock I suppose, when I heard the whirring of the camera. I opened the top of the cupboard, found the camera and switched it off. I took the video tape out and I got out of there. And I just said I hadn't seen or heard anything. The rest you know.' The drugs or whatever seemed to be relaxing their hold.

'So, what do we do now?' I said. 'Call the police?'

'No.' He didn't shout, but he still sounded very sure of himself. And he still had the gun. 'I'm going to shoot this bastard.' Halifax didn't even twitch; Andy and I were the ones who started to shake.

'I don't understand,' I said. 'This tape contains the clearest possible evidence of his guilt. There is no way that he could avoid conviction for murder. He's going straight to prison for life.'

'Oh, don't bullshit me, Parker. Man like that, killed his wife in a fit of jealous passion, some degree of provocation, lots of evidence of her infidelity and criminal behaviour. I wouldn't be surprised if they agreed to reduce the charge to manslaughter!

'But even if they did press the murder charge, think about what would happen. They would plead all kinds of extenuating circumstances, temporary insanity, diminished responsibility and every other kind of legal bullshit that is open to people like him with lots of money—and in the process Monique's name would be dragged through the manure. And let's just assume for one wild moment that the jury finds him guilty of murder. Or for that matter, he may even plead guilty. Either way he's going to throw himself on the mercy of the court with a demonstration of contrition and remorse that is bound to have the judge and everyone else in tears.

'But OK, let's go mad and assume that the judge still gives him a life sentence. What does that mean in the case of a man like Halifax? It means around fifteen years, and what with good behaviour and remission, he'll be out in about eight or nine years. It's not good enough.'

I have to admit I couldn't fault the legal reasoning, although that did not mean I agreed with the idea of shooting Halifax. 'But you can't shoot him; in cold blood just like that . . .' I could hear the meaningless clichés lining up to trip off my tongue. 'You'll end up in prison yourself, for Chrissake!'

'Leave off, Parker. Don't you think that I haven't been thinking about all this since the day it happened? I knew that I had to kill him as soon as I saw that terrible tape, and I've had weeks and weeks in which to change my mind while I watched for the bastard to come out of hospital. I've thought about it every single day from every conceivable angle, and and there's no other way that would be right in my eyes. Do you think you could convince me otherwise in a three-minute off-the-cuff argument?'

To be frank, I didn't. So I did something stupid that everyone says you should never do. I grabbed the gun and tried to prise it out of his grip. Andy did something more stupid. She tried to help me. We didn't manage to get the gun away from him, but we did manage to ensure that it was pointing at the floor, and then I screamed at Halifax to clear out.

I expected him to run for the door, but instead he uncoiled from his position on the couch, moving so slowly it was almost slow motion, and he began to walk in the opposite direction. He opened the sliding door to the balcony, and while Nathaniel was shouting and swearing at us to get off his arm, Halifax went out on to the patio and stepped up on to one of the cast-iron chairs. He looked at us, just once, with a puzzled expression full of pain and confusion, and let himself fall over the railing. There was no sound at all, and we didn't even hear the sound of his body hitting the rockery three floors below.

When we saw what had happened we broke up our frozen tableau, and I was relieved when Nathaniel showed no sign of anger at what we'd done. Halifax was gone, and that was what was important to him, I suppose.

But it wasn't finished yet. He was still holding the gun, and he had a lethargic, resigned look on his face that worried me. 'You two get out of here now,' he said softly.

It was Andy who answered him. 'Oh no, we're not letting you do that. We're staying with you, and if necessary we'll jump on you again. You can't do it!' We were both in shock and acting quite irrationally.

'You want me to go on living, remembering that video film every day of my life, remembering the details of how the only person I ever loved in my entire life was squashed out like a bug?!' The words churned my insides. 'No, you go and talk to that policeman over there,' he said gesturing with the gun towards the door.

It was, as they say, the oldest trick in the book. Andy and I looked around towards the balcony, and by the time we turned back, Nathaniel was six or seven paces away and heading fast in the direction of Monique's bedroom. He beat us to it easily, and had the door slammed and locked by the time we pounded against it. In despair I took Andy's head and wrapped my arms around it, hoping I suppose to protect her from the sound we knew would be coming. We didn't have to wait long, although the report was very much more muted than I had expected.

We sank to the floor, clutching at each other in horror and holding on tight until the worst of the shaking and trembling and awfulness of it all passed by.

Then I went to the telephone and dialled Hampstead police station. They told me that both Theo and Harrison were off duty.

'Well, find them, and tell them that Horatio Parker is at Park Vistas where there are two more bodies and another video tape and to get over here fast. You had better organize for the Flying Squad to look in, too. Oh, and get some ambulances for the bodies.' Then I hung up. They were to say later that I had not been very coherent. I was not surprised.

Then I phoned Arnie Bloch at home and got him out of bed early that Thursday morning.

'Arnie,' I said, 'it's Parker. Hold the front page.'